Imagining Violet

by

Mary E. Hughes

Mary Hughes

Imagining Violet

Part One of Three

www.imaginingviolet.blogspot.ca

Cover Design by Mark Hand

This is primarily a work of fiction, although many of the people in it were part of Violet's life.

Printed in Victoria, BC, Canada
by First Choice Books

ISBN: 978-0-2285-0164-0

To my dearly beloved husband
Alan Hughes
for his patient support and encouragement
throughout this project.

Foreword

When she was nine, one of my granddaughters asked "Why is it called *Imagining Violet,* Grandma?" as we discussed her reactions to the pages she had read.

"I like Wysiwig titles," I told her. "Violet was a real person, my grandmother, in fact. I know a few things about her life, but I have imagined the rest."

This is, therefore, a work of historical fiction. It could also be described as very creative non-fiction.

I think one should read these letters a few at a time. The epistolary format does not lend itself to speed reading.

Mary E. Hughes
Salt Spring Island
2018

Cassel

Hotel Schirmer,
Königs Platz, Cassel, Germany

Thursday, 25th May, 1891

Dear Birdie,

At last, dear sister, we have arrived in Cassel. After four long, long days of travel, Mama insists that I rest. But I am so impatient to see the town that I cannot sit still. I am not allowed to venture out alone, but must wait until Mama is ready. But I am ever so restless!

And I am all aflutter to meet my new violin teacher and begin lessons. I must not waste a minute if I am going to take the entrance examination at the Conservatory in the autumn. I know you think I am proud and a little foolish to dream of performing on a concert stage, but being accepted into the Conservatory is very important to me.

When she returns to Edinburgh, Mama will have much to tell you about our journey. But I shall write about it as well as I intend my letters to serve as an account of my exciting new life. Please keep them for me, will you, dear Birdie?

I need not write about coming down from Edinburgh to London. I am glad, though, that we took the morning train, as the rest of the journey was indeed rather arduous.

Imagining Violet

The first interesting part was the paddle steamer passage. We went aboard at Queenborough at ten o'clock at night. I was disappointed that we were to sail overnight, because by the time we embarked it was too late, in Mama's opinion, to explore the vessel as I should have liked to do. The Flushing Line runs two crossings a day, but Mama chose the overnight passage so that we should not have to spend the next night on the train.

I liked the *Prinses Marie*. She is much larger than the packets we have taken on our visits to Ireland and I believe she is the largest paddle steamer in their fleet. We shared a cabin with two large,good-natured Dutchwomen but we could not communicate very well. They smiled a great deal, but they almost filled up the small space, if it is not unkind to say so. Oh well, it was only for the one night and I am determined to treat everything as part of the adventure.

We were both fearful of sea sickness, and felt ourselves lucky to have a quiet crossing. Indeed both Mama and I slept well enough, despite the narrow bunks and the discomfort of sharing a cabin with strangers.

To wake up in the morning and find oneself in Holland, in Europe – now that was thrilling! In Flushing, or Vlissingen perhaps I should say now that I am in Europe, the Customs Officers were very nice and polite. Please tell Papa for me.

On the train, we very much appreciated the air cushions which Aunt Kate gave us as a going-away present. Although they are not quite the latest thing – a passenger in our compartment had one of the new Melon cushions – we found that ours are rather more convenient. When emptied, ours roll up and fit neatly into a pocket.

My new travelling costume served me well. I know I had complained about it, but it was very suitable for travel. And my new petticoat – the one of striped Oxford shirting – was much more sensible than a white one. I was glad I had brought my tam, so that I could remove my straw hat and rest my head against the back of the seat. What a good thing I listened to Miss Mackenzie's advice. Do you remember her? The very tall girl who was ahead of me at Mr.

Waddell's Music School? She has been at the Conservatorium in Leipsic for a year now.

There is much to learn about travelling. I was curious about the brightly coloured circles some passengers had painted on the ends of their trunks. But later I could see that it was good deal easier for those people to recognize their belongings. I shall certainly do that when next I travel by train.

I shall stop here, Birdie, as finally Mama is ready to go out and I most certainly do not wish to keep her waiting.

~~~~~~~~~~~~~~~~~

Friday, 26th May

Dear Birdie,

Mama said we must first go to meet Frau Brimmer where I am to lodge, so we have paid a call and I believe Mama is satisfied that I shall be well looked after. But I cannot yet meet Herr Kaletsch, the violin teacher, until he returns from a short trip. I should not be so impatient but passing the entrance exam means everything to me. If I fail, this is all for naught!

But before we start off sight-seeing, I want to tell you more about the train journey. Our second-class compartment from Vlissingen was comfortable, and as we had taken care to find a ladies' compartment labelled, "Für Nicht Raucher", we were not bothered by people smoking. Happily I had the window seat facing forward and I was in charge of opening and closing the window which I also liked.

In Antwerp we had an hour's delay and as we were hungry we decided to visit the refreshment room. This was not, dear Birdie, a pleasant experience. It was very crowded and there was a long queue and honestly these people do not seem to have the habit of queuing, so there was a good deal of pushing and shoving. We had a struggle to find a place to sit and by the time we had been served, it was nearly time to leave, so we ate in great haste with no possibility
~~~~~~~~~~~~~~~~~

of taking a sweet or coffee. Someone had told us to avoid the pastries "as we would the plague" – I do not know why – and the puddings looked unappetizing in any case.

I have quickly learned, dear sister, that travel is full of mystery. One is forever wondering the why of things but one cannot get an answer. Another time we could order a refreshment basket and enjoy our food at leisure. That is what I shall do when I come home at Christmas.

Indeed one of our fellow passengers had such a basket and when she was finished eating, she did the oddest thing. She took a silver toothpick from her large handbag and proceeded to use it, in public. I did not know where to look.

There was another very long stop at the German border and once again we were obliged to fetch out all our luggage. Mama had taken care to watch where our cases went and she cleverly found a porter straightaway to see our trunks and boxes through Customs, so that was all right.

I was worried about the tea. Miss Mackenzie had warned that one cannot get good tea in Germany and said she always carries tea with her when she leaves home, so Mama had packed several ounces in her valise. I had not asked Miss Mackenzie how much was allowed and I was fearful that it might be confiscated, or worse. Mama was not at all flustered and said confidently that we had nothing to declare, and we were sent on our way. I still do not know just how much tea is permitted.

Here is another odd thing. You know, Birdie, how we sit in complete silence amongst strangers in a railway carriage at home? Well, on this train, people coming and going from our carriage would nod or bow to each other, to complete strangers, when they entered or left the carriage. And they spoke to each other, although it seemed obvious that they did not know each other. Mama was rather perturbed by this but I am beginning to think that it is a more natural way of behaviour, especially when one is cooped up with others for hours in a railway carriage.

But my goodness, Birdie, how rude the guards were! At home we are used to railway guards being helpful and respectful, but at the border one guard practically bawled at us as we came hurrying along the platform after we were finished with the Customs officials. Of course we could not run!

It was late in the day when we reached Düsselfdorf where we were to spend Tuesday night. We went directly to an hotel and fell asleep straightaway. Our beds were lovely with soft feather comforters, but the breakfast was very strange. This was my first German breakfast and it consisted of cheese and cold meat and cold hard-cooked eggs and rolls and butter, but alas, no toast. I have decided that this is a part of my wonderful adventure, but I do not think Mama enjoyed her breakfast.

Düsseldorf, from the little I saw of it, was busy but scarcely a pretty place. We were happy to catch the morning express train to Cassel and leave Düsseldorf behind. The Germans are proud of their splendid railway system, but the next part of the journey seemed very long. We were nearly nine hours on the train! "Express" has a different meaning here. This "express" train did not stop at every single small station, only at the larger ones. At first we passed through town after town with endless factories and foundries. Mama napped a good deal of the time but I was sure that if I fell asleep I should miss something interesting, but I did find myself nodding off from time to time. The district is evidently dedicated to manufacturing so it is not very picturesque and I do not suppose I missed much. The spires of the numerous churches were all that relieved the view.

Towards the end of our journey, we crossed over one valley by means of a long viaduct. We were alarmingly high up; a fellow passenger explained that the viaduct is more than one hundred feet high. Do you see why at times it is a good thing to speak to strangers?

Imagining Violet

Had that gentleman remained silent, I should not have known about the viaduct. After that we were in hills and forest and soon came down to Cassel.

We shall stop at the Hotel Schirmer for another two nights. Except for that one night in Düsseldorf, I have never stayed in a proper hotel before and I am enjoying this ever so much. This is a very long letter I know, but at present I have the leisure to write and plenty to write about. There are these new picture postcards here and I am sending one to Jack and Reg.

~~~~~~~~~~~~~~~~~~

~~~~~~~~~~~~~~~~~~

Imagining Violet

Monday, 5th June, 1891

Dear Mama,

I hope you were not too tired after your long journey home and that you found everyone well when you reached Pilrigg Street. I was grateful that you were here with me for a few days and that we could enjoy some of the sights together before I begin lessons.

I have found out about the statue we saw in the Friedrichs Platz, by the way, the one of Prince Friedrich that we were wondering about. Frau Brimmer explained that it was erected to honour the Prince who sent many thousands of his subjects to aid the English in the war to suppress the American rebellion more than a hundred years ago. He was paid the vast sum of twenty-two million thalers for sending his soldiers!

Mama, I am so thankful to you and Papa for this opportunity to study music in Germany. I know I shall be content at Frau Brimmer's although it is a good thing that she knows a little English or I should be in difficulties.

I already miss you, but soon I shall be so occupied with lessons and practice that I shall not have time to be lonely. That is my hope. I know that at sixteen I am young to be away by myself, but I am glad that you and Papa agreed with Mr. Waddell that I would benefit from more study.

~~~~~~~~~~~~~~~~~
~~~~~~~~~~~~~~~~~

Imagining Violet

Hedwigstrasse, No. 7, Cassel

5th June, 1891

Dear Aunt Matilda,

We arrived in Cassel safely and I have settled into lodgings at the address above. Thank you again for your thoughtful and useful gift. We were, both Mama and I, very grateful to have *Hints to Lady Travellers* on several occasions during our journey here. It is nice to have the very latest advice. Attitudes are changing rather too quickly, Mama says. What was proper behaviour just ten years ago is now regarded as old-fashioned thinking by some, but perhaps not by my dear mother. I, for one, am glad to be living in these modern times.

Still, I feel sure that Mrs. Campbell Davidson's advice played a part in persuading Mama and Papa that it will be perfectly safe for me to travel home at Christmas time, even by myself. As she writes: "I am quite sure that no man, however audacious, will venture to treat with undue familiarity or rudeness a woman, however young, who distinctly shows him by her dignity of manner and conduct that any such liberty will be an insult." I pointed this passage out to Mama and I believe it was reassuring. Mrs. C-D goes on to say that the greater independence of women which permits even young girls to travel about entirely alone, unattended even by a maid, rarely has inconvenient consequences. So you see, there is nothing to worry about.

You asked why I came to Cassel for the summer. It might seem a curious thing to do, I agree, but the explanation is simple. One of my fellow pupils at the Waddell School of Music did the very same thing last summer and found the experience most satisfactory. Herr Kaletsch, with whom I am to have lessons, is one of the few violin masters who teaches English students through the summer months. He and my piano teacher Fräul. Hohmann were acquainted years ago at the Leipsic Conservatorium. That same pupil took lodging with the

Brimmer family and found the house entirely agreeable. And so I follow in her footsteps.

Mama was able to stop a few days with me here, to rest before the journey home, and to look at the town a little. Cassel has its old town, by the River Fulda, with narrow picturesque streets. The newer part of the city has been built higher up and is airy and agreeable. There we found the Friedrichs Platz, which is the largest square of any German town. The Elector's Palace is there too, but it is not very interesting. There are buildings on three sides of the square, but from the fourth side one has a lovely view of the valley and beyond to a distant mountain. From that side of the square, one passes into the large public gardens where we admired the pretty spring flowers and flowering shrubs.

The next day we visited the principal attraction of Cassel, the Wilhelmshöhe, which was the summer palace of the former Elector. Some call it the German Versailles. Mama and I chose to go up by the amusing steam tramway which conveniently left from the Königsplatz by our hotel.

A respectable-looking young man approached us there and offered his services as a guide. His English was excellent, and Mama accepted the offer. We agreed later it had been a good idea to do so. Otherwise I do not suppose we should have had any notion of what we were seeing.

The palace is very large and elaborate as many of the public buildings are, but it is the gardens that give so much pleasure. Behind the palace, they extend for some great distance up to the very top of a high hill. Our guide took care that we were in the vicinity of the Great Fountain at the right time, three o'clock precisely, to see the waterworks play. It is a wondrous thing, Aunt Matilda, to see a jet of water rise hundreds of feet into the air. There is also a tremendous waterfall descending from a reservoir higher up the hill. In addition, there is second cascade which I shall visit another time as it requires one to climb a long, long flight of stone steps which was more than

Mama was willing to attempt. I should not have been able to explain any of this without that nice young man who showed us around. I shall send you a picture postcard. I hope you and Uncle are keeping well.

~~~~~~~~~~~~~~~~~~

Hedwig Strasse, 7, Cassel
Sunday, 2nd July, 1891

Dear Mama und Papa,

Sunday is a good day to write letters. For the most part, I am settling in here. Frau Brimmer is rather strict and keeps a well-regulated household.

We must not be a minute late for Frühstuck – I mean, breakfast – which is just coffee with warm milk and a roll with a little marmalade or butter. Not at all like that curious big breakfast we had in Düsseldorf.
~~~~~~~~~~~~~~~~~~

I have been able to practise my few words of German with the family and I have had my first meeting with Herr Gerhard, the tutor you arranged for. I know you liked Herr Gerhard, Mama, but I am not sure that I do. He seems a little old-fashioned and determined that I shall learn a great deal of grammar. And I have a feeling that he does not much like English people. Before I know it, he will have me conjugating irregular verbs, whilst I simply want to learn enough of the language that I can speak with people in the shops and so forth.

My violin lessons have begun with Herr Kaletsch and I feel sure he will do me a world of good. For the moment, he has taken me back to the basics, scales and exercises. Also I am trying to adjust my bow hold, trying not to grip it so hard. I played my recital piece for him and I thought it went well, although I stumbled badly during the faster section at the end. For the time being, I am to go twice a week on Monday and Thursday for an hour and I am to practise no more than three hours a day. In the morning, I begin with an hour and a half practice and then go to my daily German lesson. I like to explore the town a little on the way to or from Herr Gerhard's, but I must be back at Hedwigstrasse precisely at one o'clock for Mittagessen (dinner). The German people are very punctual, and I am forever looking at my new pocket watch. Woe betide me if I forget to wind it!

Dinner is a very long meal, much longer than we are used to. We are at table for well over an hour. I do not think Papa would enjoy that, do you? We usually begin with bread soup, followed some days by a course of veal with sauerkraut and potatoes. Another time we had beef with red currants and spinach. There is always black bread and sometimes also rolls. I should like to know how you make bread black but I dare not ask. Some days Frau B. serves stewed apricots and yesterday there was a delicious cherry cake with whipped cream. So you see the food is very different from our usual fare. There are two more meals in the day: tea may be taken at 5:00 and a cold supper is served at eight.

My German lessons proceed, but I am shy to speak much German yet. I try a little with Frau B., and she is patient and helpful, but with the servant girl it is impossible. I cannot understand anything she says, so aside from "Danke Schön", we make do with smiles and sign language. This might sound ridiculous, but when I see a group of children playing in a park, I think how clever they are to speak German so well. I cannot manage it at all.

I look forward to your letters and often feel I am very far away. Margaret and Annie have both written and their news has made me a little homesick. The weather continues mild, although the nights are chilly. My new spring mantle keeps me warm enough though.

Ihre liebende Tochter – that means "Your loving daughter",

~~~~~~~~~~~~~~~~~~

Hedwig Strasse, 7, Cassel

Sunday 9th July, 1891

Dear Mama and Papa,

You will be glad to know that I went to church this morning with the Brimmers. I did not understand much of the service but it was a lovely old Gothic church. I am told there is an English service somewhere in the city so I shall try to find out more and perhaps I shall attend that instead if it is not too far to walk.

This afternoon I visited the Picture Gallery. I was surprised to learn it is open Sunday afternoon. Frau Brimmer says it has the fourth largest art collection in Germany, which is reason enough to be in Cassel. To begin with, there are twenty-eight works by Rembrandt alone. There are also seventeen Van Dyck portraits.

I push along with my German lessons but the grammar is indeed difficult. It is not always easy to remember what you were going to say when you have to save the verb for the end. When I am
~~~~~~~~~~~~~~~~~~

discouraged, I tell myself that at the Conservatorium, the classes in music history and theory will be in German and I shall have to be able to follow. Then I shall be grateful, I am sure, that I had this summer to learn the language.

I practise for one hour in the morning and for two more in the afternoon. I continue with the scales and other exercises and I am reviewing the Bach *Gavotte* that I began to play last year. It is a good thing I am a violinist and can practise in my room. It must be difficult to find lodgings where you may have a piano. I do not miss the piano very much.

Kiss Birdie for me and the boys if they will bear it. They will be quite changed by the time I see them at Christmas. And a warm hug for dear Papa. I look forward to having a letter from him too.

~~~~~~~~~~~~~~~~

Hedwig Strasse, 7, Cassel

Wednesday, 26th July, 1891

Dear Birdie,

I was glad to have your letter, dear sister, and know that everyone is well.

I can scarcely believe it has already been one month that I have been studying with Herr Kaletch. He is old, probably over forty, and he is a big gentleman, but he has such a jolly, friendly smile. I think of him as Herr Cabbage, although I would not say that to Mama. I did not mention this before, but at the end of my first lessons, he said I was doing well enough with my left hand, but he wanted to make some adjustments to my bow hold. And then he asked if I minded if he moved my right hand into a better position. That made me a little uncomfortable and also the bow hold felt awkward at first, but I had to agree that it makes a better sound. I am making
~~~~~~~~~~~~~~~~

progress, I think, because last week he gave me a study book which will make a nice change from the scales and exercises. Herr Cabbage studied at the Conservatorium years ago and follows their traditions. He is optimistic that I shall pass the entrance examination in November, but says it will take a good deal of hard work for me to be truly ready.

The only difficulty here is that I do not know anyone my age. Frau Brimmer understood that and suggested I attend the English Church service which is held in a school room, a curious place to attend church, but it is a small congregation. Of course I was shy to go by myself, but the Pastor was very welcoming and it was so nice to hear English spoken. After the service, I lingered a little chatting with him and in short order a young woman joined us and the Pastor introduced us. Her name is Ellen Kramer and as we were walking in the same direction, we had time for a little conversation. Frau Kramer is also English but met her German husband two years ago whilst they were both on a tour of the Greek ruins. She has been married less than a year and is at least three years older than I am. I hope I may see her again.

I hope your holiday at the seaside brings fair weather with plenty of sunshine and perhaps an interesting young man?

~~~~~~~~~~~~~~~~~

Sunday 27th August, 1891

Dear Mama and Papa,

I was happy to hear you had a pleasant holiday at North Berwick and that it was not too crowded despite being so close to Edinburgh. As you say, with more and more people beginning to have an annual holiday, the seaside resorts may be filling up rather more than you would wish.

My goodness but it is warm here during the day. The roads are very dusty and dry, but the water carts rumble by every morning,
~~~~~~~~~~~~~~~~~

and damp them down. That works for a while, until the wind starts to blow in the afternoon. It is best to walk out in the morning.

I continue to go twice a week to Herr Kaletch who has lately begun to nag me about my posture. Mr. Waddell would mention this in passing, but for Herr K. it is very important that I stand in a certain way. Correct posture, he insists, is the basis of good playing. He has me walk around his room, violin clamped under my chin and just lightly supported by my thumb. At first I was sure I would drop it, but little by little, I have learned to trust the chin rest. We do this for a couple of minutes at the start of every lesson and I am to practise this exercise in my room as well. I am now holding the bow as he wishes and he is pleased that my bowing is generally as straight as it is since he gave me a little exercise which is mainly intended for beginners. As he constantly reminds me, sometimes one must take a step back in order to go forward. This is an up bow action where I am to follow through and "take off like a bird flying off the water." He allows though, that since I came to him, I am making a better sound. Even so, whenever I begin to play, the first notes are often scratchy and out of tune. He says, "Take a deep breath" and I begin again.

One of the curious customs here is the bowing, not the violin sort of bowing. I keep getting it mixed up. You know how at home a woman bows first when she meets an acquaintance in the street. Well, here it is just the opposite, and the man bows first. I keep thinking this is a bit forward of them, and then I remember. At times I forget how it is supposed to be, and bow first. I passed Herr Kaletch in the street the other day and duly bowed to him and he gave me such a look and then I remembered that I should have waited. Well, no matter really, I am sure I shall get used to it before long.

Fr. Kramer, the woman I met at church, invited me to call and I have done so three times now. It is so nice to speak English without fear of misunderstanding. She speaks German fluently and has quite settled into her life as a German Hausfrau, but there is small group of English-speakers here who gather when they can. They are not all exactly English, of course, but then perhaps, neither am I. It is difficult to explain to people that one was born in Ireland, lives in Scotland, but that one really is English. At tea the other day there were two American gentlemen who are learning the railway business. There is a large factory here where they build locomotives. And I met a very nice young man from Australia as well. He asked me if I was attending the church services, so perhaps I might see him again on Sunday.

I wait for the post every day and so enjoy receiving your news. If the boys would write too, that would be grand.

~~~~~~~~~~~~~~~~

Hedwigstrasse, 7, Cassel
Sunday, 17th September, 1891

Dear Mama,

Soon I shall be packing up and making my way to Leipsic. As you say, this is rather sooner than we had planned, but it is now definite that Frau Brimmer's mother must come to her as soon as possible. She cannot return to her village until she has completely recovered from the attack of pneumonia she suffered. Therefore, I must give up my room as soon as I can. I am not fussed at all about making the journey by myself.

Still, as Mr. Waddell himself said, one of the principal reasons to go to Leipsic is to hear wonderful music every day, something that is impossible in Edinburgh and unlikely in Cassel. And to be honest, I had always hoped to be in Leipsic for the music season. I just hope Fräul. Hohmann's aunt will be able to take me in earlier than we had originally intended.

I will admit that it has been lonely here at times despite the acquaintances I have made at the English Church and I shall be glad to be in a larger city and in the midst of student life even if I am not truly a part of it yet. You were right, of course, that it was better to
~~~~~~~~~~~~~~~~

start this adventure in a smaller place and to be taken into someone's home. I shall arrive in Leipsic with a modest ability in German and eager to get to work on preparing for my audition. I trust the arrangement with Fräul. Taylor is still firm and that I may start lessons with her as soon as I arrive? I must work steadily if I am to succeed at my examination.

~~~~~~~~~~~~~~~~~
~~~~~~~~~~~~~~~~~

Leipsic, Braustrasse 4

Braustrasse 4, Leipsic

3rd Oktober, 1891

Dear Birdie,

This is my first letter to you from Leipsic. I have dreamed of this day for many, many months. Altogether, the journey from Cassel was prettier than I thought it would be. I had been fussing a little about making the journey alone, but I reminded myself of Mrs. Campbell-Davidson's advice and indeed, there was nothing to worry about. After all, it is 1891, and young ladies are beginning to travel without chaperones all the time. Mama would probably not approve but I did speak from time to time – in German!! – with the other women in our carriage and that was helpful as they were able to point out matters of interest along the way.

At first the railway line followed the river but after the town of Eisenach we climbed through hilly wooded country. From time to time I caught glimpses of the mountains in the distance. There was one delightful moment when I espied three fairy tale castles all at once on top of three different mountains. Next came the large town of Erfurt with its two citadels and then on to famous Weimar, and after that we came to the flat land around Leipsic. This part of Germany is all connected by its rivers; all the towns seem to be built on a river, which is a new idea for me as I am so accustomed to living near the sea.

Here in Leipsic, the pupils have returned for the Michaelmas term and the streets are busy with their comings and goings. Of course I wish I were one of them, and attending the Conservatorium right now. You know I will have difficulty being patient, and already I feel rather left out of things. But then I think how presumptuous I am, for I may not even be accepted; I may not pass the entrance examination. I begin lessons with Miss Taylor tomorrow and I hope with her help, I will overcome my anxiety. One hears a surprising amount of English, by the way, as there are dozens of American and British pupils in this city.

Life at Fräulein Hohmann's pension is very different from the Brimmer household where I was almost treated as part of the family. Here at Braustrasse, the large flat is on the ground floor, so we do not have stairs to climb. There are five storeys in this building though, and I am grateful I am not on the fourth floor. Every morning we must say whether or not we shall be home for Mittagessen, and generally we meet for supper in the evening around eight o'clock.

You wanted to know all about my room? Well, it is the farthest from the main sitting room and therefore the quietest. It is very small and simply furnished, a sofa-bed, a small wash-stand, a nice table by the window and one straight chair and one more cozy chair. There is a high green tiled stove in the corner which has not been lit yet, but Fräul. H assured me the servant will look after that for me. These stoves are a wonder; I'm told that they stay warm all day and night with very little fuel. On the floor are a few small rugs, but because the apartment is a Parterrewohnung – a ground floor flat – the floor is chilly.

The concert season begins in a fortnight and there will be concerts at the Gewandhaus every Thursday evening. Tickets a little dear, but the great thing is that the Wednesday morning rehearsal is open to the public and of course all the students flock to these rehearsals to hear the symphonies and the solo musicians. Tickets for the Prabe – the rehearsal – are only 50 pfennigs.

Then there are the Philharmonic concerts and student recitals and oratorios and cantatas. There will be opera companies visiting from time to time and those performances begin at 6:00 or 6:30 so there is time afterwards to meet and talk about the music. I shall need to ration my concert going. Fräul. Hohmann – my teacher, not my landlady – told me often how important it is to hear all kinds of music. Every student, she said, must attend a concert once or twice each week.

The city itself is old; its ancient walls were replaced only forty or so years ago by broad promenades which circle the old town, which in German is the Innere Stadt. However, the streets of the musik viertel – the music quarter – are in a newer part and laid out in straight lines, like New Town in a way. They have musical names, like Mozartstrasse, Haydenstrasse, Beethovenstrasse and so on. These pretty avenues are lined with grassy boulevards and young trees which over the years will no doubt grow tall and shady. The Conservatorium building is but four years old and very handsome.

I sent a birthday card to you separately. It was in German of course, but I hope you liked it. Did you do anything special to celebrate? I mentioned to Fräul H. that it was my sister's 18th birthday and she laughed and said, "I hope you do not do in Scotland what happens sometimes in Germany, that you break an egg over the head of someone who is turning eighteen!"

~~~~~~~~~~~~~~~~~
~~~~~~~~~~~~~~~~~

Imagining Violet

Braustrasse 4, Leipzig

Sunday, 16th October, 1891

Dear Mama and Papa,

I hope Birdie has shared her letter with you and that my last postcard reached you. I shall not repeat all that I wrote about my pension. I have learned that in Germany this city is spelled Leipzig, so I shall use that spelling from now on.

The date is fixed for my examination! It will be on the tenth of November which is less than one month from now. I shall have to do nothing but practise if I am to pass and even so, I may not succeed. I do not know what I shall do if I fail.

My tutor, Miss Taylor, is very plain spoken. She is a dedicated student who says proudly that she never visits cafés or mixes with the Anglo-American students. We shall meet twice a week for the next month. Apparently it is the usual thing for senior pupils like Miss Taylor to tutor younger ones. This is how she can gain some experience of teaching since mostly everyone who graduates from the Conservatorium goes on to teach at some time.

I am working hard on my audition pieces, and Miss Taylor has already made several suggestions for small changes. Fräul. Hohmann told me that I must not be disappointed if Herr Sitt puts me off until the start of Easter term which is when the new courses usually begin. And because I am not yet seventeen, she says I should not be in a hurry. In any case, Herr Sitt is very famous and of course only teaches the most senior students. Mr. Waddell's letter of introduction was flattering and I hope that might help my case. I hope I do not disappoint.

I assure you that Fräul. Hohmann is very strict with us here at Braustrasse, as I know you would wish it to be. You must not worry. The house is comfortable enough and I feel cosy in my small chamber. I shall have to be very tidy indeed if I am going to have room to work on my drawing. My window faces north and that is a good light for drawing, I believe. Whilst I practise, I confess I am often distracted looking down at the street where there is a good deal of traffic with carts and carriages rattling along all the time. In the evening, Fräul Hohmann's large sitting room is always welcoming and warm with a fire on chilly nights in the big porcelain stove in the corner. I must say these stoves are a brilliant invention and we should have them at home. There is no smoke and no dirty ash and they simply radiate heat all through the room.

There are three other young ladies besides myself in our pension. Miss Lily Foster is a friendly English girl in her second year of piano studies. Her home is London and I hope she may become a friend. Miss Annabelle Donaldson hails from Boston. She is over twenty and has been here three years and like Miss Foster, she is studying piano. Fräulein Frieda Hilz, who studies voice, comes from Hamburg and is living in our pension in order to practise her English. Sometimes we three English speakers try to have a "German" supper, but we rarely get through the meal without lapsing into English.

I hope you will not object, but I have decided that I shall try out the different church services that are conducted in English. Miss Foster prefers the All Saints Church, but I am curious to attend service at the American Church as well as the English services at the Alte Thomas Schule. If I feel very adventurous, I may go to the Union Evangelical Church as well.

I have found a new tutor for German lessons thanks to my landlady's help. She is accustomed to having English-speaking boarders, so it should be no surprise that she could recommend someone. She sent me to meet one gentleman who did not have time for me, but then he sent me along to someone I think I shall like much better, a young man by the name of Herr Joseph Schneider who is a student at the university. I had my first lesson with him last week and I believe I am going to make very good progress. He takes an interesting approach to our lessons, escorting me on pleasant walks around the city. He teaches me the names of places and things and asks simple questions which I must answer in German. It is a great deal nicer than conjugating verbs with old Herr G.

I shall tell you a little more about Leipzig, and you can tell the boys if they are interested in what their big sister is doing so far away from home. It is not a very big city, but it seems always to be busy in the streets. Like Edinburgh, the old quarter has many cobbled narrow lanes and winding passages. There is also a splendid wide ring road that was built when the walls were taken down in 1840 and it is always chancy, crossing over into the Innere Stadt. Around the Ring are many squares, or Platz, with cafés, hotels, restaurants. And there are canals here and there where one can watch the ducks. The new Conservatorium is in a newer section of the city with straight broad streets. It is a large and impressive building with a concert hall of its own. When I imagine that one day I might be playing in that hall, well I get goosebumps.

The large Johanna Park is close by with its grassy meadows and ponds and woods and paths all around. The trees are attractive and well cared for and one can ramble about for an hour. Fräul. H. discourages us from going out alone, but I am sure it is safe to do so. One sees many young ladies walking about on their own here. The atmosphere is less restrictive than at home which I like very much.

It has been some time since I had a letter from Margaret or Annie or Catherine, although I confess I was slow to reply to their last letters. I hope they are well, and should you happen to see them, greet them for me.

~~~~~~~~~~~~~~~~
~~~~~~~~~~~~~~~~

Imagining Violet

Friday, October 27th, 1891

Braustrasse 4, Leipzig

Dear Birdie,

Did the boys like the picture postcard I sent? They are a new thing here and one may purchase them at the post office. Are they permitted in England yet?

The music season has begun and there is suddenly too much to do. We dress one or two evenings a week and at this rate I wonder if my blue silk will last the winter as I am wearing it so often. Dare I ask Mama to send a nice length of material for a new evening frock? I would be content with benzaline, especially if it were a pretty lilac shade or pale green. Fräul. H. has a dressmaker who could run up a gown for me at not too great a cost, and I could do the trimming myself. Fräul. H. has a solution for everything; it is quite wonderful.

And then there is all the trouble of putting up one's hair. At first, I admit, I was trying to look older and I began putting my hair up before society required it. Lately I have been getting lazy, reminding myself that I am not obliged to put it all the way up until I am eighteen. So most days, I pull it back neatly in a ribbon. But for an evening out, it's pins and combs, and Lily and I help each other.

I should tell you about Sundays here. Do you remember how dull and dour we found Sundays in Leith when we were first there, compared to Suffolk? Thank goodness Mama and Papa did not adopt Scottish customs. I had friends at school who were not allowed to do anything on a Sunday except go to church, attend Sunday School, read an improving book or go for a walk. We are used to everything being closed on Sunday, aren't we?

Well, Birdie, here it is not like that at all. The cafés in the squares and in the parks are all open and thronged with people. There is a village called Connewitz about four miles down the river which seems to be a popular destination for Sunday boating and in winter the river will freeze over and people will skate there .

Life here is different in many little ways. The way Fräul. Hohmann keeps house for instance. She is constantly cleaning and washing and is proud of her spotless table. The Germans seem even more thrifty than the Scots. The other day I went into the kitchen to ask for a candle and found her stirring a large pot at the stove. To be friendly, I asked "What kind of soup are you making?" To my astonishment she answered that she was boiling up the potato peelings from the past few days to make starch for the linen. Can you imagine Mama going to such lengths?

The Conservatorium public practice evenings – we call them "Abends" for short – have begun, and I went with Lily on Friday last and my goodness how well the musicians played. First the young men play and then the young ladies. Of the ladies in our pension, Miss Donaldson has been here the longest and she has already performed at two Abends. It is thrilling to hear so much music, so many composers I do not know. The "moderns" are very much in favour with the pupils. I made a sketch of the concert hall for you, so you may imagine me performing there one day.

It was funny to see one older gentleman – I found out later that he is the Director – who nodded off during each performance. He would wake up in time to clap his hands in approval, read about the next number in the programme, then relapse into sweet slumber. After the performance, we went to a café on the RossPlatz.

I hope I shall be good enough to play at an Abend once I am enrolled in the Conservatorium. At that first Abend we heard a violin sonata by Henryk Wieniawski – you will not know him – which was so dramatic and stirred up the emotions so that my heart was thumping. Oh how I wish I could play something like that, or at least begin to learn it, but for the time being I keep to my scales and studies and my audition pieces.

We have been to our first Gewandhaus Orchestra concert in the grand concert hall. It is all upholstered with plush seats and is all sparkly with vast chandeliers of electric lights which light up the whole huge hall magically. I wonder if some day there will be electric lights in our homes? I was surprised to find that ladies here do not wear hats to the theatre. The programme was very long, with several vocal numbers. We had paid for standing room and were rather tired out by the end of it.

The day before we had attended the public rehearsal, which all the students attend faithfully. I cannot describe how thrilling it was to listen to Herr Adolf Brodsky perform the Brahms *Violin Concerto*. It is the most wonderful piece of music I have ever heard. Miss Taylor told me that Herr Brodsky is friendly with the great Brahms. I should write about the rest of the concert, but it is late. When I recollect how we attempted to play the Beethoven *C Minor Symphony* at Waddells, I blush.

I like my new tutor, Herr Schneider, very much. He is rather good-looking with light blond hair, bright blue eyes, and a ready smile. He is also very tall and a good companion for our walks through the old city during our lessons.

For myself, I scarcely stop to eat, I am practising so much. I try not to worry, but it is difficult to get to sleep some nights.

~~~~~~~~~~~~~~~~~~

10th November 1891

My own dear Mama,

I have had my examination! I played for Herr Sitt today and my goodness, I was all aflutter. My mouth was so dry I could scarcely speak and I was even a little lightheaded. I think he could tell what a state I was in and he was only a little gruff with me.

We began with scales and then the Schradieck études I have been learning since the summer. At first my playing was harsh and scratchy which is always upsetting. Then I played the Bach, and finally the Seitz and that was all right. The Master only nodded and said "sehr schön" a few times.

By the time I finished playing, my heart was not beating so fast, and when he asked about my education and theory studies, I was able to answer correctly. Of course all of this was auf Deutsch, but I understood most of it, I think. At the end he declared, "Fräulein Courtenaye, I believe you will be ready for us by Easter." As I came
~~~~~~~~~~~~~~~~~~

out of the Conservatorium I did a little dance on the pavement, probably amusing the passersby. I will sleep well tonight.

I asked Fräul. Hohmann why he had inquired about my schooling. It seems that there is a requirement that foreign students have a general school education and familiarity with normal classroom procedures. She explained that many young ladies come from England and America who have never been inside a school room. They are not always rejected, but it is a serious disadvantage. What a good thing that I spent three years at St. George's.

As you know, I had hoped to be allowed to enrol in January, but I suppose it is for my own good that I have another three months to study German and to continue with violin lessons. I am disappointed, but not desperately so. Generally the Conservatorium year proper begins after Easter and hardly anyone starts in January.

I am not feeling at all well, Mama, so this will be a short letter. I shall write again soon.

~~~~~~~~~~~~~~~~~

19th November, 1891

Dear Mama,

Right after my examination, I came down with a beastly cold which has kept me indoors for a few days. As well it has been damp and drizzly. I am still somewhat seedy, but by the time you receive this, I am sure I shall be completely recovered. Fräul. H. had cautioned me not to overdo the practising but perhaps I did too much during the past few weeks. She kindly gave me chamomile tea and that has helped me to sleep, but I surely missed my dear Mama. Chamomile tea seems to be a favourite remedy here. Herr Schneider has kindly come to the pension so we could continue our lessons. He truly is very charming and very nice and helpful and I enjoy my lessons with him very much and I am sure I am making great progress with my German.
~~~~~~~~~~~~~~~~~

Imagining Violet

I am grateful that Papa has agreed I may look for a new violin but I shall not be in a hurry. Fräul. Taylor said I should take the time to find an instrument that I love. And it need not be the most expensive one; that is the best part.

Herr Sitt has arranged for me to take lessons from Miss Bessie Doyle who has nearly finished her work here and has been tutoring for some months now. Lily and I heard her play some tremendously difficult *Caprices* by Paganini at an Abend and it was marvellous. She is from Australia and is so talented and pretty and such a wonderful performer and dresses beautifully. I doubt that I shall ever be able to give myself so completely to the music as she does, swaying and bending and enjoying herself so much. Miss Doyle has already toured all over Europe with Herr Sitt and she has yet to graduate from the Conservatorium. And she won the coveted Mendelssohn Prize a few years ago when she was only fifteen.

Now that it is getting dark early our explorations of the old city take place on Sunday afternoon. Miss Foster is familiar with the Innere Stadt and happily she is willing to be my guide. But even she gets lost sometimes in the narrow winding streets and passages. Fortunately her German is better than mine. The other day we went as far as the Thomaskirche on the far side of the old city. It is an impressive building and very old. It was built in 1212, although there have been many changes over the centuries. I tried to read the pamphlet in German but it was too difficult. But I have sent a post card.

We sat for a while inside and tried to imagine Herr Bach at the organ. Probably this is not the same organ that he played, but nevertheless, we enjoyed imagining him playing it and we agreed we could hear in our minds his wonderful music.

As you likely know, Mama, Bach was musical director here for many years so we felt we should visit his grave which is in the choir of the church. And out in the platz there is a wonderful statue of him put there by Felix Mendelssohn back in 1843. We did not leave the kirche through the same door by which we had entered, and when we emerged we did not know where we were. Lily was able to ask, "Wo ist die Hochschule für Musik, bitte?" A helpful Frau pointed us in the right direction and thus we found our way home.

Living in a German pension, I am always learning something new. For instance, the proper German hausfrau never spends money on anything she can make or grow herself. Did Birdie tell you about the potato peelings being boiled for starch? Convenience is not regarded as a reason to cut corners, nor is it done to buy from the shops that which you can make at home. I do not think I would be a success as a German hausfrau.

As you suggested, I have arranged to begin drawing lessons on the 24th inst. with Herr Martin Falonisch. I have been away for six months now and it feels much longer. I am grateful that it is possible for me to return home this Christmas.

~~~~~~~~~~~~~~~~~~

~~~~~~~~~~~~~~~~~~

Imagining Violet

2nd December, 1891

Braustrasse 4,

My own dear Mama,

Thank you for the dress goods which arrived earlier this week. What a pretty shade of pale green. The dressmaker has already started on the frock and I shall go for a fitting before I leave to come home. It will be very nice to have a choice of gowns to wear to all the concerts we attend.

The Christmas markets are beautiful and merry and not like anything I have ever seen. All around the large Marktplatz in the middle of the Innere Stadt people have set up wooden stalls where they sell such lovely things. I have purchased a few small gifts to bring with me but I shall not tell you what they are. The country people come into the city with their wares and there are many stalls offering delicious warm baked goods. I especially like the Lebkuchen which are very tasty ginger biscuits and the Glühwein, which is spicy and warm and so delicious. Christmas decorations are everywhere.

We go every week to the Gewandhaus public rehearsal. To hear such glorious symphonic music every single week is truly wonderful. In Edinburgh we have little opportunity to hear good music and of course that is one of the reasons Mr. Waddell encouraged you and dear Papa to send me to Germany even though I am only sixteen.

Now that the weather is poor, we have given up long Sunday walks in the parks and city. Our most recent expedition was to the fine art museum, die Bilderkunste Museum. I have sent the boys a postcard of it. Miss Foster and I went Sunday afternoon when admission is free! See how practical we are. The gallery has mostly modern work and I am not sure you would like it. There are several large and dramatic paintings of mountains and gorges by a Swiss painter named Alexandre Callamé. The images are fierce, almost threatening and you feel you could almost be swallowed up in them. There is nothing at all like them in our Edinburgh gallery.

We dutifully admired the two Murillos and they also have a small self-portrait by Rembrandt which is very good. Having had the opportunity to view so many Rembrandts in the gallery in Cassel, I was especially interested to see a self-portrait. One of the famous treasures of the gallery is a huge painting called *Germania.* It is of a large lady who supposedly symbolizes the German nation. I keep forgetting that Germany has only been a proper country for about twenty years.

There was a helpful guide who spoke some English and told us that M. Callamé is of the Düsseldorf School, which is a group of painters who favour 'plein air' painting which means painting out of doors right at the scene. I should like to try that.

Since I last wrote I have had a few lessons with Miss Doyle. And what an experience it was. She is but a year or two older than I am, but goodness me, I felt quite the shy young miss and stumbled badly when I first began to play. She started right in to correct or change all manner of things, the way I stand, how I hold the bow, how I hold my head. Truly, it is impossible to alter all these things at once. She is keen for me to start with a more modern piece and that will make a nice change. I like her, I think, but at the same time, I am a little afraid of her.

Our plans for Christmas are settled. Lily and I shall travel together as far as London and I am invited to spend the night at her family's home in South Kensington. Then I shall take the morning train to Edinburgh and will reach you on the 21st. Lily wants to leave before the end of term as her mother is not well and Lily is anxious to get home. Last year she did not go home at the Christmas holiday as it is a great deal of travelling and of course an expense. Very likely I shall have to make the return trip by myself.

~~~~~~~~~~~~~~~~
~~~~~~~~~~~~~~~~

10th December, 1891

Dear Birdie

Is it horrid of me to say I am not brokenhearted that my time with Miss Doyle was so brief? Honestly, I do not think she will make a good teacher; she is so full of herself. She did not seem much interested in a young girl from Scotland and spent most of our lesson time showing me how she would play such and such a phrase. As it was an étude by Reinecke we were working on – a very conservative étude – her flourishes and embellishments were rather extraordinary. It seems to me she would rather be on a platform, not stuck in a wee practice room. She certainly has the gumption and energy to go along with the talent and ambition.

Still, I was quite taken aback when she announced that she would be leaving Leipzig within the week to go on a tour of Germany. Possibly Herr Sitt expected this, as he was quick to tell me that he has already arranged for a new tutor. She is Canadian and her name is Evelyn Street. Her family live in Toronto, where her father is a high court judge and she's ever so nice.

My goodness but it is cold here, ever so much colder than Leith. The ponds in the Johanna Park are already frozen and "bearing" as they say, and crowded with children and students skating every day. It looks like such fun! At home we never get the chance to skate, do we, because the lochs do not always freeze hard enough. I may be able to hire skates and I want to attempt it as soon as I can. Herr Schneider assures me it is not difficult to learn; he has even offered to combine a skating lesson with our German lesson. He is so patient with me that I think it would be jolly nice to learn to skate with his help. He gives me two German lessons a week and we often seem to go past my allotted time.

Please do not tell Mama, but I am thoroughly tired of Fräul. Hohmann's perpetual stew. There is scarcely any meat in it, just potatoes, onions, cabbage and carrots. Thank goodness that Papa pays the extra charge that allows me an egg a few times a week.

I am looking forward to Christmas at home especially as it will be my last Christmas with you for a few years. I feel I have been away for such a long time. I have not wished to whine or complain, but I miss you all very much and am grateful that I may come home even if it is only for a short visit. Next year when I am enrolled at the Con, I shall have only the usual eight day break. It is getting very cold here and I am a wee bit homesick.

~~~~~~~~~~~~~~~~~

13 January, 1892

Very dear Mama,

One week ago I reached seventeen years and here there is not one person who knows it. I might have told Lily but I was shy to do so. I did not open my gift, for which I thank you, until the day, but it was not easy to wait. A pair of opera glasses all my own is a wonderful present. And goodness knows I need the dictionary. Seventeen is not a very important birthday, yet I wish I could have stayed with you until the 7th inst, but Lily had to be back for the
~~~~~~~~~~~~~~~~~

beginning of term a few days ago. And I was happy and I dare say you were too, that I was not travelling alone.

The Registrar of the Conservatorium asked me to come to the office this morning to tell me he had received your telegram giving permission for me to enrol. Many thanks for sending it so speedily. It means I shall be allowed to register for Easter term.

It was wonderful to be at home for Christmas and New Year's. It was grand to see the boys who grow bigger all the time, but are just as mischievous as ever. They still think it is a good joke to apple-pie my bed and now I laugh with them instead of getting annoyed. And I am very thankful that our family celebrates an English Christmas with a tree and a proper Christmas dinner. The caroling was enjoyable and a pleasant way to spend some time with old school friends, but it was too bad Birdie was not well enough to come out with us. It is a worry, that she feels so poorly so much of the time. The Germans make quite a fuss over Christmas, so different from the Scots. They are sure that they celebrate better than anyone.

Our return journey went well enough without any unpleasant incidents. The crossing was rather choppy and we arrived a little late, so had to hurry to make our train in Flushing. But once aboard, we could settle down for the long journey to Berlin. The countryside looked very pretty all covered with snow.

I was telling Miss Donaldson, the American who is in our boarding house, about how tiresome it is managing one's luggage on a long journey and she told me that in America there is no trouble at all with luggage, as the express office wagon comes right to your home, collects your trunks and boxes, gives you a duplicate check and that's the last you see of your things until you arrive at your destination. Then within an hour of your arrival, along comes the express wagon with your luggage delivered to your door. I must say that sounds ever so much easier than here. Just fancy if my boxes could be taken away in Leith and magically arrive at our pension just days later.

Oh how wish I was starting at the Conservatorium now as I see the pupils arriving back for the start of term. I know I shall be busy with German lessons and violin lessons with Miss Street and drawing lessons but I am still on the outside.

You will enjoy this, Mama, another sample of how I go on learning to live in a German household. Fräul. H. has these pretty embroidered towels, known as “überhandtucher”, roughly translated as over-hand towels, which are used all over the house to cover things, even other towels sometimes, like tea towels, or to conceal corners containing brooms and mops. I found this out the hard way when I went to dry my hands on one and metaphorically got my wrist slapped. “Was machts du, Fräulein?” she asked impatiently. And then she said I must never ever use these towels, as towels. I apologized as abjectly as I could, given that I was trying so hard to stifle a laugh.

Thank you again for the pocket dictionary. I dare not leave home without my Chamber’s.

~~~~~~~~~~~~~~~~

Braustrasse 4, Leipzig

Tuesday, 26th January, 1892

Dear Birdie,

I hope you are feeling better and can keep warm through the chilly nights. Will Papa let you have a fire in your room? My little room is cozy indeed with its own tiled stove, which stays warm for ever so long. Good for you, keeping on with your history studies. Sitting in on the lectures could be quite satisfying, I expect.

I believe I shall get on very well with my new tutor, Miss Street. I played my examination piece for her; then she showed me how she would play it, with little crescendos before the ends of a phrase and I tried it and my goodness the piece suddenly made more
~~~~~~~~~~~~~~~~

sense. She said that I must think beyond the notes to the story the music is telling. She also speaks about her family and her life in Toronto. People in Canada do not seem to be as fussed about matters of class and manners. In the new world, old fashioned ways have partly given way, and women seem to have more choices. They can even become musicians if they want to! Miss Street will return to Canada in the summer and she is definitely planning to perform in public. It is heartening to know that such a thing is possible. It allows me to dream.

I am glad now that I was not with Miss Doyle for long, so that her ways did not become mine. Miss Street has also been working on how I hold the bow, but she says I do not need to grip it so intensely and I must break the habit of pressing with my little finger. I do not mind her manipulating my fingers, trying to get them into the right position. I was uncomfortable with Herr Cabbage doing that and I suppose I never did get it right.

The whole business of formal manners does become tiresome. Do you agree? I think it would be wonderful if one did not have to worry about being introduced before speaking to a person, especially to a young man. Here is an example of what I mean. Lily and I and Miss Donaldson were taking coffee in a café the other afternoon. At the table next to us, there were two respectable young men, speaking English, and one of them is in Lily's music history class, but as she has not been introduced to him of course we could not speak to them nor would they dare to address us. Miss Donaldson thinks our concerns are exaggerated, even ridiculous. In America, people are not so formal and stuffy. She says that after two years at the Con, if she meets someone in the street whom she recognizes from a class, she simply says hello and even shakes hands straightaway. That seems very sensible to me, the saying hello part at least but perhaps not the shaking hands right off.

Another thing about the cafés is you see so many young men smoking cigarettes. And one day last week, we saw a young lady smoking as well!!! It seems very unladylike to me though, and besides that it must make your fingers smell and probably your hair and clothes too. Still, I wonder what it's like.

I have had four lovely skating lessons with my nice German tutor on the ponds in the Johanna Park. I hope Mama does not object that I accepted his invitation as he is such a pleasant and polite young gentleman. The ponds are busy and crowded later in the day so we go before dinnertime when it does not seem so frantic.

One can easily rent skates for a few pennies, and the management will also rent a beginner a chair to push along the ice. The ice is as slippery as you might imagine and I took a few tumbles on my first attempt. But kind Herr S. was there to give me hand up.

Of course we are supposed to be speaking German all the time but when I take a sudden tumble all the German vanishes in an instant.

~~~~~~~~~~~~~~~~~

Sunday, 21st February, 1892

My dear Mama,

Sunday evening is such a good time for writing letters. But what can I write about as this icy cold German winter goes on and on. Perhaps I should try harder to describe the amazing Gewandhaus which we attend every week. And I shall also attempt a small sketch which will probably convey more than my poor words can. I wrote earlier about the plush seats and the brilliant electric lights. The grand foyer is also lavish. That is where the audience promenades up and down at the intervals walking about in twos and threes. The foyer has handsome marble pillars and busts of the great musicians. The floors are inlaid and highly polished, the staircases are very grand and even the garde robe is imposing. Everyone leaves their cloaks at the garde robe and the staff has an amazing ability to fetch them all out in minutes after the performance.
~~~~~~~~~~~~~~~~~

Imagining Violet

I have had some drawing lessons now from Herr Falensch and I realize how much I have missed it. We mostly work with pencil and charcoal but I hope to work in water colour soon. You may remember that I tried my hand at watercolour at home with dismal results. My drawing lessons are held in the new Academy for Visual Arts which is just across from the Conservatorium. I should write "Conservatory" as that is what they say here.

Aside from an occasional hour on the pond with Herr Schneider, it is too cold to go exploring in the old town. I should be visiting the violin shops, but I think that will have to keep until spring. Lily and I have made a few more Sunday afternoon visits to the Art Museum and always stop to gaze at our favourite paintings of the Swiss mountains.

Snow has covered the streets for a few weeks now, but people get around on horse-drawn sleighs which are delightful with their tinkling sleigh bells. When it is very cold, the stoves in our rooms scarcely keep up and I shiver through my morning practice. In the evening we all spend more time in the general sitting room huddled up in robes, reading and talking or sometimes playing duets. A gentleman friend of Fräulein Hilz comes to visit her some evenings. She is from Hamburg but chose this English pension so that she is obliged to speak English. Her friend is also interested to practise English and so he asks Miss Donaldson to talk about Boston and I must tell him about Edinburgh.

An important part of the conservatory calendar is upon us, a set of concerts which are the Prüfungs or examinations, although they are in fact the public performances of some of the best graduating pupils. The concert hall of the Conservatory is packed with family and friends and every pupil strives to play something brilliantly. The crowds wait for an hour before the doors open at half past five, and then everyone rushes in to get the best seats. These are in the front row of the gallery that runs all round the concert salon. Everyone from our pension attends together which is very jolly.

We have been going to the Anglo-American church most Sundays, Mama; please do not worry. There has not been anything very interesting to say about it, and that is why I had not mentioned it.

One thing the Scottish have in common with the Germans: extreme thrift is seen as a virtue. Well, I am not really a Scot, and I am not always as thrifty as I might be. Fräul H. saw me putting marmalade and butter on my toast at breakfast the other day and scolded me for being so extravagant. So you see, I am not falling into many bad habits here.

~~~~~~~~~~~~~~~~~

Braustrasse 4, Leipzig

Sunday, 27th March, 1892

Dear Mama and Papa,

At long last we are seeing a few signs of spring. First though, the snow turned to horrible wet slush and one's feet were forever wet. But now the snow has all melted away. Skating is finished for this year but on our last outing I did rather better. Herr Schneider has been a patient skating teacher, I must say. Next year I hope to be able to skate all the way to Connewitz. For now, Herr Schneider and I have resumed our German lessons whilst walking around the city. I
~~~~~~~~~~~~~~~~~

am sure I am learning a great deal of the language. Last week he took me to a café for chocolate after my lesson.

The Germans love Easter and Easter weekend will be a long holiday and the Conservatory will be closed for eight days. In the shop windows one sees the prettiest decorations; they call them Easter Egg trees. These are not real trees but rather they are branches placed in vases and hung with fancy painted eggs. At first I was not sure if they were real eggs, raw or boiled, or if they were made of wood or what. But they make a lovely sight with all the bright colours. Grey old Edinburgh could learn from Leipzig.

The egg trees are everywhere, not just in shop windows. A few of the smaller trees in the Markt square are also decorated with dozens of eggs hanging from the branches, rather like Christmas baubles. At the Easter market there are flower stalls and other booths with all manner of Easter decorations and chocolate in the shape of bunnies. And there are children's shows too. The Punch and Judy show was the funniest I have ever seen.

I wrote a few weeks ago about some of the concerts I have been to, but one last week at the Gewandhaus was truly remarkable. The conductor was the composer Richard Strauss himself. He composes pieces he calls tone poems which seek to tell a story in music. The music was thrilling, especially Strauss' own *Tod und Verklarung*. In English the title means Death and Transfiguration and it tells the story of an artist who is dying and looking back on his life, his childhood and so on. I tried to follow the program notes in German but it was all more than I could take in on a first hearing.

We have been going regularly to the Prüfungs. The most exciting has been Miss Street's. She played a concerto by the French composer Charles de Beriot accompanied by the student orchestra, which must have been exciting for her as the rest of the time the orchestral parts are played by a pianist. I have learned a great deal from Miss Street who will be here until July but after I begin at the Conservatory next month I shall not need to take lessons from her any longer which in a way is too bad as I like her very much and she has been very helpful. Perhaps it is easier to learn from someone closer to one's own age.

She has told me much about Toronto where in winter there is usually a great deal of snow but she insists it is not as bitterly cold as it has been here in Leipzig. It sounds as if Canada is a place where young women are not so constrained by convention and people are more friendly. She does not concern herself very much with matters of class, whether someone is appropriate to befriend or not. Understandably she is eager to return home. She has been a little grumpy with me lately, and now I think I know why. Her parents had intended to come from Canada for her Prüfung, but her father, who is a judge, was not able to leave for so long a journey and her mother did not wish to travel alone. I am glad that you and Edinburgh are just a few days distant as I cannot imagine being as far away from home as Miss Street is.

Now that the weather has improved, there are many young people riding about on bicycles, and indeed there are just as many young ladies riding as young men. I do not suppose one could manage one's German lessons whilst riding a bicycle though. As the land is flat it would be easier getting about to the parks and such rather than on foot and less expensively than by bus. If I can find a way to hire one, perhaps I shall have a go.

There is also a wonderful zoo here and Lily and I will make an excursion there one day soon. Fräul. H. tells us there is a kind of charabanc or excursion bus that leaves from the Central Station on a Saturday morning, returning to the city in the afternoon. The weather is so fine, one wants to be out of doors as much as possible.

~~~~~~~~~~~~~~~~~
~~~~~~~~~~~~~~~~~

Imagining Violet

Braustrasse 4, Leipzig

Wednesday, 6th April, 1892

Dear Birdie,

I wrote to Mama about the wonderful Easter trees in the shop windows, but for you I saved the tale of how Lily and I helped Fräul Hohmann make one for our sitting room. A few weeks ago, she asked if we would care to help her by blowing the eggs. We had no idea what she meant by that but nevertheless we said were willing to try. On Saturday afternoon, after classes were over, Lily, Miss Donaldson and I sat down at the kitchen table in front of a large bowl of raw eggs. Miss Donaldson was sceptical about the whole exercise, especially when Fräul H. showed us how to poke a wee hole in each end of an egg. Well, we did try, Birdie, but goodness,what a mess! Talk about scrambled eggs. On my first go, I crushed the egg in my hand I was gripping it so tightly. The second attempt was more successful and the egg survived. Lily fared a little better than I, but she too crumpled one of her eggs. Finally we figured it out and produced half a dozen or more ready to decorate.

After we washed and dried those precious objects we got down to painting them and I was ever so much more at ease with a paint brush in my hand. In the end we had made ten lovely eggs for "our" Easter tree. We poked a bit of string in the holes to hang them on the branches Fräul. H. had brought indoors and then she unwrapped another dozen eggs which she had carefully saved from other years. Guess what we had for our supper that night! All along the street now, people have Easter trees in their front windows and it surely is a cheerful sight. As we are on the ground floor, ours is very visible and we can point to it with pride when we pass by with friends.

I hope, dear Birdie, that you are not as poorly as you were when you last wrote, and that you can get out and enjoy the spring weather that surely has come to Leith by now. Did you see the doctor this time? Perhaps you need to take more fresh air and to spend less time in the library with your history books. But I doubt you will listen to a younger sister's advice.

Have you and Mama attended any good concerts this winter? I know there is not a great deal of symphonic music to be heard in Edinburgh, but Mama has not written a word about it and I would like to know. Perhaps you will go to the Waddel School recitals and tell me about them.

My German lessons continue, but now that skating is over for the season, my nice tutor Herr Schneider has somehow become more formal. When we see him with his friends in the cafés he nods a greeting, but he no longer suggests that we sit down with him for a chocolate. I admit I am a little disappointed as I thought we had started to become friends over the winter, and now I am confused.

~~~~~~~~~~~~~~~~~

Braustrasse 4, Leipzig

Sunday, 24th April,1892

Dear Mama und Papa,

We went to the English church this morning, dear Mama, and it was a very nice service. One sees all the American students at the English church; it is amazing how numerous they are.

I have held on to the dream of being a real pupil at the Conservatory for so long it is hard to believe that finally, after all these months, the great day has arrived. Classes began immediately after Easter and it has all been a little overwhelming. Even though I have been in Germany for almost a year, I still pinch myself that I am really enrolled.

This term marks the beginning of the Conservatory year and new classes have begun in theory and other subjects. We have classes from Monday to Thursday and on Saturday but for some reason there are no classes on Friday. As a new pupil, I have a one hour violin class four days a week, as well as a piano lesson twice a week. With that many classes I should improve quickly, don't you
~~~~~~~~~~~~~~~~~

think? I also have a class in Italian, but that is mostly to learn musical terms. Our theory classes are taught in English for which I am very grateful. Practice pianos are readily available; one signs up for an hour's practice here and there; thank goodness I am not obliged to hire a piano. Where on earth would I put it? In the Conservatory, the women are taught separately from the men, but at the university which is where the music history classes are held, I do not know how it is done.

I shall describe our violin class. We begin by playing all together some warm up exercises. Our master, Herr Rüther, assigns a new study at our Monday class which we sight read, each taking a turn. We have started with the studies of Violin Master Sitt. Herr R. spends a few minutes with each pupil and it is helpful to hear how the others get on. There are four in my class, two older German girls and one American girl who is even younger than I. Herr R. tells us why he has given us this piece and we go away to practise it. It is a different way to study after this year of private tutoring, so it will take some getting used to.

I practise scales and arpeggios and trills and double stops for hours on end, as well as the new study. The Conservatory is very strict about this. When the teacher agrees that I am sufficiently proficient in all these exercises and studies, I shall move on to pieces. My aching right shoulder is a little better, thank you, since Miss Street suggested I take a short rest every quarter of an hour and walk around a little. Last summer Herr Kaletsch kept telling me I must try to be more "entspannter", to be more relaxed and not to be so stiff with my arm and my wrist.

I have not had much chance to play the piano for most of this year so I must work a little harder at technique at the moment.

Last week Lily and I went to one or two of the violin shops but there is so much to look at and try, that I could not make up my mind. I shall have to devote more time to this or I shall never have a new violin.

Well now you have a good idea of what I am doing. I hope the boys are working as hard in their school as I am with my music. It would be nice if they would write to me once in a while. I do not want them to forget me. And please tell me honestly how Birdie is, as I am sure she will always say she is just fine. I wish I knew just what was ailing her but there does not seem to be a simple answer to that.

Please write about the music you have heard in Edinburgh this season. I want to know what I am missing.

~~~~~~~~~~~~~~~~~~

Braustrasse 4, Leipzig

30th May, 1892

Dear Mama und Papa,

I hope you are enjoying your walks on the Links now that it has stopped raining. Have you begun to think about your holiday yet?

I do not think I told you about my favourite class which is Ensemble Class on Wednesday afternoon. At this time I am only permitted to listen as the pupils play their trios and quartettes, but it inspires me to practise more so that one day I may take part in these classes. And perhaps one day, I might be able to join a real orchestra.

There was an important event here the other day when a new statue of Mendelssohn was unveiled in a great ceremony. You know he is revered as the founder of the Conservatory. It has been installed in front of the building and is very handsome. Part of the ceremony was a performance of a *March* played by the pupils and led by Herr Sitt. I hope that when I am a more senior and accomplished pupil I may have the chance to play in such a ceremony. It would be an honour to be sure.

That same evening there was a special concert at the Gewandhaus. The great violinist Dr. Joachim was performing and I badly wanted to see him. The tickets were expensive and we had not
~~~~~~~~~~~~~~~~~~

bought them in advance, thinking we would take standing room places. Lily and I went early and were in the queue when a nice older couple came by and asked if we were seeking tickets and of course we said yes. They said they had two extra because their friends could not come after all and we looked like nice young ladies and would we like to have them? Weren't we lucky? You can imagine our response. We watched the amazing Joachim play the Mendelssohn Violin Concerto from excellent seats and it did not cost a pfennig!

Next week three of us plan to go to the opera, and Mama, I hope you will approve as I am sure I am old enough now, and Lily does want company, and Miss Donaldson likes opera very much. We will see Herr Direktor Reinecke's *Der Gouverneur von Tours* which is a new comic opera. Fräul. Hohmann is sure it will be suitable for young ladies.

For the past two months we have been working in water colour at my art class and I will enclose one small piece. Do you think I am making some progress?

~~~~~~~~~~~~~~~~~
~~~~~~~~~~~~~~~~~

Sunday, 26th June, 1892

Dear Mama,

I wrote a long letter to you last week and yet I forgot to tell you about the opera.

We all liked it very much. It was very amusing even if we did not understand many of the words. It is quite a different matter to follow German when it is sung. The theatre was completely full and Herr Reinecke received a great ovation at the end. I have added some new trim to my summer evening dress so it felt almost as if I had a new gown.

Another evening – and of course it remains light until quite late at this time of year, the same as at home – we went as far as the Arienwald Park where a band was playing. That was delightful to hear, but it is a little embarrassing to see how the young couples behave in public. They were sipping their beer, and nibbling their cake and caressing each other with such abandon. We were taken aback to see young ladies drinking beer in public. I know it was rude, but I simply could not help staring and wondering. Lily says I will get used to it. Later I asked Fräul. Hohmann about this, but despite her ready explanation, I remain confused. She said that in Saxony the conventions forbid a young lady from receiving calls at home or from walking or having any companionship with gentlemen except at general receptions. I did not wish to be argumentative, but it did not make sense to me that such a display of tenderness in public places is therefore somehow acceptable. If conventions are so restrictive, how can these public displays be proper?

The annual student picnic outing is next week, but I do not think I shall go. I scarcely know anyone and Lily does not wish to go and Miss D. is preparing to return to America. In any case, classes will be over in a few weeks and I shall be coming home.

It seems that almost everyone leaves Leipzig for the long holiday. All the conversation is about travel. Some students will go tramping in the Black Forest or the Harz Mountains, especially the Americans and Canadians for whom a trip home is costly and takes so much time. The English and Scots will mostly return to their homes and the Germans of course just go home as well. I heard one young woman talking excitedly about her forthcoming trip to France. A summer in Paris – wouldn't that be wonderful?

I shall be on my way to you in a very few weeks so do not look for any more long letters. They might not reach you before I do.

~~~~~~~~~~~~~~~~~
~~~~~~~~~~~~~~~~~

7 Pilrigg Street, Leith

25th July, 1892

Dear Lily,

Thank you once again to you and your mother for having me to stay with you when we returned to England. My mother has asked that I pass on her gratitude. She was much relieved that I had somewhere safe to stay in London.

It is always nice to be home with the family, but it has been a little strange visiting with my old school friends after an absence of these many months. Have you had a similar experience? My world seems to be – well it is – so very different from theirs that we found ourselves with very little to talk about. They did not seem interested in all my tales of Leipzig, of travel, of speaking German, of the Conservatory. I know I have not written often, but neither have they. I am a little sad about this, but at the same time I confess myself the tiniest bit annoyed.

We go next week to the seaside, just to North Berwick this year, and I hope the weather stays fine. Enjoy your holiday at Eastbourne. I expect the sea is warmer on the south coast than it is here.

~~~~~~~~~~~~~~~~~~

Braustrasse 4, Leipzig

Thursday, 8th September 1892

Dear Mama,

We have arrived safely back and in good time. The journey has become quite familiar now.

Things are somewhat unsettled in our house at the moment. Fräul. Hohmann took a bad fall while I was with you in Edinburgh. I believe she uses the long vacation to do a complete cleaning of the house and she was up a ladder to clean the high windows and
~~~~~~~~~~~~~~~~~~

slipped off. She did not break anything but she is limping badly. We are all trying to help where we can. Even her brother, whom one scarcely ever sees, has appeared in the kitchen to make his own coffee.

Our new pensioniste, Miss Susanna Armstrong, is another American, from Virginia somewhere and she speaks very differently from Miss Donaldson. She will be studying the pianoforte, but I think she is already very advanced. I thought I was doing well with six years of lessons behind me, but in comparison I have a long way to go. She likes to talk about the numerous recitals she has given in Richmond and speaks with enthusiasm about this past year at a fine music school in New York City. Well, everyone is different and we shall all try to get along. I dare say we may miss Miss Donaldson more than we expected to.

It is still very hot and dusty here, even though summer is practically over. The leaves on the trees are brown and dry. The pavements are warm underfoot and water-carts move up and down the streets dodging pianos, scattering and spraying water to keep down the dust, just as they did in Cassel. But every few days a fierce thunderstorm blows through and in the morning, all is fresh and cool again, at least for a few hours. Perhaps I should explain about dodging pianos.

It is the time of year when students return to the city and many take up new lodgings for one reason or another. The piano students usually hire their pianos, so the piano movers are kept busy at the beginning of term taking pianos from one house to another. I have watched with amazement to see them hoist a piano up the outside of a building and maneuver it through a window into a fourth floor apartment. At times they even have to remove the window. I wondered if they ever dropped one, but Lily assured me this rarely happens.

Michaelmas term is underway. I am to remain in Herr Rüther's violin class which is supervised from time to time by Herr Sitt, the Violin Master. I have a new piano master and I must add more piano practice hours. I am supposed to begin voice lessons for one hour a week, although I do not know exactly why this is necessary. How I shall find time to practise singing and piano and violin I do not know. Then there are classes in theory and harmony in which I am doing well as it seems I studied more theory at Waddell's than many pupils have done before they come here. It is also helpful that Herr Jadassohn's harmony book has been translated into English. There are about twenty of us, all young American and British ladies, in the theory class. Actually, there is one Australian and one may be Canadian, but I cannot always tell the Canadians from the Americans. It is easier to become acquainted in these harmony classes as we simply introduce ourselves. In violin class we are working all the time, and there is little chance to converse. In piano lessons, everyone just comes into the piano room, waits their turn to play and then leaves when they are finished.

The concert season will begin in a few weeks and we are all looking forward to a wonderful feast of symphonic music in the months to come.

Dear Mama, I would like to ask your advice about continuing with German lessons. What I have discovered in my months here is that I am speaking English most of the time and the English-speaking pupils do tend to stick together. I have a good understanding of basic German grammar from my lessons last year so now it is a matter of vocabulary. With all my extra classes this term I do not know if I should go on with German. My tutor from last year, Herr Schneider, is nowhere to be found and in any case, I would not care to continue with him so I would have to find someone else. Please write and tell me what you think.

~~~~~~~~~~~~~~~~~
~~~~~~~~~~~~~~~~~

Sunday 16th October 1892

Dear Mama and everyone,

Thank you Mama for sending on that box of warm clothes which I left behind in August. It will soon be getting chilly and I shall want them. The material for a new skirt is also very welcome. It's such a pretty shade of blue and will go nicely with the shirtwaists we bought at Jenners.

The weather has remained fine so we are having a good ramble in the Johanna Park whenever we have time. It will seem an odd thing to say, but we look forward to winter when we can take up skating again.

You will be glad to know that Lily and I are regular in our attendance at the Anglo-American service on Sundays. People chat for a short while afterwards and some of them were talking about the dances that take place a few times in the year which they referred to as Anglo-American dances. These are organized by various groups but Lily and I do not understand if we need an invitation or how it is that one manages to go.

One of my new acquaintances from violin class, Miss Charlotte Davis, has had an amusing idea. She thinks it would be an interesting challenge if we were each to learn the piano part and the violin part in the next piece we are given, so we could accompany each other. Herr Rüther has not exactly forbidden this, although he did not approve of our choice of music. We proposed to learn a Romance by Clara Schumann but Herr R. wants us to play Bach. It will be enjoyable to work in this way with a friend. Romantic music is not much in favour here.

Thank you for your advice about taking more German lessons. I shall try to find a new tutor. Oh, and I forgot to tell you thank you for asking after Fräul. Hohmann who is now quite recovered. She was grateful for your concern.

~~~~~~~~~~~~~~~~~
~~~~~~~~~~~~~~~~~

Braustrasse 4,

Sunday, 12th November, 1892

Dear Mama,

Thank you for allowing me to look for new lodgings. Now Lily and I may begin to search for rooms where we may be more independent. I am glad that you and Papa agree that I am old enough to take this step and indeed, Fräul. Hohmann is most understanding. She agrees that I do not need as much "mothering" as I did last year, and besides, her pension is in demand. There are always younger ladies and their families looking for a place such as this. We had considered putting an advertisement in the local paper, but now we plan to search the neighbourhood streets looking for signs in the windows saying "Zimmer vermieten". We do not wish to move away from the music quarter, as we do not want to walk any further than necessary in the cold winter weather.

Truth be told, Fräul. H. rather peevishly asked how soon we will be leaving as she has two young ladies waiting for our rooms. We must choose a new place soon. I expect that by the time you receive this letter we shall have made a choice and removed ourselves from Braustrasse where I have spent a happy year

~~~~~~~~~~~~~~~~~
~~~~~~~~~~~~~~~~~

Imagining Violet

Sunday, 27th November, 1892

Dear Birdie,

Finally Lily and I have found rooms. It feels as if we have been searching for days and days, tramping up and down the streets of the music quarter in the rain, growing ever more pessimistic. You see, Birdie, we had to find a landlady who would allow Lily to practise the piano. Some landladies will not have more than one piano pupil on their premises at a time. Some will not take music students at all. But at last, we have succeeded!

Our new home will be in a house nearer to the Conservatory. It is at Grassistrasse, Number 34 and is a handsome tall building, all stuccoed and so on the way the Germans do. Our rooms are on the first floor and we pray it will be possible to get Lily's piano into her room.

Our landlady, Frau Gibson is a widow and is not English, although you might think that from her name. I believe she went to England to attend school, and married an Englishman who died there and so she returned to her native city. We shall remove on Friday when we do not have classes. It is just as well that I gave up drawing lessons this term, as my days are very full.

I suppose I ought to be grateful that Mama took the time to write Fräul. H. asking her to locate a new tutor for me, and I suspect she hinted that this time he should not be so young. Obliging Fräul. H. went with me to meet Herr Becker who is decidedly not young and I am to go to him twice a week for a half hour. Oh well. Still, he is a good-natured sort with a smile and a chuckle and at our first meeting we talked in German about my classes and my life here.

It is grand to have the Wednesday morning Gewandhaus rehearsals to go to again. I watch the string section intently and have a greater appreciation for what they are doing than I did at this time last year. I cannot wait until I am allowed to play with others at ensemble class, and perhaps next year I will be good enough to join the student orchestra and who knows where that might lead. Still, society generally does not approve of women playing with men on stage, although I have heard of women's string quartettes and I believe there was an all-women's orchestra here some years ago. I confess I dream of performing somehow, somewhere, once I have my diploma.

The Christmas Markets have opened and as I must post my Christmas box soon, I went straightaway and did my little bits of shopping. The principal squares are set about with fir trees of all sizes and filled with booths and stalls. In some of them you can purchase special wooden crafts from the Ore Mountains. That is where I bought that nice candle-holder for Mama last year. The shops and stalls are brightly lit until late in the evening, every one crowded with shoppers. Then there is all manner of baking with various Saxon specialties like Lebkuchen and Christstollen, which is an egg bread made with candied fruit. It is very delicious but I did not think I should put that in the post.

As my budget will not stretch far, I had the idea of making small sketches for presents and framing them with pasteboard frames covered in green felt. The sketches are of Leipzig sights, as I do not do people very well.

I am sorry that I cannot come home this Christmas and I do miss you all, but in Mama's last letter she suggested that you and she might come here at Easter time which would be wonderful. I should love to show you Leipzig. Fräul. Hohmann has kindly invited Lily and me to spend Christmas at Braustrasse, so we shall not be alone in our new lodgings.

~~~~~~~~~~~~~~~~~~
~~~~~~~~~~~~~~~~~~

Leipzig, Grassistrasse No.34

Grassistrasse, No. 34, Leipzig
10th December, 1892

Dear Mama and everyone,

I have not had a moment to write, what with packing and unpacking, and practising and shopping for Christmas and everything else. But I want to tell you all about our new lodgings.

Lily and I each have a small room with a sofa-bed which makes up easily for the night, and in the morning, while we are at breakfast, the maid quickly turns it from a bed back to a small sofa so that my room becomes a cozy sitting room. Is that not clever? There is a small table by the window where I keep my music and I can sit or stand to play. I do not mind that my window looks to the rear of the building as I am less distracted by the goings-on in the street below. I am fortunate that there is a large wardrobe in my room, and one trunk serves as a sort of table as well. There is a small wash-stand with basin and jug and for heat there is a large porcelain stove which one finds in every student room. The room has pretty wall paper, just a little shabby, of small roses on an ivory background. Lily's room is larger which she needs in order to accommodate her piano. She has a beautiful Oriental screen which hides an alcove where her washbasin and a small bureau are located. However, she does not have a wardrobe, so I share some space in mine for her gowns.

You know that we do not take our meals here. It is not a boarding house in the same way as Fräul. Hohmann's, but we are permitted to make tea in Frau Gibson's kitchen. But my goodness, she is strict about bathing; we are allowed one complete hot water bath a week. Also we are not supposed to have food in our rooms. She would not admit plainly that food can attract rodents but we suspect that is why she has these rules. Still it is expensive to take our dinner and our supper at a restaurant or café, so for supper at least we manage with some cheese and sausage, a roll and apples and we are very careful not to leave any crumbs. We take our dinner at a nearby restaurant but we order very little.

Lily and I agree that we miss the evenings when we all sat together in Fräul. Hohmann's general sitting room. If Lily were not across the hall, I am sure I would be lonely.

~~~~~~~~~~~~~~~~~~

Grassistrasse, 34

Thursday, 29th December 1892

Dear Mama und Papa,

Thank you and everyone for the lovely gifts which arrived in good time. I am always grateful for books in English and I have not read either of these. I am very glad to have new leather gloves as well.

Our Christmas celebrations began a few days before the day itself when Fräul. Hohmann's brother brought in the Christmas tree and stood it in the corner of the general sitting room. Lily and I had been invited to tea and helped to set it in place.

Little by little, small wrapped presents appeared and were put about on tables in little piles. On the 22nd, we went with Miss Armstrong to a Christmas fète given by the Schumann Verein which is a club or society. This one was a temperance fète as I am sure you are relieved to know, but some of them are beer fètes. They generally commence with a short concert, and of course there is a Christmas tree, and everyone gets a silly small gift and afterwards there is dancing. There seems to be dancing all the time. Lily and I did not
~~~~~~~~~~~~~~~~~~

know what to expect and did not take any presents, but we were made welcome all the same. My gift was a clever wooden puzzle.

At Braustrasse we helped to decorate the tree which we covered top to bottom with gilded nuts, glass icicles, wax candles, flowers and ribbon, marzipan and chocolate. Until Christmas Eve the sitting room was forbidden territory, but at precisely 7:00 o'clock on the 24th all the lights were turned out, the doors to the parlour were flung open and there the glorious tree stood, ablaze with candlelight. We were a large group, as Fräul. H. extends her Christmas spirit to former pensionistes like ourselves who have moved into their own apartments. Before we were allowed to open presents - and somehow there were little packages for everyone – we sang carols. I did not know the great favourite, *O Tannenbaum,* and I sang the English words to *Stille Nacht*. Being a musical sort of pension we had plenty of people to play the piano. Miss Armstrong taught us two new carols from America; one is a jolly song called *Jingle Bells* and the other is a very pretty thing called *O Little Town of Bethlehem*. Have you heard that in Edinburgh yet?

Then came the Christmas Eve supper which is not a large meal. The traditional meal in Saxony includes roast carp so I was relieved that Fräul. H. broke with custom and gave us bratwurst and potato salad and a special cucumber salad.

For our Christmas dinner, we had roast goose just like in England, with boiled potatoes and a dish of red cabbage mixed with onion and apple. I must say I missed the plum pudding which is not part of the tradition here at all. I should have been longing for shortbread, Mama, had you not included some in my Christmas parcel.

I did miss you all and thought of you all and wished you a happy Christmas in my mind, but to say the truth, we did have ever such a jolly time and so I have had my first German Christmas.

~~~~~~~~~~~~~~~~~~
~~~~~~~~~~~~~~~~~~

Sunday, 15th January, 1893

Dear Mama und Papa,

Thank you for the birthday card and the lovely warm muffler which is very welcome on these wintry days especially when skating. And I send new year's wishes even if they reach you somewhat late. Your letter came too and I was glad to hear the boys liked their German nutcrackers which I had found in the market and that you and Papa also liked your small gifts.

Margaret McKay sent a nice long Christmas letter, the first letter in many months. She wanted me to know that she is practically engaged, although they will not marry for a year or so. Her betrothed, Gerald Farquharson, is the son of a colleague of Papa's. My friend Annie writes that she is training to be a teacher. Thank you for passing on greetings from Catherine Stirling. She has not written to me once.

As in Scotland, the New Year's celebrations here are ever so lively, to put it delicately. Frau Gibson. discouraged us from joining in, saying that everyone gets tremendously drunk and it would not be safe for young ladies on the streets. Therefore we watched from Lily's window and felt rather left out of things. The streets were thronged with people, most of them students, and there was a good deal of riotous dancing and running up and down. Perhaps next year we will dare to participate. The celebrations went on very late and indeed they kept us awake, but at precisely three o'clock in the morning, the police appeared and everyone went home quietly.

We have found a solution to the problem of dining in an economical fashion. A classmate of Lily's told her of a lady who keeps a dinner-table for a few respectable young people. We plan to call next week to see if she has space for us and if it is not too far from our house or from the Conservatory.

Everyone is happy that the pond in the Johanna Park is bearing. We have taken up our skates again and it is almost as if I had been practising in my sleep. I found to my surprise that I was rather better at it than when we had to stop last spring.

The routine of the Conservatory has started up and I shall not tire you with all the details. My piano master is introducing some of the modern masters like Grieg and Debussy. We do not prepare for performance, but simply try to improve our musicality and our technique and also to experience new music. Harmony and theory and composition classes take up a good deal of my week and I rather enjoy how they make me think. And I continue with German lessons as well with Herr Becker, going to him for one hour every Friday instead of two shorter lessons.

The experiment with Miss Davis was only partly successful, as we probably did not devote enough time to either part, but we enjoyed it. It was a good exercise in understanding how the music fits together. Now our junior violin teacher is allowing us to work in the same way on a delightful duo of Mendelssohn's. Herr Klesse is much less conservative than his older colleagues. He will listen to us in a few weeks and might even recommend us for an Abend later this term. That would be worth working for.

At the skating pond this year, there are a few young men who practise impossibly complicated jumps and turns. And they skate round and round in circles, over and over again. These manoeuvres they call their figures. It is most entertaining to watch as they can do the most amazing things on skates. I wonder if ladies will take to this figure skating some day. Do you know if there is a figure skating club in Edinburgh?

There are numerous concerts to attend and I continue to be impressed by how much music there is and what variety. I believe I have heard more music here than I ever will hear in my whole life. For something different, there is a comic opera by Bizet coming next week. Lily, Miss Davis and I shall go together.

Please tell me your plans for your Easter visit. I am ever so impatient to see you! Easter was festive last year with the Easter trees and it will be awfully jolly to show it to you and Birdie.

~~~~~~~~~~~~~~~~~
~~~~~~~~~~~~~~~~~

Imagining Violet

Grassistrasse, 34

Sunday, 19th February, 1893

Dear Birdie,

I was delighted to read about your Sunday walks with Mr. McFadden. How pleasant to have an interesting companion and something to do on a Sunday when everything is so quiet in Edinburgh. It took me a while to adjust to how different Sunday is here, but now I like it very much, and do not relish the thought of returning to Scottish Sundays.

I mentioned to Mama about the Bizet opera *Djamileh*. To be frank, we did not think much of it, especially the plot, although the music was, dare I say, sumptuous. Very melodic and lush. It was a silly story about a slave girl and a sultan set in Egypt so the music was of the oriental type. The soprano played the sultan's mistress-of-the-month, a troubling idea I thought, and she was foolish enough to fall in love with her sultan. Then there were dances of which I am sure Mama and Papa would not approve – they were almost naughty, to tell the truth – although I was imagining Papa might secretly have enjoyed them. There was a comic servant named Splendiana who made us laugh out loud, but the soprano was a little too corpulent for my liking. And here I am, after going to half a dozen operas, pretending the critic.

Our arrangement with Mrs. Ingham is working splendidly. For 50 pfennig we now have a proper dinner every day. I was curious as to why this nice lady was offering such a service and had the temerity to ask. It seems she came to Leipzig several years back with her young daughter, and when the daughter took her diploma and left for further study in Berlin, Mrs. Ingham decided to stay here rather than return to her native Australia. Of course I did not presume to inquire further. She adds to her income by cooking good English food for traditionally poor but hungry music students.

Everything goes well with my studies, although I find one of my violin classes rather discouraging. Herr Rüther seems to devote most of his time to the young American girls, and Charlotte and I are left to wait around. Between ourselves we call him Herr Rooster, because he struts around rather and has reddish hair. Lottie is considering a course of private lessons but I would not want to ask Mama and Papa for that in addition to everything else they pay for.

Perhaps because we all live in boarding houses and such, students spend a good deal of time in cafés, so one might as well join in. This is especially true in winter when it is dark by late afternoon and too cold for walking, but one wants to be warm and to enjoy a little company. Practising can be a little lonely sometimes. I am even learning to like beer and coffee.

I am counting the weeks until you are here. I should not allow myself to become so excited, but I cannot help it.

~~~~~~~~~~~~~~~~~

Grassistrasse, 34, Leipzig

12th March, 1893

Dear Mama,

It has been an important time here, with the celebration of the 50th anniversary of the founding of the Conservatory. Imagine! That was before even you were born. There have been special recitals and other events, but the best of all was on the 10th inst., when the King and Queen of Saxony came to Leipzig for the Jubilee Concert. Lily and I went along to the station to see their arrival which we barely managed to do as we were a little late. They looked very stately and regal but nice. He is very much the military man and was wearing a fancy bemedalled uniform, and he is quite old now. She is about sixty and a little stout, but wore a lovely crimson travelling costume and thankfully a small hat so one could see her face. They
~~~~~~~~~~~~~~~~~

must be very popular, because there was a large crowd of Leipzigers lining the streets, waiting to welcome them with cheers and flags waving.

That evening we queued up for the longest time to get a standing room place for the concert. Herr Prof. Reinecke led the student orchestra and chorus in a fine performance of his new *Festival Overture* composed for the occasion. The chorale was beautifully sung and we all clapped until they sang that section a second time. Audiences here clap for a very long time. I am hopeful that I shall be asked to join the student orchestra next term. It looks like great fun to make music with a group of your fellow students. The concert ended with that most extraordinary symphony of Beethoven's, known here simply as *The Immortal Ninth*. I heard it for the first time last year and do not mind if they play it every year which in fact I believe they do, to finish the Gewandhaus season. The *Ode to Joy* is the most thrilling piece of music I have ever heard.

The King is not much of a concert-lover though. He appeared to nod off from time to time, but the Queen was on the edge of her seat throughout, very splendidly gowned, wearing a sparkling tiara and a sparkling gown as well. Lily and I wondered if they were real diamonds on the tiara. He, the King, was so weighed down with medals, it is no wonder he fell asleep. In any case, I had never seen a real King before, so it was quite exciting altogether.

The ponds are slushy now, but I did not have time last letter to tell you about our great skating expedition to the village of Connewitz, which is about three miles along the river from here. We were a party of eight – Lily and I and Charlotte Davis as well as a Mr. Puddicombe who is a friend of Miss Davis and also some new friends from church. You will be pleased to know we prudently went early on Sunday afternoon so as to be back before dark and had a jolly good skate and warm-up in a café in the village. It seems as if every house along the riverbank there has become a café. There was a huge stove to warm us, although we did steam somewhat. We had hot chocolate and coffee and pastries and recovered enough to skate back against the wind. Our noses and cheeks were rosy pink but our toes were like chunks of ice. Still, it is a great pleasure to be able to skate so freely whenever one wants.

I am working steadily and the Mendelssohn duo is coming along nicely. Miss Davis, whom I now address as Charlotte, and I are crossing our fingers that we may be given a spot at an Abendunterhaltung this term. It would be a big step forward to perform for my fellow students, but I believe I am ready for it. Normally the repertoire that is assigned for an Abend is something the student can perform well. The programme consists of about a dozen pieces, a mixture of duos, trios and so on, and usually finishes with a movement from a concerto with piano accompaniment.

For sight-reading, we have been playing Herr Reinecke's own *Sonates Miniatures* and I keep up fairly well with the class. I know I should balance my time between my violin and the piano but to be honest, the violin gets more of my attention. I can practise at home instead of facing the cold wind and snow, walking to the practice room at the Con.

You and Birdie will be here in just a few weeks and I do so long to see you both. Birdie simply must recover from her cold in time to travel.

~~~~~~~~~~~~~~~~~~
~~~~~~~~~~~~~~~~~~

Imagining Violet

Grassistrasse, 34, Leipzig

9th April, 1893

Dear Birdie,

I was bitterly disappointed that you could not come. I wept many tears, but when I dried my eyes, I thought how selfish I was. Of course it would have been dangerous for you to travel when you have been ill. And naturally Mama did not want to make the journey by herself. I suppose I take my good health for granted and I know I should be more grateful.

Easter was pleasant enough but I was sad that you were not here so I did not enjoy it as much. I wanted so badly for you both to see the Easter trees that make the city so pretty. Oh well, just one more term and then I shall make my way back to you for six whole weeks.

Now is the time of the huge Easter Fair when thousands and thousands of foreigners visit Leipzig to trade. The squares are filled with the usual temporary stalls and shops and I am told there is one entire section devoted to pianos. It seems like a curious place to purchase a piano, but I believe they sell a great many during these three weeks. However, Frau Gibson has practically forbidden us to visit the Fair with the dire warning that there are many unsavory people about, strange people from all corners of the world.

In violin class we have a new pupil from the United States who is very young but also very talented. She is accompanied everywhere by her mother, and I do mean everywhere. Miss Dorothy Shields is quiet, delicate and pretty enough and she plays brilliantly, but her mother is in many ways her opposite. Mrs. S. is not delicate and not quiet and frequently interrupts the Master whilst her daughter is playing. The Master looks impatient but remains polite. Mrs. S., of course, speaks no German and like so many English speakers seems to think that if she speaks loudly enough she will be understood. Young Miss Shields is obviously embarrassed, but what can she do?

I have finally been accepted into the ensemble class and I am still smiling about that. I have been watching and listening many an afternoon when I should have been practising piano. Now on three afternoons a week I shall be practising quartettes and other ensemble pieces with my friends. Some of the pupils in ensemble classes are practising to play at an Abend and Charlotte and I have not abandoned our ambition to play our Mendelssohn at one of the Friday evenings.

I hope you will soon be yourself again and well enough to resume your walks with Mr. McFadden. I am glad that Mama and Papa like him.

~~~~~~~~~~~~~~~~

28th May, 1893

Dear Birdie,

What a lovely time of year it is here when we can open our windows wide to the fresh air, and along with the breeze comes the sounds of students practising in every room in every house along the street.

When I have a half day to spare, which is not often, I persuade Lily or Charlotte to come with me on a tramp through the Rosenthal. We take the tram for half an hour and are soon in the country. The meadows are green and the trees on the allées are nearly in leaf. There are paths like spokes on a wheel which cut straight through the forest and are intended to provide vistas. The paths are often crowded since many students wish to be out of doors in fine weather, even though at times they are very muddy, the paths and probably the students as well. We have found to our chagrin that if one leaves the main pathways, it is altogether too easy to lose one's way. I want to try cycling but I do not have the right costume for it. One can hire bicycles at the Rosenthal Park; it looks very sporting and surely it is healthy exercise.
~~~~~~~~~~~~~~~~

Imagining Violet

I have not written yet about music history class which I have been attending for some weeks now. These are held on Saturday morning in one of the university buildings on the Augustinum Platz. You know that my violin classes are ladies only but for the history class they have a different solution. The men sit on one side of the lecture theatre and the ladies on the other and there are many smiling glances back and forth. So far it is very interesting although it is taught in German. I am forever peeking into my dictionary for words I don't understand. My little Chamber's is quite thumbed over. In German one can wait a very long time for the verb and by the time it arrives one has forgotten where the sentence began.

The professor began our first class by talking about the music of Ancient Greece. He explained that since no one ever wrote it down, it is difficult to be sure what it sounded like. We have also had lectures on early medieval music and the examples of scores that he showed us were impossible to decipher. I think I must look in the English book store for a second-hand copy of an English history of music.

Charlotte and I continue to grumble about the mother of Miss Shields who persists in coming into our class. Whilst I am in a complaining sort of mood, I shall tell you a little more about this class. We are expected to follow Herr Rooster exactly and what he says must be accepted without question. We are to play just as he plays, to stand as he stands and so on. There is some muttering about this with some saying they wish to express their <u>own</u> feelings, and not slavishly copy the master. We have Herr Rooster for two classes and Herr Sitt for two other classes or Herr Klesse when Herr Sitt cannot come, and as their styles are all somewhat different, it is difficult to satisfy them all and that is thoroughly confusing. That is the end of my grumbling.

I have saved some good news for last. Charlotte and I have been assigned to an Abend before the end of term. It is wonderful to think I will have this opportunity to perform before an audience. If I am going to succeed as a violinist, I must have more experience in performing.

This year I will surely go to the student picnic in July. It is funny to think back and remember how I was so shy last year that I did not want to go.

~~~~~~~~~~~~~~~~~

Grassistrasse, 34

July 8, 1893

My own dear Mama,

Charlotte and I have survived our Abend debut. Charlotte graciously played the piano part. I was a little breathless and trembly, but I recalled how I should take a few deep breaths before beginning to play. We had taken care to arrive in good time in case something went amiss with either of the two performances ahead of us. On occasion a pupil falters badly and cannot continue and has to leave the stage. Thankfully when our turn came, the Direktor was still awake; he does not always manage to remain alert through to the end of the evening. All our friends had come and they clapped generously. I wore my good green gown with new ribbons and the lovely piece of lace you sent me for luck and Lily helped put up my hair with a flower in it.

When we came on to the stage, which seemed vast, I was so jittery that I stumbled a little but continued on down to the front of the platform where two grand pianos nested. Charlotte took a minute to adjust the piano chair and but when she went to lower the piano lid to the peg for chamber music, her hand slipped and she let it go and bang, it hit the piano case, just missing her fingers,which might have been squashed and then where would we have been! I took another deep breath and tried to ignore my fluttering heart.

Charlotte was not as relaxed as she appeared to be. She raced through the first movement, and I had quite a job to keep up. I did
~~~~~~~~~~~~~~~~~

not dare to look out at the audience before we began, but when we took our bows, I could see that our friends were sitting in the front rows applauding heartily. Then we bowed again and I felt proud to stand on that stage; I did enjoy the applause and I was happy that I did not suffer very much stage fright. If one is going to become a performer, as I wish to do, one should not be too nervous. We remembered to walk slowly and sedately all the long way back up to the exit, although secretly I wanted to run.

I meant to write you about a concert that was put on by the Sterndale Bennett Society, a new group organized by the English-speaking community. They plan to present English music only, although it seems Australian counts as English, as the highlight of the evening was a sonata by an Australian composer. It felt quite novel to have English music, as almost all the music we hear is German. The opera is always in German and much of it comes from Vienna. We long to see some of the wonderful Italian operas we hear about.

We keep promising ourselves to take up cycling but never seem to find the opportunity. Soon it will be time to make the journey home. A year is a long time to be away from family.

~~~~~~~~~~~~~~~~

12th July, 1893

Dear Birdie,

We had an absolutely wizard day for the student picnic. We all met at the station to board a special train. There were hundreds of us, not just pupils but all the teachers too, and friends like Mr. Puddicombe who studies privately.

I guess it was a special train or perhaps they added cars for us. We left promptly at nine o'clock for the short journey to Bad Kösen which is a pretty little spa town on the Salle River west of here. There is a lovely large park in the centre of the town with colonnades and an impressive "Kurmittelhaus" – a health resort. The park is well wooded and there are two ponds. I have sent each of the
~~~~~~~~~~~~~~~~

boys a postcard. One of them has a picture of the "Kurmittelhaus". We were quite a sight I expect, all singing loudly as we marched from the station across the bridge to the park. Some of the young men had band instruments and played them to great effect.

Charlotte, Lily and I had time for a ramble before the picnic supper and climbed up to the ruined castle that stands high over the river. We were all at serious risk of a tumble on our way down as we did not have the proper footwear.

Our picnic was very simple – just bread, sausage, cheese and beer. I have become quite fond of the taste of beer. After our meal, the Direktor spoke and then there was dancing. Lily and I attempted the polka, but our feet did get tangled up dreadfully and we laughed so much that we had to sit down. A pleasant young man asked me to dance but as we had not been introduced, I felt obliged to decline. I know that was the proper thing to do, but I should have liked to say yes.

~~~~~~~~~~~~~~~~~

~~~~~~~~~~~~~~~~~

7 Pilrigg Street, Leith

2nd August

Dear Lottie,

Thank you for yours of the 23rd ult. Like you, I have been giving myself a holiday from my fiddle.

I was longing to meet my sister's friend Mr. McFadden who seems a gentle sort and is obviously very fond of Birdie. He has come to tea several times and would spend even more time with Birdie if she would permit it. He is an affectionate chap and I am not at all sure that Birdie enjoys that. Perhaps she simply thinks it is something that should be kept to private moments?

Mama is happy to have her family together even for a few weeks, and is planning a tea for later this month so that her friends can hear me play. I do not like to be on exhibit, but it is one way I may show my gratitude I suppose.

My brothers are off on their own adventures. They wriggled about at tea the day I arrived as Mama insisted they have a good visit with their sister, but as soon as they could they were off out the door.

We leave in a few days for North Berwick for Papa's holiday. All too soon it will be time to return to our studies.

~~~~~~~~~~~~~~~~~~

Grassistrasse, 34, Leipzig

Sunday, 17th September

Dear Mama,

I apologize that I did not get a wee note off to you immediately to assure you of our safe arrival. It was ever so nice having my new sandwich box and our food was in much better condition than on previous journeys. The customs officials at the German border were particularly fussy this time, and wanted a good
~~~~~~~~~~~~~~~~~~

look through all my boxes. Fortunately, I was not hiding a big quantity of tea, and the few ounces I had with me were allowed. I still do not know exactly what is permissible. However, after two years, my German is almost adequate for such a situation; at least I understand what they are asking me and it is not so intimidating.

There has been a good deal of rain this past week, although I am sure it is welcomed by Leipzigers who suffered an unusually dry August.

Classes have begun and my week is full with violin and piano classes. It is wonderful to have my beautiful new violin in its beautiful case. I cannot say adequately how grateful I am. I am sure I am playing ever so much better with this wonderful instrument. I should have made up my mind about this months ago.

Theory and music history continue and I have begun to study counterpoint which is complicated. I have done fairly well with harmony and basic theory but counterpoint is a new challenge. Also I am to be allowed to join a class in composition which is normally only taken by senior students. It has been made clear to me that this is a privilege. Now that I have my copy of the *History of Modern Music* I shall do better in music history, too. I was lucky to find that at Jenners.

I should have attended voice classes last term but I never found time for it. Our violin masters say that singing a violin piece a few times helps one to hear it in one's head and that should result in a more musical performance. All in all I suppose this is preparation for a life in teaching which is the fate expected for most of us. I hope that is not my destiny as I enjoy performing very much and want to do a great deal more of it.

A few of us ventured out to the Rosenthal on Sunday last, after church, just to have a taste of country air, but we should have stopped at home. As I said, it has been raining almost daily here these past weeks, and whilst Sunday was merely cloudy, the paths and lane ways were very muddy indeed. One of our party had the idea that we should go to look at the artificial hill they are building north of the park, but try as we might, we could not find our way. One person would spot it in the distance, and we would take that path only to wind off in another direction. After an hour of this and with very muddy skirts we gave it up and retraced our steps. One of the outdoor cafés was open, though, and we were able to stop for chocolate before taking the tram back into the city.

I found a pretty birthday card for Birdie this year; I hope she liked it. It was difficult to know when to send it, as I agree with the Germans, that it is bad luck to wish someone happy birthday before the proper date.

~~~~~~~~~~~~~~~~~

3rd October, 1893

Dear Birdie,

I enjoyed your letter and I am glad you are well. It must be all the fresh air on your Sunday walks with Mr. McFadden? Well perhaps I may tease you a little? I am impressed too with some of the history books you are reading. It seems like heavy material to me.

My days are busy as I try to play at least one hour at the piano on the days I do not have lessons, as well as two hours with the violin. We do not have classes on Fridays and as I no longer go to Herr Becker for German, on Fridays I have some free time. On Friday evenings, after the weekly Abend, I go with friends to the Café Seyffert and we often stay out until after ten. If I were still at Braustrasse, Fräul Hohmann would not permit that.

Are you enjoying the classes at the university? If only you had had the chance to go to St. George's, you might have enrolled at the university. Still, when you sit in on a class, surely you get the benefit of the learning without the necessity of preparing for examinations.

Since you asked, I shall write a little more about the music history we have been studying. Last week, Herr Professor Paul gave a most interesting lecture on the origins of forms of music. He
~~~~~~~~~~~~~~~~~

explained that the symphony may be traced back to the arrangements of various dances and their placement in a certain order. As he said, "Dance is, in a sense, the mother of musical form." Apparently, in the middle ages, there were two kinds of dances. Those of the aristocracy were stately and slow, and those of the peasantry were generally quick and hearty. Back in 1287, there are some *Songs of the Troubadours* which are more or less a suite of contrasting dances. You would start with a fast one, followed by a slow one, and so on, finishing with a fast one.

Then he went on to describe more than a dozen different dances, explaining where they came from and so on. One of them struck me as particularly interesting. The Sarabande, which Bach includes in his Suites all the time, comes from ancient Spain – it is not German at all – at the time when the Moors were in possession of the southern part of that country. In fact, our teacher insisted that the Sarabande has Arabic origins. "We can confirm this," he said, "by reference to a Turkish dance called the Ser-a-Bende, which is performed to this day." There is your music history lesson for today.

~~~~~~~~~~~~~~~~~~

Grassistrasse, 34

28th October, 1893

My own dear Mama,

I am having such an enjoyable time since I joined the student orchestra. It is not, however, any tribute to my ability with the violin as I had imagined it to be. There are so many more pianists than string players here that we fiddlers are encouraged, almost required, to play in the orchestra. Of course, the pianists often study violin or violincello as everyone must study a second instrument. But those of us who prefer to be dedicated string pupils are accepted into the student orchestra at an earlier stage. We rehearse for one hour and a half on Monday afternoon and we work on the concertos which the
~~~~~~~~~~~~~~~~~~

senior pupils will perform at their Prüfungen. That will be the first and only time they are accompanied by an orchestra.

There are two new English-speakers in our house whom we met whilst coming and going to the Conservatory. A boy of perhaps fifteen and his older sister have rooms on the third floor here. They have enrolled this term and are both very nice. Mr. Donaldson Heins is, I suspect, something of a prodigy on the violin and his sister Florence plays the piano. They are from Hereford, where their parents are very musical but there father is also a businessman with a number of music stores.

Mr. Heins has already joined our ensemble class. He is young but very sweet and plays the violin like an angel. He studies viola and cello as well and sometimes tries his hand at those parts.

In violin class, I am learning the first movement of a concerto by Vivaldi. In Ensemble class, we have started on trios and quartettes. It is very rewarding, practising with friends and making music together.

I shall close now as I want to write my congratulations to Birdie.

~~~~~~~~~~~~~~~~

Grassis Strasse, No. 34

2nd November, Thursday, 1893

Dear Birdie,

I was thrilled to receive your exciting news, dear Birdie. You are verlobt!! I liked your Mr. McFadden very much and now he is to be like a brother to me and part of our family. Is your ring very beautiful? When will you marry? Will it be soon?

I have decided that the German custom of socializing in cafés is a delightful one. At the Café Seyferrt of an afternoon one can always find a friend or two sipping coffee. And thus the circle of one's acquaintances grows, and one can have as much company as one
~~~~~~~~~~~~~~~~

likes. These days Lily is practising six hours a day as she hopes to make her Prüfung next term and does not have much spare time. She has started a course of private lessons with her piano master and thinks he will take more of an interest in her progress because of that.

Charlotte and I continue to complain, to each other, about Herr Rooster. who gives us very little attention. It has become exceedingly tiresome. Charlotte has inquired about changing to another class in January and if she succeeds, perhaps I shall do so as well. At every lesson he begins with the other two pupils and suddenly three quarters of the hour has passed and he has to hurry to listen to us in the last fifteen minutes. At least that dreadful Mrs. Shields and her little daughter are no longer in this class. Some days, it hardly seems worthwhile going.

The dramatic elocution class is just plain silly. We are a mixed group of English and German girls and we read passages from Shakespeare in both languages. Did you know that the Germans are crazy about Shakespeare? Half the time I do not understand what I am saying in either language and feel quite in a muddle.

Here we eat, drink and sleep with music. There is nothing else of importance in our lives. You might think this odd, and likely it is not admirable, but no one here is much interested in what is happening outside our own small universe. Once in a while I feel a little guilty about that. We do not read the German newspapers or magazines and as there are none in English, we know little of what is going on "at home". I expect you know more about the events of the day in Germany than we do here. Although young ladies are not supposed to take an interest in politics I begin to think I should have a better notion of what is going on in the world.

Still, at the cafés, the talk is not always of music; a good deal of it is just plain gossip. Who did what in a class, how so-and-so stumbled in an Abend performance, how some girls flirt outrageously, but also at times we hear the young men from the university speak with great pride of the growing strength of Germany. They insist Germany will not take second place to England.

Perhaps you could write to me a little about that if indeed there are reports in the Edinburgh newspapers. Here we agree that Germany takes first place in music, but surely Britannia rules the waves.

I should tell you about an interesting concert we attended a few weeks ago when the orchestra played three short symphonies, one by CPE Bach, one by Haydn and the last was the Mozart G minor – not the later one, No. 40 – but an earlier one which he wrote when he was seventeen. Listening to the three of them one right after the other, we could clearly hear how the symphony had developed over a hundred years which helped immensely to make sense of the music history we have been learning.

I must hurry to a class now; I shall try to add to this later....

~~~~~~~~~~~~~~~~~~

Grassis Strasse, No. 34

12th November, 1893

Dear Mama,

I thought that I would take some time to write about the concert season. I have written enough about my studies.

Last week we attended a most extraordinary pair of concerts. Professor Carl Halir, one of the most distinguished of German violinists, played <u>six</u> famous violin concertos in two evenings. Quite a tour de force, people were saying. Of course he played the Brahms and the Beethoven. How I wish they had written more than one concerto apiece, they are so wonderful. He also played the impossible Paganini, plus concertos by Spohr, Lalo and Tschaikowsky and finally, one from his own pen. Dr. Halir himself was an imposing figure, very, very tall with blond hair and beard, a Nordic giant if you will. In his hands, the violin looked like a toy. He teaches of course but has mainly American students at his studios in Berlin.
~~~~~~~~~~~~~~~~~~

The most important event here in Leipzig was the 150th anniversary concert of the Gewandhaus Orchestra. Did you know that there has been an orchestra here since 1743? That seems a very long time ago. We attended all the rehearsals as well and liked very much the most recent Festival overture by our Dr. Reinecke, his second such overture this year. The orchestra also played Mendelssohn's *Scotch Symphony* which I heard for the first time. It is rich and melodic. Have you heard it in Edinburgh?

Earlier this month, Eugen d'Albert came and played <u>five</u> Beethoven Sonatas at one sitting. Can you believe it? Lily quibbled a little about his tempo in first movement of the *Waldstein*, which he played almost presto, not *allegro con brio* as the master intended, said Lily. She is preparing the very same sonata for an Abend so I guess she knows it well enough to comment.

I am struggling a little with the Vivaldi as it has so many fast passages, but Herr Sitt says it is within my abilities. I wish I would have another Abend assigned as I need much more experience performing in public.

We get along well enough at Frau Gibson's. We wish we could have hot water in the morning to wash, but the good Frau is reluctant to accommodate us. And she is not always welcoming to visitors. A friend came by the other evening to borrow some music, and Frau G. grumbled about answering the door at such a late hour, although it was not quite nine o'clock. I thought it was rather tiresome of her but there you are. However, the rent is reasonable, and she does give us two rolls at breakfast most days and is usually generous with the jam.

We have had our first fall of snow and are eager to hear that the ponds are bearing so we can get out skating once again. I have promised our new friends Miss Heins and her brother, that we will take them skating. Mr. Heins practises all the time and his sister says he needs some diversion. Sometimes I think she is here more to keep an eye on him than for her own musical ambitions. He frequently has pain in his shoulder although I believe he has been trying some therapy or other. It would be too bad if he were forced to give up playing for weeks or months as sometimes happens. I appreciate more than ever your wise counsel to be moderate in all things, although I do not always follow it.

~~~~~~~~~~~~~~~~~

26th November, 1893

Dear Birdie,

My regards to Mr. McFadden; but of course you call him Ernie. Your ring sounds so beautiful. There is something so luminous about moonstones.

Last week the American students gave a dance at the Hotel de Prusse to celebrate their Thanksgiving holiday and what a grand time we had. There are more than a hundred Americans studying here, both at the Conservatory and at the university. For some reason Saxony has a special appeal for them. Our Conservatory is well known to be superior and many music students come here from the United States, but I do not know why they favour the university.

In any case, Thanksgiving is an important holiday in the American calendar, as Miss Armstrong explained. She lived with us at Braustrasse and I see her often striding about the halls and she invited us to go along to the Thanksgiving Dance. Well Birdie, this was much more than a dance. There was a good deal of speechifying, then a funny comedy performance put on by some students, and finally a short concert. Miss Armstrong took care to introduce us to some of the nicer young men, so when we were asked to dance, we were able to accept.

I had a little time to refurbish my green gown with a cascade of silver ribbons but I was obliged to purchase some dancing slippers and new gloves. I have been economising on meals, what with Mrs. Ingham's dinners and our home-made suppers, and have saved a little of my allowance. Mother would find it shocking, I am certain, but some of the young American ladies were wearing the latest
~~~~~~~~~~~~~~~~~

fashionable bright red and purple cotton stockings. Not that one could actually see them, but one could catch a glimpse during the faster polkas and schottisches. Some also use a touch of rouge and rice powder on their faces.

The dancing commenced with a Grand March up and down and all around the ball room, which was handsomely decorated for the occasion. Then there was a quadrille. As I do not know the steps, I had to sit out. A Lancers came next on the programme and that I do know, thanks to all those dancing classes Mama made us attend. Did we miss the quadrille lesson? There was a very handsome Master of Dance who kept things moving along, and tried to ensure that everyone who wished to dance was invited to do so. Miss Armstrong explained that the young gentlemen are often just as shy as the young ladies and need chivying along or they would be inclined to wander out to the balcony to smoke.

The whole matter of introductions is easily managed at a dance and all in all, we half-filled our dance cards. The large room was hot and crowded as this was the first big Anglo-American dance of the year. Sometimes the various music societies host a dance party, but we have not been invited to one of those yet. You do not need a formal invitation, but I think it is nicer if someone at least suggests you might come along, as Miss Armstrong did. Lily and I are certainly not the kind just to appear.

You might expect there would be more young ladies than gentlemen at these affairs, but the university here attracts many American students, and as it only admits men, you can see that things are nicely balanced. One meets philosophy students and theology students and one has little to talk about with them but since everyone is there to dance, not to talk, this is not at all the obstacle it might be.

I am sure you are right that a long engagement is a good idea. Selfishly I hope you will set a date for a summer wedding when I may be sure to be there. If the bank offers Mr. McFadden a better position in another town, will that make a difference to your plans? Is a transfer away from Edinburgh likely?

I write in haste, before Frau G. comes round to tell me it is time to turn the lights down. She is forever trying to save a pfennig or two on gas. And I have run out of candles.

~~~~~~~~~~~~~~~~~

Grassistrasse, No. 34

26th December, 1893

To all my dear family,

Christmas greetings from your loving daughter and sister. Many thanks for the generous Christmas gifts. The fan is exquisite and so much nicer than the plain one I have had until now. I shall be quite elegant at the next dance I attend.

I miss you all very much. I hope my Christmas parcel arrived safely and that the Lebkuchen survived the journey. My gifts were home-made again this year but I hope you liked the sketches and the pomanders. Of course I had to send those Pflammentoffel again. The children who sell them in the markets look rather needy and sweet, and I like to help them out. You will think the fur collar extravagant, but truly that was not the case.

Christmas at Grassistrasse is a skimpy affair with a small thin tree and few decorations. Lily and I were grateful that we were once again invited to join in the merrymaking at Braustrasse. Despite the late evening, we went church on Christmas morning promptly at ten o'clock. We knew we should arrive early, as we recalled from last year that the church would be very full. The Germans, even if they have not attended a single church service in the whole year, always go on Christmas and at Easter, so the church was packed. We squeezed in at the back and vowed we would come even earlier in future.

As I mentioned in an earlier letter my friend and violin classmate Charlotte Davis is keen to visit Berlin during Christmas break. She has friends there and one of them is to perform at a
~~~~~~~~~~~~~~~~~

recital, so tomorrow we will be off on the morning express train. Her friends will meet us and take us to their apartment. Charlotte and I will have to share a bed, but we shall be comfortable enough and of course we cannot afford a hotel.

I shall be sure to tell you all about our adventures when we return. In the meantime, happy new year or Prosit Neujahr to all of you, my dear family.

~~~~~~~~~~~~~~~~~

Grassis Strasse, 34

Friday, 5th January, 1894

Dear Mama und Papa,

Charlotte and I have had an exhilarating but exhausting trip to Berlin. On our first afternoon we simply walked about getting our bearings. The wide streets of Berlin would remind you of New Town, and after the narrow lanes of old Leipzig, they seemed very broad indeed. The principal street, Unter den Linden, is a double avenue with two rows of lime trees on the central boulevard. On each side of that boulevard is a wide carriage road, busy with traffic of all kinds.

All the important sights are close together except for the Zoo. From the Brandenburg Gate to the the Schloss – the castle – and the Museum Island, it is only three quarters of a mile. Just west of the Brandenburg Gate is the Thiergarten, a large park with ponds and coffee houses where we stopped for a warm drink at Kroll's Wintergarten. These winter gardens make a charming oasis in the generally bleak winter landscape. They are large glass buildings, filled with exotic plants and are all warm and green inside. Kroll's has an immense dining room and a concert hall as well.

We spent much of the next day at the New Museum where the most interesting exhibits are in the new Egyptology rooms. I shall write more about them to Birdie who is so fond of ancient history. Charlotte's friends took us around the cafés our first evening,
~~~~~~~~~~~~~~~~~

and the recital occupied us on the second. Berlin's Café Bauer – the one in Leipzig is a smaller copy – was utterly dazzling with its electric lights and lavish décor.

We had good intentions of visiting the Palace, with its six hundred rooms and its silver throne, but the morning proved sunny and mild so we changed our minds. Neither of us having appetite for another day of galleries, we took the tram out to the Charlottenburg area to the amazing Zoo, the first in Germany, and much the best we were told with almost as many animals as the London Zoo.

The Germans do seem very competitive, do they not? They seem to want to be the biggest and the best all the time. Almost as interesting as the animals themselves were the pavilions built for them. The Antelope House with its four minarets, an Indian style elephant house and the Egyptian Ostrich house were the most exotic. There are also music pavilions and an enormous restaurant.

We were off early the next day to return to Leipzig, very impressed with all we had seen but a little intimidated by such a large and busy city. The population is well over one million people and we agreed we much prefer our little Leipzig.

Ensemble class is still the favourite part of my week. Right now I am working on a violin trio by Haydn. Mr. Heins is playing the violincello, whilst I am playing the second violin part. Most of our classes are segregated, but they make an exception for the ensemble classes.

I have persuaded Mr. Heins and his sister Florence to take up skating. They come with me on those mornings when we all have leisure to go. It does seem silly to have to go on calling him Mister when we have become quite good friends and he <u>is</u> younger. Charlotte comes along too on occasion and yesterday Mr. Puddicombe joined us. It is not surprising that he is an excellent skater and he was most willing to give Florence a hand.

I shall try to add some more later on, but I must practise before my lesson this afternoon. I sent a postcard from Berlin. I hope it reached you. Of course in winter the Kroll Wintergarten did not look as pretty as the picture, but that was the only one I could find.

~~~~~~~~~~~~~~~~~~

Tuesday, 9th January, 1894

Dear Sister,

Prosit Neujahr to you, my dear sister. And to your Mr. McFadden as well. I hope you have enjoyed some fine times together over Christmas and had a jolly New Year's Eve.

New Year's here was more than jolly, it was positively boisterous, even rowdy which is a word that Miss Armstrong uses. I do like her American way of talking. As usual the streets were thronged with people – all kinds of people – including small children! At midnight the bells rang out all over the city and everyone shouted "Prosit Neujahr"on the streets and from the windows.

I understand now why Frau G. kept us in last year as the crowds, the pushing and dancing were alarming at times, but everyone was good natured. We even joined in the dancing up and
~~~~~~~~~~~~~~~~~~

down the street and in the squares where bands were playing. The Germans certainly do make a night of it.

I did not tell mother, but we had a close call at the museum in Berlin. I must have put my handbag down to take up my sketchbook, and I guess I was absorbed in sketching and distractedly moved along to the next room. When I realized I did not have my handbag I raced back whence we'd come, but no handbag to be seen. I did not have much money with me, but I was terribly frightened of losing my passport. In a panic we rushed to the Lost and Found office, but nothing had been turned in. The person in charge suggested that we wait and we did so, fretting all the while, I can tell you. Finally, after what seemed like hours, a guard appeared bearing my bag. He explained that he was not permitted to leave his post until his replacement arrived. That was why it took so long. You can imagine my relief when I found there was nothing missing. The guard had noticed it, seemingly abandoned, and picked it up for safe-keeping. So all was well, but we were certainly in a state for a while.

I trust Mama will relate the other news of our trip to Berlin, but I thought I would save for you some of the details of the Egyptian "apartments" in the New Museum.

There are five large rooms whose walls are covered with replicas of real Egyptian paintings. One of these rooms is arranged to represent the forecourt of the Temple of Karnac with sixteen huge, coloured pillars. These are copies, but the Chamber of Tombs is a restoration of part of the actual necropolis of Memphis! Fancy, Birdie, three whole tombs have been brought all the way from Egypt and rebuilt within the museum. The contents of one were on display; that rather unpleasant and we did not remain for long. Then there is a large collection of all manner of things, arms, utensils of all kinds, ancient garments and sandals and everything that encourages you to imagine life in ancient Egypt thousands of years ago. To my mind the most interesting things were the decorative items, mirrors of brass, pins of brass and ivory, and necklaces. In another part of the same museum there is a large collection of Greek and Roman pottery and bronze, but it was dimly lit and difficult to see anything well.

Imagining Violet

Classes have started up again. I practise, and go to my classes and practise. Matters have not improved in violin class but at least Charlotte is still with me. Her request for a change was rejected. Herr Rooster has given us some music by Wienawski this term, a Mazurka called *Chanson Polonaise*. It is certainly lively and more fun than Bach. Someone will be invited to perform it at an Abend and I want that someone to be me. He played a little of it for us and it is showy and impressive but perhaps not terribly difficult. The possibility of a performance will keep me motivated.

In ensemble class we are playing quartettes. Learning to watch your fellow players and take your cues from them is a different way of playing and is occasionally very satisfying but often frustrating. It can also make us laugh when one of us gets hopelessly tangled in the notes. As well, we practise the orchestral parts we are to play at the Prüfungen.

Of course there are the usual skating parties and often we go all the way to Connewitz; it no longer seems as far as it once did. But the hot chocolate is just as welcome when one reaches the village with its brightly lit cafés and their glowing hot stoves.

There have been a few uncomfortable moments of late with Frau Gibson who is growing suspicious about our suppers. I am afraid that Hilde, the general servant, has been telling tales, and we shall have to be ever so much more careful. As it happens, I know that young Hilde likes chocolate, so I shall be generous and share some chocolate with her and perhaps she will be more inclined to overlook certain things in future. It's that or go hungry at night. Well, I exaggerate, but at this time of year, we cannot picnic in the park, can we?

I hope Mr. McFadden enjoys his new position as assistant branch manager in Aberdeen. I know you will miss him and trust that you can stay close through letters and an occasional visit. But honestly, Birdie, how do you feel about moving to Aberdeen?

Imagining Violet

Sunday, 18th February, 1894

Dear Birdie,

I am grateful that you take such an interest in my music history classes and I want to tell you a little of what we have learned lately. I am copying from my notes so if I sound a little teacherish, that is the reason.

Professor Paul has been discussing the evolution of the orchestra and the different instruments. I did not know that our word orchestra comes from a Greek word meaning "I dance", because in ancient Greece singers and musicians always combined their music with dance. Isn't that a lovely idea? He said that in ancient Rome, the orchestras were composed mainly of flute players and that was also the case at the beginning of the Christian era. In medieval times trumpets and drums were the main instruments of musical bands.

The first opera was printed in 1600 and that is how we know which instruments were in the orchestra at that time. There was a harpsichord, a large guitar, a viol, large lute and three flutes. What was so different in those early works was that each character in the opera was accompanied in his solos by one special instrument.

I was surprised to learn that in the ancient world the violin was completely unknown. The saying, "Nero fiddled while Rome was burning" is in fact utterly impossible according to Professor Paul, since Nero and the ancient Romans did not have fiddles! The violin came into Europe from India, more than a thousand years ago, and it has gone through many changes since then, but that is a long time after the Roman period. The golden age of violin making was about 1650 to 1750 when the craft reached perfection. My new violin is a Copy of Joseph Guarnerius, who was one of the very finest violin makers of that time.

I especially like the story about Nero, don't you?

~~~~~~~~~~~~~~~~~~
~~~~~~~~~~~~~~~~~~

Imagining Violet

Grassistrasse, No. 34

3rd March, 1894

Dear Mama,

Thank you for sending news of the boys and of yourselves. In these dark winter days it seems a very long time until I shall be home again in August. It is also a very long time since I saw you all so many months ago. I am sorry Reg has been ill with la grippe and I hope he is now fully recovered. Papa's nice letter arrived in the morning post. I know he is busy at his office and that he does not care much for letter writing, so I was particularly grateful.

We have had some fine music lately. One of the best concerts took place last month, when the famous composer Edvard Grieg, who has Scottish ancestors by the way, conducted his own work at a Gewandhaus concert. It was three short movements of some new music written for a drama. And also at the Stadt Theater there was a premiere of a new opera by Puccini about a young woman named Manon who is a most interesting heroine. She is not the most virtuous of young ladies, but somehow one is sympathetic with her plight. Puccini's music has such beautiful melodies. But the story was sad – so different from the usual mix of Viennese comic operas that tour here.

Prüfungen season is upon us and our pupils' orchestra is rehearsing concertos to accompany the senior students. There is a great deal of repertoire to learn and we are simply told to do the best we can. As the master says, if you miss a note or two, just keep playing. The rhythm is everything! One senior pupil will give a Paganini Concerto which many have said is impossible to play. I cannot even imagine being able to play it, which rather puts me in my place.

My friend Lily is to graduate soon, but alas, she was not nominated for a Prüfung. She had been working so very hard on her Beethoven. But there are many, many talented pianists here and not everyone can make a Prüfung. Naturally she was greatly disappointed, especially as her parents had planned to come to Leipzig for the performance. Also, when one makes a Prüfung, the local newspaper critics come and often write something about one's debut, and one can use those kind words later when one is starting out as a performer. Her piano master told her that she would be ready next year but she must return home. We are such good companions and I am going to miss her very much.

I know it is selfish to be too dedicated to one's own ambitions, but here one <u>must</u> be self-centered. Everyone is. It is very competitive, especially when senior pupils are vying for selection for the Prüfungen. Music is everything and everyone wants to shine. If I want to succeed, I must put myself forward. Someone will be chosen to play the Wienawski we have been playing this term. Why should it not be me? When it comes to our violin and piano classes, if I want to do well, I have to be noticed, not let myself be lost in the crowd. I only have one more year here and I must forge ahead.

Next week, we have examinations in theory and history so I must study. I enjoy studying for the history and I have been doing well in harmony but I do not have much aptitude for counterpoint. I guess I am a wee bit down in the dumps, as I have had a beastly cold for several days and have been wishing I could have a good old fashioned hot toddy to relieve it. Honey and lemon in my tea help but a spoonful of Papa's whiskey would fix me up straightaway.

~~~~~~~~~~~~~~~~~

8th April, Sunday,1894

My dear sister,

I am desolate that you and Mr. McFadden have decided to end your engagement. Although I should say that it is tremendously brave of you to do this if you have accepted that you are not well suited. You say he was simply too affectionate? I suppose one might be uncomfortable with that.
~~~~~~~~~~~~~~~~~

Imagining Violet

But you know, Birdie, I am coming to think that it is too bad that there is such pressure in our society to marry. A life of childbearing and housekeeping should not be the only choice for women. Will you think perhaps of taking some training to become a teacher or would you possibly try to enrol at the university? I hope you are not terribly upset, although I am sure one cannot help but be disappointed. At least you will not have to move to Aberdeen! But please, do not say you will never marry. It may not be for everyone, I agree, but still, you may meet someone you like much better.

Let me distract you a little with the latest from our music history class. This term our professor has turned his attention to what he calls the "aesthetics" of music, an expression I did not understand at first. He asked us, for example, "Why should one tune please, another prove indifferent and another offend?" I would not have thought there was a clear answer to such a question, but many of the pupils said something like, "some tunes are nice and melodic, others are dull, and still others almost ugly."

Our Herr Professor agreed that these questions have been asked many times and suggested that no one has answered them satisfactorily. From my notes, "We have seen that the human ear welcomes the sounds to which it has been attuned by nature. We like to hear familiar sounds, and we shrink from combinations that are new or strange. But tastes are acquired by innovation and confirmed by habit, and with persistent and long continued schooling, the ear may be molded to fit any succession of musical intervals however disagreeable they may seem on first hearing." I had never thought about it that way before. Perhaps with persistent and continued schooling I might come to find the music of the pipes more agreeable? Or is that a ridiculous idea?

All that you have been writing about Ireland in your recent letters is so interesting. I am grateful that you are a student of history and that you can find books about Irish history in Scotland. The Celts sound very romantic; please tell me more in your next letter.

I mention this because at a café the other day a Miss O'Byrne was introduced and we got to chatting about where we were from.

Miss O'Byrne is from Dublin and when I told her I was born in County Mayo, she exclaimed, "Ah, but then, you are Irish too!" and whilst I demurred, saying that I rather think of myself as English, it set me to thinking about whether or not I am actually Irish, and what that means. Our parents have not spoken a great deal about Ireland, and you and I have only been there a few times on holiday to visit Mama's family. What is your opinion? Do you think of yourself as Irish? Or Anglo-Irish? Or just plain English? Or does it matter?

We have had some amusing entertainment lately. Some friends in the pupils' orchestra organized a small dance party to celebrate the end of the year. It was shortly after Lily left and I was reluctant to go without her, but Flo Heins agreed to come with me. Flo and I have become quite friendly over this winter.

Truly, Birdie, a small dance soirée is much more agreeable than a large ball, being less crowded and one knows most of the guests. Donald came too and looked quite the stylish gentleman in his evening clothes. He brought Mr. Puddicombe who was very amusing, but is more talented at the piano I think than on the dance floor. Not for the first time I was introduced to Mr. Jackson, an American, who is a lovely dancer and ever so nice. He is tall and fair haired and cuts a fine figure. He is a piano pupil but does not strike me as a very serious person. Still, I have not liked anyone as well for a long time.

Another piece of pleasant news. At Easter Flo's mother came from England for a visit. Whilst Mrs. Heins was here, she took us to supper at the large and elegant Café Bauer. It is four storeys high and the ground floor and the first floor are given over to the café and restaurant. Mrs. Heins explained that the facade is a combination of Renaissance, Rococo and Baroque, but I honestly could not tell one bit from another. Inside it is luxurious too with ornate ceilings and columns and all lit brilliantly with electric lights. The only difficulty is the smoke, as everyone smokes and it does get very thick and smelly. Nevertheless, it was a rare treat to have supper in a fine restaurant.

This has become a rather long letter, so I shall stop here. I hope I have cheered you up just a wee bit. Again, dear sister, let me say how sorry I am that you have given up Mr. McFadden.

~~~~~~~~~~~~~~~~

Grassistrasse, No. 34

Sunday, 13th May, 1894

My own dear Mama,

What can I write about that I have not written a dozen times.

Mr. Heins is rehearsing a quartette – the Schubert No.13 known as the *Rosamunde* – and he generously hoped I would be permitted to play with him. Herr Rüther said I was not ready, but agreed I could learn the part if I cared to, as an understudy as it were. It is a lovely piece and while I do not wish anyone ill.......

April was, as always, an extremely busy month with several wonderful concerts. One rare treat was hearing the *Scandinavian Symphony* by the British composer Mr. F. H. Cowen. Then the violinist Miss Edith Robinson gave a farewell concert at the old Gewandhaus, before returning to England. It is always inspiring to see a female violinist on the concert stage and I like to imagine myself in her place. Her extraordinary programme included three double concertos, one by Bach, one by Mozart and one by Brahms.

The third concert did not cost us a pfennig. Anton Rubenstein gave a recital of his own music and all we music students were admitted free! This was much appreciated as you can imagine. Finally, Verdi's new opera, *Falstaff*, was performed here for the first time. We do not see much Italian opera, and this <u>was</u> sung in German, but nevertheless it was very funny. It is too bad that one month can be so full, then there is very little that is worthwhile to go to, or write about, for weeks. Of course, the bands will soon start up
~~~~~~~~~~~~~~~~

in the parks and the outdoor cafés, but after such a full diet of symphonic music, it will be a musical desert from now until October.

Birdie seems bent on telling me she is not truly unhappy. I hope that is the case and that she is not simply being brave. In truth, she did not tell me much. It is difficult to be so far from home when there is trouble and unhappiness in the family. Your news about young Jack was not encouraging either. I am sorry to hear he is being so lazy at school.

Lily has returned to London, and I miss her smiling face and the companionship we had. A Miss Linklater has taken Lily's old room. She is from Bristol, and I hope I do not sound too unkind when I say that I do not find her congenial. She is given to knocking on my door at any time of day, to borrow something or other which she then neglects to return without a reminder or two, or she simply wants to ask how she looks in such and such a frock. I am a little fearful that she will want to borrow money but as I have very little, it will be easy to discourage that sort of request. Thank goodness Florence Heins lives upstairs.

Now that I have been a pupil for two years, I have begun to notice that much of the harmonious atmosphere at the Conservatory is superficial. Little by little, one becomes aware of tensions amongst the faculty members. The older teachers assign us the old masters, Beethoven, Haydn, Schubert and the like, as you might expect. The younger masters are more interested in the romantic composers like de Beriot and Spohr and still others are devoted to the Belgian-French School. The German composers have always dominated but de Beriot in particular is slowly gaining acceptance. His duets for two violins are within our abilities musically which is something I cannot always say about Beethoven.

I am of course very disappointed that I was not chosen to perform the Wienawski in June. I have worked hard on it and I need more experience in performing if I am to move on with my music. Still, I hope to play in one more Abend. But as I hear more of my fellows playing so brilliantly I begin to have doubts about my own abilities. I might not even be nominated for a Prüfung.

It seems that one's friends are constantly coming and going. We promise to write, but after a letter or two, well, we are all a little guilty about letting friendships slide away. I am determined that I will remain friends with Lily.

However, on a more positive note, it is possible to enjoy oneself in Leipzig with very little money. And there may be an opportunity to do a little tutoring come autumn. I should like to save some money for travelling or for a new evening gown. My poor old blue is barely presentable and I have been wearing the green for two seasons.

I shall hurry home to you in a few weeks and look forward to the long holiday and seeing all your dear faces again.

~~~~~~~~~~~~~~~~

Sunday, 10th June, 1894

Dear Lily,

I thank you for your letters and hope you have received mine. I will say it again; it is very different here without you. And believe me, Miss Linklater is not improving with time, as you optimistically suggested. I cannot write of such things to my family, but one of her most irritating habits is the unconscionable amount of time she spends in the Klo, if you don't mind the German expression. You would think she would realize that first thing in the morning, there are others who need the conveniences. I may move to new lodgings if she is still here in the autumn, but for now, I shall stay put. Thank goodness for Donald and Flo, who are such good companions.

I am indeed enjoying the aesthetics class which you took last year. It is opening up many new ideas and ways of thinking.

Mr. Jackson continues to make frequent appearances at our favourite café. He <u>is</u> amusing, and handsome too. We meet "by accident" in the park every few days and have a nice walk together. He seems to like me, but when we are in a group he flirts with everyone and I realize that I am not at all special. Still, he is a very
~~~~~~~~~~~~~~~~

good dancer, and we danced together perhaps more often than we should have at the year-end dance..

Mr. Puddicombe invited us to his private recital last week. I thought he played terrifically well, and Florence Heins was ever so enthusiastic, but he confessed afterwards that he had the most dreadful case of stage fright. He is beginning to think that a performing career may not be possible, although he is certainly talented enough. I do not get particularly nervous before performing and in that I suppose I am fortunate. Unlike Mr. P. though, I know I do not have an extraordinary talent. How terrible it would be to have to abandon one's dream because of nerves.

There are signs of spring everywhere and it is again a pleasure to be out of doors, rambling in the woods and parks. You can see that I am not as dedicated to my music as I ought to be if I am going to succeed on the concert stage.

Charlotte and I continue to talk of bicycling and we may do something about it. At least we have promised ourselves to find out if we can hire them in the city. We thought we could do so at the Rosenthal, but they are not available there this year. I suppose it would be awkward to ride wearing a skirt, but not impossible. I have not yet seen young women in Leipzig wearing those daring bloomers that Miss Armstrong talked about.

I told you that my sister has broken her engagement. She will only say that she realized after some months apart, that they were not well suited. Well, there must be more to it than that. I hope you do not object to my speaking openly, but I wonder if the physical side of marriage and the dangers of childbirth may be frightening to Birdie who has never been strong.

You will remember about the quartette Mr. Heins was leading? The second violin came down with pneumonia and must rest, so Herr Rooster agreed, without much enthusiasm I might add, that I could step in. It is a good thing I had been practising it on my own. We perform it in two weeks and I am glad to have this small chance of performing.

Thank you for the invitation to stop with you on my way through London. I hope you are will consider a visit to Edinburgh later in the summer?

Are you still searching for a suitable teacher? I hope you decide on someone soon. How fortunate you are to live in London where there are so many fine teachers. I am not likely to find anyone to go on with in Edinburgh. But once again, it is time to turn down the lights, so I shall say Güte Nacht for now.

~~~~~~~~~~~~~~~~

#7 Seaview Villas, Leith
3rd August, 1894

Dear Lily,

How delightful to see you on my way through London. The long holiday does not seem very long this year and I seem to be rushing about rather. In a few days we shall be away to Oban for our week's holiday and after that you will be here.

I have been round to see Catherine, a friend from my school days who is already married and recently became a mother. She finds it difficult to get out now what with the baby and only having the one servant and no nurse. We had an agreeable visit, although the cake was not fresh. Oh, that is rather mean of me. For Catherine has her hands full keeping house and looking after baby, who is a sweet little thing, I suppose. Even so, like Margaret, she did not seem much interested in my stories of Leipzig, and my goodness, she did go on and on about the infant who was brought in to be introduced, all wrapped up and virtually invisible. It is unkind of me but after an hour of this, I had heard enough. We were good friends at school, although we did not write often. I shall invite her for tea as soon as she is able to come on her own.

Please send a postcard to the Caledonia Hotel in Oban and let me know which train you will take.

~~~~~~~~~~~~~~~~~

Imagining Violet

5th September, 1894

Dear Lily,

Once again, thanks to you and your dear mother for your kind hospitality. I have, of course, written separately to your Mama, whom I like very much. I hope you will not object to a friendly admonition – what a big word – but I think you could be a little more patient with her. She is not nearly as strict as my mother, as you yourself have seen. Fancy not wishing to let us go alone on our *Columba* excursion at our age!

I hope you have happy memories of your time in Edinburgh. It surely is a beautiful city which I am only now beginning to appreciate. We moved there when I was eleven and what eleven-year old takes an interest in old buildings? The only one we liked as children was the castle.

I am to play the Wienawski at an Abend in a fortnight! Another pupil was to perform it in June, but as the date approached he decided that he was not adequately prepared. I may be second choice but I do not mind, very much. Still, I am in a bit of a stew now because in the long break I foolishly gave myself a holiday from my fiddle. Now I must practise ever so hard; yet if I do too much, I feel the cramped nerves in my left hand.

I have saved my best news for last. The nicest young Canadian has arrived in Leipzig. He is in the same pension as Donald, so naturally Donald brought him along to the café for a drink and we were introduced. His name is Frank Welsman. Like you he is a pianist, but he also plays the violin and the viola and has been studying German back in Canada. Imagine that! He has arrived here ever so much better prepared than I was, but of course, he is not as young as I was when I arrived, and in fact he is a little more than a year older which makes him nearly twenty-one. He is tall enough with wavy light brown hair. It is a little odd that I am a senior student and he is in some ways a beginner, but only in that he is beginning his time in Leipzig.

I do think I like Canadians in general; is that a foolish thing to say? You have met Mr. Puddicombe and liked his warm sense of humour. But if one might generalize, Canadians are quieter and more polite than Americans, or at least the Americans I have met, and they do not appear much concerned about matters of class which I find entirely refreshing. Mr. Jackson seems to have found a new set of friends and all things considered that is just as well.

We did have a jolly outing on the *Columba* didn't we, despite the frightfully early start. Getting to the west coast even for a day is a rare treat, and I was glad that Birdie was up to coming with us.

Write soon, please. I want to know how you are getting on with your new teacher and whether you are still considering taking some pupils or whether you are thinking about preparing a recital, or both!!

~~~~~~~~~~~~~~~~~

14th September 1894

Dear Birdie,

I am glad that you do not seem to have had much difficulty putting Mr. McFadden out of your thoughts. I will tease you a little and ask if perhaps someone else may be hovering on the edge of your affections?

But I am sorry that Jack continues to plague dear Mama and Papa about staying in school. One of these days he is likely to take to the road or do something else drastic, because I fear he is not going to conform to their idea of a proper son. Reg is not so adventurous and may be the ideal son.

It is always agreeable to see my old school friends in the summer, but I feel I have outgrown them. They see nothing but marriage in their future, whilst I am still devoted to my fiddle and my studies, although my hopes of becoming a concert violinist are fading. In the company of such talented pupils like Mr. Heins, I believe I am becoming more realistic. I realize there is not much else
~~~~~~~~~~~~~~~~~

a young lady from a respectable family may do except marry, but it seems such a waste, to spend one's days paying calls, visiting one's dressmaker, worrying about being invited to this luncheon or that soirée, as if these are the only things of importance in life.

I was interested in what you said, Birdie, about a life of study and I wonder if Mama and Papa will encourage you to follow that path. I suppose I shall marry eventually but there is much I want to do before I am restricted to home and hearth and babies. I still carry the vision of playing my violin on a concert stage some day.

Last week I was introduced to a fine young pianist recently arrived from Toronto, Canada who has moved into the same pension as Donald and Flo. He is a little older than I am, but has already spent four years at a college of music in his home city so comes here rather more advanced than most. I have not heard him play yet, but Donald says he is very talented. Certainly he is amiable. He has decided to study privately rather than enrol in the Conservatory where he would be obliged to take many courses which he has taken already. He has made arrangements to study composition with Herr Schreck though, and piano with Herr Krause.

Now that I have had the chance to ride a bicycle at home I shall try it again here. It took a few attempts before I could stay upright didn't it, but I'd rather have had those mishaps in Leith than in Leipzig, where one knows so many people. But once I managed it, I found it completely exhilarating to go flying along on two wheels.

I shall close now as I am to play in an Abend soon and must put in as much time with my violin as I can. I was so disappointed last spring when another pupil was selected, and now I am to do it after all, I admit I am thrilled. But I am also chewing my nails. Still, if I perform very well, I might get a Prüfung after all.

~~~~~~~~~~~~~~~~
~~~~~~~~~~~~~~~~

Imagining Violet

Grassistrasse, No. 34

10th October, 1894

Dear Mama,

All is well this term. My disagreeable neighbour did not return after the long holiday and even better, her room remains empty.

I played the *Chanson Polonaise* at an Abend at the end of September and I thought that it went fairly well. But Herr Sitt shook my hand afterwards and said, "Well played, Fräulein Courtenaye", which was decidedly guarded praise. Even so, it is good to have some kind of performance to work towards, otherwise I find myself too easily distracted from practising

In fact, no one tells me these days what tremendous progress I am making as they did a few years ago.. I must be honest with you, dear Mama, and say there is little point in my having extra lessons. Thank you for offering the opportunity but I know it would be an additional burden for you.

Our pupils' orchestra has started up again and I am more comfortable there this term because I am familiar with some of the repertoire.

I know you enjoy hearing about the musical world here and of course October is the beginning of the season. One event of interest was the fine recital last week by a Belgian violinist, Mademoiselle Irma Sethe. She is a year younger than I am! A year or so ago I would have found her inspiring, but now she serves as a reminder that I am unlikely to succeed as a virtuoso. Mlle Sethe was a child prodigy who performed all over Europe as a little girl. I used to think that travelling around and playing concerts would be rather glamorous, but now I think, "What a life for a child!" Mlle Seth has been studying since she was five, and she is but eighteen now.

The dress goods I brought with me have made up into the loveliest deep rose gown and I can retire once and for all my faithful blue which really is shabby after all its outings. Perhaps I shall attempt to dye the green one and give it a new life and I shall save the rose for special evenings. My lilac, is still serviceable.

I have become quite friendly with a young Canadian pianist whom I met through Mr. Heins a few weeks ago. He is from the city of Toronto in Canada where he attended the Toronto College of Music over the past four years. He is already nearly twenty-one. His parents are from Devon, but they emigrated to Canada thirty years ago. His father has a shop, so, yes, they are in trade, and the shop, but it would seem they are prosperous enough to send their son to study here.

You kindly inquired after Mr. Heins and I realized I have neglected to mention him in letters lately. He is such a brilliant player and has already moved into advanced classes, so we are no longer in the same ensemble group. Flo keeps a good eye on him and does not let him over-do it.

My violinist friends are debating these days about the growing use of vibrato. Some young players seem to use it to excess. Do you remember one of my early tutors, Miss Bessie Doyle who was so dramatic? Well more and more, at the Abends, the string players are adopting this more demonstrative style. The masters do not all approve, but a few agree that with larger orchestras and bigger concert halls, the restrained and intimate approach cannot be appreciated from the upper galleries. And so the controversy rages. For myself, whilst I may not suffer from severe stage fright, I fear I am not a natural performer and I cannot play with such temperament as do some of my friends.

My violin master has spoken about my doing some tutoring, but nothing has come of it yet. Otherwise life goes on much the same as ever and as always, we look forward to winter and skating.

~~~~~~~~~~~~~~~~
~~~~~~~~~~~~~~~~

Imagining Violet

Grassistrasse, 34

14th November, 1894

Dear Lily,

Thank you for your thoughtful letter. I am grateful that we can have this discussion even if it is by post. You have always been such a staunch friend, encouraging me when I was downhearted. But Lily, I simply must accept that my talent is a small one. When I hear what my fellow pupils can do with their violins, after two and a half years of study, I know it is impossible for me to achieve the same quality of performance. My notions of a performing life begin to seem a trifle foolish. You and I have often discussed whether one can succeed with talent alone. Is it just talent, or is it ambition, or some combination of these? Or is it something else again? Persistence? Stamina? Luck? Plain good health?

We both knew pupils who suffered serious pain from over-practising, possibly even serious injury. We heard of that young pianist Mr. Hoben who damaged his right arm so seriously he could only play pieces for the left hand. He went home to New Zealand for a rest cure, but he never returned. Everyone says he would have had a brilliant career. And yet, if you do not work all the time, you do not impress.

But it's not in me to devote myself completely to practise. Even if I thought it were healthy, I cannot stick with it eight hours a day. In winter, the ice is calling, in spring and fall, the woods and pathways demand a ramble. I tell myself that seeking balance is the right approach, but that will not lead to a life on the concert stage. I feel I should somehow be flattened by this realization, but curiously, I am not upset.

My respect and liking for Mr. W continue to grow. You know that he came here hoping to pursue studies in both violin and piano. Well, Herr Krause insists that he make a choice of which instrument to go on with full time. He plays the violin so well and we have been having a lovely time with some de Beriot violin duos. There is a large and attractive general sitting room in Frau Schwabe's pension where there are also young ladies in residence, so in the evening, a few of us gather there and take turns playing. At Frau Gibson's as you well know, one has one's own room and that is all.

It is good to hear that you have a few young pupils. Having a little money of one's own is important I agree. I hope to get some tutoring soon, perhaps in time to buy Christmas presents.

~~~~~~~~~~~~~~~~~

18th November, 1894

Dear Mama,

I have a new neighbour, a Fräul. Hauptmann, from München. She is quiet and rather shy, and we have our little conversations auf Deutsch. I do not get much opportunity to chat in German so it is good practice. I do miss Lily, but with a nice group of friends I am not lonely. A small pension such as Frau Gibson's is better for practising as there are not the sounds of many people playing to distract and annoy. I shall be content to stay here until I complete my studies in April.

Whilst it is becoming grayer and colder, we always have some marvelous concert or other to lift our spirits. Last week we went with eager anticipation to hear Mr. Antonin Dvorak's latest symphony called *From the New World* so-called because he has been in America. We thought the rehearsal performance was excellent, but other friends attended the concert and said the audience did not care for it. I have come to the conclusion that Leipzigers are overly critical. A few weeks back, many people left in the middle of a performance of Brahms' *Fourth Symphony*, and that is a completely wonderful piece. At the Dvorak concert, the American soprano, Madame Nordica, amazed everyone by singing in four different languages in one programme. I was not able to get a ticket to see her in *Lohengrin*, but we adored her performance as Violetta in *La*
~~~~~~~~~~~~~~~~~

Traviata. Even though la Nordica was much older than her tenor, one could still feel how much they loved each other. I expect I am repeating myself, but thank goodness we are seeing a little more Italian opera.

My friend Mr. Welsman has not yet made his decision. In Canada he had been studying and performing both violin and piano and at his final concerts in Toronto he performed on both instruments in one programme which is impressive, don't you agree? However, here his piano master insists that he make a choice between the two, saying he cannot excel at both instruments. Mr. W does not want to give up either. I wish I could think of something helpful to say.

The skating season has begun at last. Everyone is delighted as for weeks it has been damp and dull but not cold enough for the ponds to freeze. I like it very much, especially when one can skate with good friends. From time to time I have to stop and remember that this will be my last winter to skate on the ponds and the river. When I am home again I shall make a much bigger effort to go to Duddingston Loch.

I have begun to tutor a young girl from Belfast who is preparing for her entrance examination. Miss Hearne is sixteen, as I was, and misses her family and she has not had the good fortune to find such a homelike pension as we had at Fräul. Hohmann's. It seems very long ago that I was in the same position, studying first with Miss Doyle, then with Miss Street. Goodness knows I am not in their league, but Herr Sitt evidently believes I can be of help to Miss Hearne. It is generally expected that I shall move on to teach violin to beginners when I finish my studies here, and the Conservatory likes to provide these opportunities to exercise one's teaching skills. I am happy to earn a little money of my own, and hope I may be more generous with my Christmas shopping.

~~~~~~~~~~~~~~~~
~~~~~~~~~~~~~~~~

Sunday, 2nd December

Dear Birdie,

Lately Mr. W. and Mr. Puddicombe have been coming to concerts with Flo and me and it is so interesting to experience them through their eyes. There is no permanent orchestra in Toronto and he finds the musical offerings here almost overwhelming in their variety. In fact, he has scarcely ever heard a symphony played through from beginning to end. It is the custom in Toronto for an orchestra to perform a single movement only in an evening's programme. We heard the Schubert *Fifth* last week and he was very moved to hear how all four movements work together to form a whole. Mr. Puddicombe has been here for three years so is accustomed to the very full calendar of concerts.

Things have become a little awkward with Charlotte of late. I did not realize that she thought her friendship with Mr. Puddicombe was something deeper than it was. I should have noticed sooner how much he enjoys Flo's company, especially on the ice.

We were surprised at how the audience behaved at one concert last week. It was a work written by the Kaiser himself, called *Song to Aegir*, Aegir being an old Norse god of the sea. The director had provided an elaborate scenic background which added to the effect, but that was not enough to stop many in the audience from hissing energetically while others applauded the performance. We four thought the music pleasant enough and agreed that it did not deserve such a rude response. We thought it was odd that the audience did not feel the need to show respect for their Emperor's creation. If the Queen were ever to compose something, would we not applaud it, whatever its merits?

Skating with Mr. W. is wonderful and it is very nice indeed that we may hold hands in public provided we have our skates on. Off the ice, we are circumspection itself. Dancing, however, he is not fond of, but he has on one or two occasions agreed to be my partner.

A young man who attends a dance is obliged to dance whether or not he is familiar with the pieces, and Mr. W. makes the effort, for my sake, which is very sweet of him. A group of us went to the Mendelssohn Society's annual soirée and had a wonderful evening. And the Americans' annual Thanksgiving dance was very pleasurable as always. It is ever so much nicer when there is a special friend to dance with.

Flo and I persuaded Mr. Welsman to come to church with us, which he did graciously and said politely that he found the service interesting. I believe his mother belongs to a new sort of Protestant church called the Church of Christ's Disciples. Frank was taken there as a lad, but did not care for it.

It will be very jolly to show him round the Christmas Markets which start up soon. And as I have been earning a little money with my tutoring, I shall enjoy shopping all the more. We shall see how he likes the pastries and Glühwein. Then there are Christmas dances in some number which will be ever so much more fun this year.

It is time for me to be realistic. I am coming to accept that what talent I have is a small one. I can see that I am not as dedicated to my music as others are. I cannot make myself devote every waking minute to practising. Surely there is more to life.

Thank you for your news about Mr. Hamish MacCunn's new opera. I am glad you and mother were there for such a great occasion. And that Papa went too, even though he insists he does not like opera. I can well believe that it was the first such premiere in Edinburgh in a generation. We have a steady diet of opera here, although I know now that not every offering is worth hearing or seeing.

I wish you and everyone a happy Christmas. This time next year we shall all be together again.

~~~~~~~~~~~~~~~~~
~~~~~~~~~~~~~~~~~

4th January, 1895

Dear Mama and Papa,

New Year's greetings, and many thanks for your thoughtful, generous gifts, both for Christmas and for my birthday. It is hard to believe that this is the fourth birthday I have had in Leipzig.

Christmas Eve was different this year and pleasantly so. Frau Schwabe,the landlady of Miss and Mr. Heins and Mr. Welsman, invited me to join in their Christmas Eve festivities. For three years Lily and I enjoyed Fräul. Hohmann's hospitality, but I have not seen much of the latter in past months, and when Frau Schwabe said I should be welcome at her house, I happily accepted and took small bags of toasted almonds for everyone. There are about eight pupils living in Frau Schwabe's pension, three of them being young ladies, so it is entirely proper for me to be there. Frau Schwabe has rooms on both the third and fourth floor of this building. Some of them are "dachzimmer", which means rooms under the roof. If a person is very tall, can he stand up straight?

Frau S. is a warm and friendly woman, but I would have to say she is not a very good cook. Perhaps we were spoiled by Fräul. H. Nevertheless, though the sausage was tough, and the cabbage was mush, there was a lot of laughter and singing especially with the tradition of silly small gifts after the meal.

On Christmas Day, as we always do, we attended service at the Thomas Kirche. And for once we arrived in sufficient time to find a place. Mr. W. was very moved by the pure young voices of the boys' choir as they sang Bach's Christmas music. Then, as the day was not too blustery, we joined the crowds of Leipzigers making their traditional Christmas Day walk. We ventured all the way to the Rosenthal which truly was a winter wonderland, with sun sparkling on the snow-covered trees.

At one point the conversation turned to the various Christmas rituals our families enjoy. I was surprised when Mr. W. said he did not think there were any Christmas customs that were particularly Canadian. They celebrate much as we do at home, with the Yule logs, Santa Claus, carol singing and turkey. We agreed that what we missed here was having Christmas crackers to pull at the table and plum pudding.

I must tell you about Dr. Joachim's performance. He plays almost every New Year's Day at the Gewandhaus. It is fascinating to watch him and see and hear how he varies his performance style according to the composer. You remember that we saw him in Edinburgh some five years ago, but now I watch with greater appreciation of his extraordinary technique. Most violinists approach all their repertoire with the same style. But not Dr. Joachim, who is rather old now and yet so vigorous. When he performs Bach, he keeps to the simple clean style. It is impeccable, one might say. But when he turns to more romantic repertoire, he puts his heart and soul into it. This year he again played the Beethoven Violin Concerto and finished with the Romance from his own *Hungarian Concerto*. I cannot imagine anything more wonderful than to create a piece of beautiful music and then perform it to an adoring audience. I think that when Mr. Welsman heard Joachim play, he felt a little better about giving up his ambitions to be a violinist. He said to me after the concert, "I could never have played like that."

I continue to work with Miss Hearn who will have her examination in a few weeks. I recall that I found it helpful to have a tutor who was closer to my own age, and Herr Sitt, who arranges these things, has been complimentary.

It was kind of you and Papa to assure me you are not too dreadfully disappointed that I am not to make a Prüfung. You know that I came to Leipzig with such hopes and ambitions, the hopes and dreams of a young girl, in truth, and it has taken a while to find my place here amidst such talent, such ability, such musicianship and such ambition. I shall be forever grateful that you and Papa have allowed this experience, encouraged me to do my best and to develop what ability I have. Probably you are both relieved that I no longer imagine myself gracing the concert stage but see a more conventional life ahead. But I shall have to devote myself to something when I am home in Scotland. Perhaps, with your permission, I might resume drawing classes. I did try here, for a little while, but it was too much with all the music classes.

~~~~~~~~~~~~~~~~~~

January 4th, 1895

Dear Birdie,

Happy New Year. May 1895 be a happier year for you than 1894.

I wrote a little about my Christmas time to Mother, but forgot to mention New Year's Eve which was even livelier than last year. It was unseasonably mild that evening, and rain had cleared the snow away, which made the ponds unbearable I regret to say, but the weather brought out vast crowds of Leipzigers of all ages.

As expected, it was a great lark visiting the Christmas markets with Mr. Welsman. We stuffed ourselves with Lebkuchen and candied almonds and had large mugs of Glühwein. He had a grand time buying small gifts for his brothers and sisters. He is very modest, but I begin to suspect that he is the only one of his family who is truly talented.

I am happy to know that your Epsom salts baths are giving you more energy. I cannot enjoy similar benefits, I am sorry to say, as it is out of the question here to soak in the bathtub for any length of time and more than one hot bath a week is frowned upon.

Tomorrow I shall be twenty years old, the start of my third decade, and I feel quite grown up. As my last few months at the Con. commence, I must think about life after Leipzig and I have mixed feelings, Birdie. On the one hand, I shall be content to return to the real world. It is all very well to live a life where no one talks of anything but music, of their next performance, of their injuries and their landladies, of problems with Herr Professor this or that, but it is after all, a somewhat narrow existence. My goodness, how I would like to have time to simply read a novel, or to have some slight idea of
~~~~~~~~~~~~~~~~~~

what is going on in the world outside the Conservatory. I know a good deal of music history now, and masses of theory, and I suppose I may say I am an accomplished violinist, but oh, how ignorant I am about just about everything else. At least I had a few years of high school with classes in English history and geography. Many of the young ladies who come here at the age of fourteen or fifteen do not have even that.

On the other hand, leaving will mean leaving friends and one in particular as you know, and giving up a good deal of freedom which I do not expect to find under Papa's roof. Here one can make friends with anyone one likes. You know how it is at home, where any acquaintance must come from a certain level of society. One cannot mix with those above, and certainly not with those from lower classes. What a shame it is that these things are so fixed and rigid. My Canadian friends rejoice in a society that seems to be much less strict.

When I try to write about life in general, I find myself starting each sentence with Mr. W and I, did this or that. We have taken to meeting one way or another almost every day. We often just happen to arrive at our favourite café at about the same hour of an afternoon. I am glad he has taken up skating, but being Canadian, he has been skating all his life.

I asked him to tell me about his family and his city on Lake Ontario. The Great Lakes sound like inland seas, and not at all like lakes as we know them. He has two brothers and two sisters; sadly one younger brother died of typhoid a few years ago at the . His oldest brother, Fred, is a jeweler and watchmaker with his own shop and he is also a bandleader in a military band. Then his older sister Olive has married a pharmacist, also named Fred, which will be endlessly confusing, and the younger sister, Alice, sounds like a fun-loving sort. She is also very musical, according to Frank. The youngest, Arthur, works in the family dry goods business. To pursue music as a profession is a great change of direction for this family.

I suspect that Mr. W has something special planned for my birthday. I shall write to you later but right now, thank you for your good wishes and the pretty birthday card.

~~~~~~~~~~~~~~~~~

15th February, 1895

Dear Lily,

Thanks for yours of last week and I hope your dear mother is feeling better. Please give her my best wishes.

I am sure you will want to know the latest gossip about Mr. Jackson. I wrote you, I think, about the rumour that he was taking an untoward interest in one of the younger pupils? Well, as the story came out, it seems that the young pupil in question, was Miss Dorothy Shields. She was in one of my classes last year and her mother was utterly irritating. I suppose it is fair to say that Miss Shields, young and pretty as she is, does not know much about the world, and found the attentions of Mr. Jackson flattering. Naturally, he was rather pleased with himself and boasted that he was able to persuade her to take walks with him, walks which she kept secret from her mother. Well, the worst thing happened. The mother suspected that her daughter was up to something unsuitable, managed to get it out of her and complained to the Registrar, and except for her classes, Mrs. Shields has confined her poor misguided daughter to quarters and chaperones her absolutely everywhere.

That is too bad for Miss Shields, but she will no doubt get over it; we all suppose she imagined herself in love. But the Registrar called Mr. Jackson – who <u>is</u> a terrible flirt, but a good fellow for the most part – into the office and gave him strict instructions to curtail his misplaced gallantry or risk suspension. As it <u>is</u> a first offense and as Mr. Jackson was abjectly apologetic and took all the blame, the Registrar felt moved to give him a second chance. It is quite a chastened young man who joins our table and there are no more mysterious disappearances and unexplained absences. I am relieved,
~~~~~~~~~~~~~~~~~

as you can imagine, that my acquaintance with him did not develop into a real friendship.

We have had good skating so far, although things went rather amiss last Friday when the group of us – Donald, Flo, Harry and Frank and a few others – set off rather later than usual to skate down to Connewitz, and stayed late singing and larking about at our favourite café. Charlotte never did like skating very much and has pretty much given it up. Outside of our classes, I do not see as much of her as I used to.

When we emerged from the toasty warmth of the café, a howling blizzard had set in. Fierce winds were gusting down river directly at us. It was a struggle, I can tell you, to skate against that wind into the blowing snow. We all held hands in a line and skated together so no one would become lost. Flo had a time of it keeping up but we kept pulling her along until we made it back to town. Luckily no one suffered frostbite, but oh my it was painful as our toes thawed out and how we were shivering! One can bundle up in cloaks and so on, but there is nothing I know of that can keep your feet warm.

You missed the most extraordinary set of concerts the last week of January, Lily. Brahms himself was in Leipzig and what a feast! On the 27th, he gave his new clarinet sonatas with Herr Muhlfeld. Two nights later, Eugen d'Albert took part in a performance of the great *F Minor Pianoforte Quintet*. Oh Lily, you would have loved it! D'Albert is sublime. Then the grand finale, when Herr Brahms led the orchestra and d'Albert played not one but both pianoforte concertos with the *Academic Overture* to top things off. As the newspapers explained, "The grand old master had not been in Leipzig in over seven years, and the people of Leipzig indulged in a good deal of hero worship." Honestly, it was almost worth your staying an extra year.

Perhaps I should not say that, as I know you are moving ahead happily with your new teacher. I am sorry, though, that your plan for a recital did not go forward. Are you seriously thinking about going to Paris? "They" say, as you know, that lessons in Paris are invaluable for smoothing off the rough German edges we evidently acquire whilst we are here. "They" should not always be attended, but in this case I wager "They" are correct.

The tutoring keeps me busier than expected, but I am not sure if I shall make a successful teacher. I have finished with Miss Hearn who was easily distracted and far from punctual. Indeed, I often found myself waiting for her, having finished my own practice session early on her account. I thought it inconsiderate of her to keep me standing about. My new pupil, Miss Ellerby, is from one of those New England states with the unpronounceable names. She has acquired some very odd habits from her teachers in America and now needs regular coaching as she tries to adopt what are thought here to be the correct ways of standing and holding her bow and her violin. We have met twice, so we shall see how we go on. But it is very nice indeed to have a little money of my own

I have done well to get this far without mentioning Mr. W. once. We get along so very well; I suppose you could say we are keeping company but naturally there is no talk of the future. We do not talk about our feelings. If we were at home, I dare say we could not spend so much time together without raising eyebrows but thankfully, we are here. Where will it all lead, you ask? Well, Lily, it is early days and I do not allow myself to dream very much. Well, not very much. Whilst he is not registered as a pupil, he intends to study here for at least two more years.

~~~~~~~~~~~~~~~~~
~~~~~~~~~~~~~~~~~

Imagining Violet

2nd March, 1895

Dear Mama,

I have not written sooner because last week I caught a chill after a skating expedition. Perhaps we were out too long, and it was exceedingly cold and windy. I heeded your oft-heard advice, and took to my bed for a day or two and missed rehearsal for a trio I am playing in. Someone said the other day that a young woman of twenty never listens to her mother, but I hope I am not typical as I do miss my dear Mama when I am poorly.

Of course, you have been a good deal colder in Leith, or so I hear. Lily has written about the extreme cold weather Scotland suffered last week. I hope you were able to keep warm and did not have to venture out in it very much.

Since the Brahms' concerts at the end of January there has not been much music worth writing about. Oh there is plenty of it, but do you think that perhaps after four years I have begun to take it for granted that something amazing will happen every week? My friend Mr. Welsman continues to be impressed at the large number of famous performers who regularly visit Leipzig, along with all the musical organizations that are resident here.

Flo and I go about together a good deal with Charlotte too if she is free. Flo is less dedicated to her studies than her brother. Indeed, she has taken the time to write and stage a clever little play about student life called, *Looking Backward*. In it she imagines a time twenty years hence when various students look back on their time at the Conservatory. It was very witty and a great success with the audience. She has become quite adept at skating and spends a good deal of time with Mr. Puddicombe on the ponds. I would not be surprised if they became engaged.

From what you have been telling me lately, it appears that the musical season in Edinburgh is much improved in the last year or so. How delightful that Mr. Henschel's Scottish Orchestra has performed the *Symphony from the New World*. It is in their favour, in my opinion, that the audience in Edinburgh enjoyed it with more enthusiasm than people here. If Mr. Henschel's orchestra goes forward, there will be more music next season when I am home.

The tutoring is going well. My first pupil, Miss Hearn, passed her entrance examination with excellent results. Herr Sitt seemed satisfied and asked me the other day when I would be returning to Edinburgh. When I told him I would be finished with my studies at Easter he paused for a moment and asked whether it might be possible for me to stay on for a month or so. He did not say anything further, but Charlotte thinks he might ask me to continue on as a tutor. If I could contribute to my board, and of course there would be no fees to pay, do you think you and Papa would agree to my staying until July if that is indeed what Herr Sitt has in mind?

I shall write my very last examinations in theory and history toward the end of the month, and I am studying hard for them. I would like to see some favourable remarks on my certificate about my work in theory, at least. I keep going with the piano lessons, but my heart is not in it.

There is some talk at our table at the café about a walking trip during Easter break. As I approach the end of my time here I realize how unadventurous I have been, sticking close to my violin, my classes and studies. It would be grand to see a little more of the Saxon countryside, and I like to think I am strong enough to tramp in the mountains as the men do. It may all simply be talk, but something may come of it.

~~~~~~~~~~~~~~~~~
~~~~~~~~~~~~~~~~~

Imagining Violet

2nd April, 1895

Dear Birdie,

I hope you are enjoying a spell of good health now that the severe winter weather is over. Did that new tonic help? And I like to think that you follow doctor's orders and get some fresh air every day.

My final examinations – there were just two of them – were not too difficult. I had worked diligently at the history and aesthetics so received a respectable mark. The harmony exam is more of a practical nature. You are given a set of tasks to complete within the two hours of the examination and you simply do your best, trying to remember all the complicated rules. As I had studied harmony at Mr. Waddel's, I have had an advantage here all along compared to the other young ladies.

You asked how I feel about coming home. And that is a good question. I am rather in a muddle, if you want to know. On the one hand, I shall be glad to be home with you all, and also, I am ready to be finished with my studies here and thirdly, I will not mind being somewhere where everyone speaks English. On the other hand, it may be difficult to return to a society where class is everywhere and everything. It has been wonderful here, where student society is almost completely classless. This may be particularly true of music students who revere talent above all and for whom money is of little importance. The size of one's allowance does not affect one's standing in the least nor does one's wardrobe, thank goodness.

And it will be difficult to leave the music behind. For my very last Gewandhaus concert, we treated ourselves to a ticket to the concert, not just the rehearsal. Herr Hilf played Arnold Spohr's *D Minor Violin Concerto*, and the orchestra performed Herr Direktor Reinecke's new *Symphony in G Minor*. I marvel that Herr Reinecke composes as much as he does and still has the full responsibility of directing the Conservatory and the Orchestra. Just last year he completed two different festival overtures. He is not a young man either and will soon retire. It will be interesting to see how the Con. will change under a new director.

Mother has written writing about the numerous concerts in Edinburgh this past winter which cheers me considerably. I hope you may go often and that Papa is willing to purchase tickets. Sometimes he displays an almost German sense of thrift. I like his Irish side better.

In the meantime, I am glad that I may stay here through June provided there is enough tutoring to keep me busy and employed. I wish I knew what I wanted to do after I return to Edinburgh.

But first, we are taking a little holiday the week after Easter. A group of us has organized an excursion to a town called Wernigerode, which is a two hours journey by train, going by way of Halle. The town is supposed to be very attractively sited on a river in the foothills of the Harz Mountains, and the North German guide book makes it sound thoroughly charming. There are a great many walking paths and one can climb to the very top of Mount Brocken, although I am not sure I am capable of such a climb. If we had heaps of money, we could hire a carriage, but we do not, so we shall not.

Let me know what you are reading in your next letter. Have you given any more thought to becoming a teacher?

~~~~~~~~~~~~~~~~~

19th April 1895

Dear Mama and Papa,

This will be a short letter to tell you of our Easter outing which was a great success. There were six in our party and we set off by the early train and changed in Halle to a slow train to Wernigerode which is an interesting old town as well as the start of a good many walking paths and trails. Friends had recommended the Goldener Hirsch, a small country inn, where the food was very plain, but at least it was hot. I have sent a postcard.
~~~~~~~~~~~~~~~~~

I shared a small room with Flo Heins, and after a restful night in our lumpy bed, we set off the next morning under a bright blue sky, mild temperatures and brilliant sunshine. And yes, Mama, we took care to wear broad brimmed hats so we would not have sun on our faces. Our hostess, who is accustomed to student lodgers, lent us haversacks for the day as well as walking sticks.

Wernigerode has an ancient town centre which is very charming with its timber-framed houses and famous medieval town hall. The town is also the starting point for a good deal of tramping about in the mountains, so it is doubly attractive to the visitor. We spent our first afternoon exploring the old town's sights and admired, from a distance, the fairy tale castle atop the hill where the Count Stolzer-Wernigerode lives. I wonder if some day it will be possible to visit such places.

The principal attraction for most visitors is Mount Brocken, the highest peak in the Harz Mountains at 3700 feet. They say it is about ten miles to the top and back but Flo and I did not think we could manage that so we chose a pleasant but less strenuous walk up a long winding forest road to the Forsterplatz. There was a restaurant there but our landlady had packed us a good box lunch, so we simply rested on a bench before going further on up the hill to the famous viewpoint from which we could gaze down at the town.

Despite our preparations, I fear my footwear was inadequate and unfortunately on our way back down the hill I tripped over a stone and over I went, with some injury to my ankle I regret to say. I was able to hobble the rest of the way using two sticks – how lucky we were to have them – but by supper time my ankle had swollen alarmingly. Our host wrapped it tightly and advised me to sit with my leg up all through the next day. It did hurt a good deal if I put weight on it. The rest of the group had planned another day's tramp, so left me behind with my book. It was good practice, in fact, to be obliged to spend the day chatting in German with our hosts, and the ankle is much better already.

It was grand to see something of the countryside in this beautiful part of Saxony and I am very sorry that I had not made the effort earlier. Now I am eager to see more and would like to go to Dresden when I leave in early July. I am told it is an exquisite city and that it would be a great shame to miss it. I shall be saving what I can over the next weeks with hopes of going there. And no Mama, I will not travel alone but hope to find a companion for the trip.

~~~~~~~~~~~~~~~~

23rd April, 1895

Dear Lily,

We had a jolly good outing to Wernigerode last week. There were six of us but I was vague in my letter to Mama as to who made up our party. I did not mention that Frank and Don were with us. You know it is common for students to make these short journeys in mixed groups, but my parents would think it improper.

Mount Brocken, as you know, is the chief attraction, and Flo and I chose a shorter walk up to a viewpoint. The rest of the group climbed all the way to the top of Mount Brocken. They could not boast of the view however, as apparently it is often shrouded in thick mists, and that day was no exception. And they were sacked by a heavy rain which falls most days at the top of the mountain. Flo and I were not disappointed to have missed that aspect of their adventure. Their downhill journey took three hours on a good mountain trail and they complained a good deal about aching knees.

Flo and I returned to the village along a simple roadway, yet I managed to trip and twist my ankle and had to stay behind the next day. Mr. W. offered to keep my company and oh, Lily, I was tempted to accept, but I did the right thing and declined, graciously, insisting he must go with the others. But was that not sweet of him? It was a long dreary painful day I can tell you, sitting about at our lodgings by myself. But I was forced to take his arm all the way to the station and then on to the train. He says two days of tramping have whetted his appetite for such activity. There are no mountains near Toronto, so
~~~~~~~~~~~~~~~~

these dramatic and beautiful landscapes are new and exciting. As they are to me, of course.

To quite change the topic and tell you some other news, Lily, you would be sad to see that the old Gewandhaus with its wonderful Concert Saal has recently been razed to the ground. The original old Conservatorium next door was demolished at the same time and no one is shedding tears for that, but that old concert hall had a special feeling, don't you agree, although perhaps I am being too romantic. I do not know what they plan to do with the property, but it was too bad to see that grand old building come down.

There has been little of interest musically of late. The Tschaikowsky one act opera *Yolanth* was given at the Stadt Theater. The audience did not seem to like it and for once I was in agreement with the general response.

I must prepare for my pupils so will close for now. What a change in my daily life though, with no classes of my own to attend, no assigned music to study, no ensemble rehearsals. I am becoming lazy as warmer spring weather arrives and enjoy dawdling through these more leisurely days. It was good of Mama and Papa to allow me to stay on for these extra weeks and of course I am especially pleased for more than pecuniary reasons as I expect you are aware.

I shall have to leave Frau Gibson in a week's time as she had previously promised the room. I shall find somewhere perhaps little cheaper where I can accommodate my pupils. It is tiresome to remove for two months, but it is practical. It has been nice here, especially to come and go from Frau Schwabe's upstairs.

I suppose you will be somewhat at leisure during the summer months as well? I look forward to a few days with you and your family on my way home early in July.

~~~~~~~~~~~~~~~~
~~~~~~~~~~~~~~~~

Imagining Violet

Haydnstrasse, 8, Leipzig
28th June, 1895

Dear Lily,

This will be my last letter to you from Leipzig. Soon we shall be chatting away as we always have. The room at Haydnstrasse has been suitable for my needs but it was a little lonely as I did not know anyone else in the house.

Of course, I wanted to take part in my last student picnic. It is such a fine conclusion to the Conservatory year, and I also thought that Mr. W. should have the experience. The destination this year was Grimma which is an hour's train ride from the city. I well recall feeling too shy to attend, just three years ago! How foolish that seems now.

Grimma, like Wernigerode, has been a market town for centuries, but it is surrounded by attractive woodlands. There are the usual stately old buildings in the historic centre and of course, an impressive town hall. There are also ruins of a convent which are mainly of interest because Catherine de Bora, who married Martin Luther, escaped from it. Her story sounded frightfully romantic, but of course we did not have the time to see everything.

We all liked the old town, but for myself, all the singing and marching and drinking and dancing were not as appealing as formerly. Too many of the younger pupils take the opportunity to consume more beer than is good for them with occasional unfortunate, even unpleasant results. Two years ago, I thought it all tremendous fun. Goodness, am I getting old?

I suspect Frank, who is such a dear quiet unassuming man, was a little uncomfortable with such boisterous behaviour. What he has taken to is wandering the countryside and lately he has been compiling a list of places that offer tramping opportunities. There are said to be pretty walks on the Gattersburg near Grimma, so perhaps he will go there another time. Mind you, he may not have much opportunity this summer as I believe he plans to return to Canada for the long holiday.

Well, I did not mean to sound critical. Because there are certainly aspects of the famous picnic which I would not want to miss. To hear hundreds of voices raised in song; that is fine indeed, as you know.

I have finished with Miss Ellerby, my pupil, and have begun to say my goodbyes. That is difficult, isn't it? We all promise to write and for those of us who come from Britain, we swear we will visit each other. Too many promises to keep perhaps? Certainly we never did hear much from Miss Donaldson or Miss Armstrong after they left us. Saying good-bye to Mr. W. will not be easy. But if I promise to write to <u>him</u>, that is a promise I shall keep most faithfully. Flo is going home too and we shall travel together from Berlin after my visit to Dresden.

What does the future hold? I do not know and I try not to worry too much. In the meantime, I have the glimmer of a little plan for later this summer which I shall share with you when I see you.

~~~~~~~~~~~~~~~~~~~~
~~~~~~~~~~~~~~~~~~~~

Imagining Violet

4th July, 1895

Dear Birdie,

I write this from the train to Berlin, where I shall post it along with the postcards I bought in Dresden. Oh, why did I delay in making this trip? Dresden is the most fascinating city.

My companion was Miss Ellerby whom I had been tutoring for several weeks. Her family allowed her to come with me and for the most part I was content with her company. I suppose I was her chaperon and for that, her family paid for our modest lodgings. We were up early to take the eight o'clock train, which brought us into Dresden a little after noon, so we had two and a half days, and we managed a great deal of sight-seeing.

I headed straightaway for the Picture Galleries. Miss E., who has not travelled at all, had promised her mama to stay with me at all times, but unfortunately she had little interest in the paintings. I teased her and said we must see every one of them. Well, Birdie, there are 2,450 paintings for goodness sakes, so that was a poor joke. One entire room is set aside for Raphael's master piece, the *Madonna di San Sisto*, and it is truly extraordinary. We admired the Titians and Veronese as well.

The next morning, Miss E. wanted to visit the Historical Museum. Whilst I would have preferred another few hours in the Picture Gallery, she had accommodated me in that respect, and so I went along. They have an enormous collection of armour -- all the weapons of warfare plus all the trappings of the mediaeval tournament -- which was more interesting than I had expected.

I must tell you a little about the tilting suits. In one gallery, there is a display of the equipment that two knights on horseback would wear for the "battle ordeal". The little card explained that this was a judicial combat in which the first man thrown from his horse usually died of a broken neck caused by the great weight of the suit, which was more than two hundred pounds. It added that it was impossible for the knight to move about at all, and that was easy to believe. Oh, the age of chivalry was in some ways ridiculous.

As it was lovely summer weather, it was a great temptation to spend time out of doors, and we did take coffee at the Café Réal on the Terrace of Bruhl. The Terrace is a favourite promenade for Dresdeners and there is an entrancing view. Then we went to the Frauenkirche, an 18th century Italianate church which was fully restored just thirty years ago. It is fitted up with tiers of galleries that make it look more like a theatre than a church. One can climb up to the cupola from which there is said to be the most excellent view all round the city. However, as the climb involved ladders and narrow walkways, I did not think it was safe or practical to attempt it. Wasn't that sensible of me? I took my chaperoning duties seriously, as you can see.

Miss E. wanted also to visit the Zoological Museum, and reluctant as I was at first, I found it fascinating, at least the ethnographical collection was, where we looked at the garments and weapons of various barbarous nations like Borneo and Java. There were hammocks, clubs, poisoned arrows, shooting tubes and robes made of coloured feathers.

The gardens of the Japanese palace were a welcome respite from all those museum cases. On our second afternoon, we took a nice walk in the Grosser Garten, a park rather like our Rosenthal, with wide paths and vistas as well as cafés and restaurants. And like the Rosenthal, there were bands.

Oh, Birdie, I wish I had taken the time to visit Dresden before, with a good friend, not a young girl. It was only 83 miles away all this time, but chances are that I shall never be there again. I saw Miss E. onto the train back to Leipzig, where her landlady was to fetch her from the station and I continue on to Berlin, from which train I am writing this. I shall soon be home, forever!

Dresden.

DRESDEN
Frauenkirche

~~~~~~~~~~~~~~~~~
~~~~~~~~~~~~~~~~~

Leith, Scotland

Seaview Villas No.7, Leith

12th July, 1895

Dear Lottie,

Thank you, dear Lottie, for your excellent suggestions for our trip to Dresden. Your recommendation of the Misses Lindners' boarding home was spot on. What dear old ladies they are and they did all they could to make us feel at home.

We saw a good deal of what you suggested, although Miss Ellerby's appetite for the fine arts was limited, so I am sorry to say we missed the Green Vaults and spent too much of our museum time at the Historical Museum instead. About the only thing I could summon any interest in were the tilting costumes, which I expect you have seen. But the rest of it just reminded me of man's appetite for violence and war. How can war be thought of as chivalrous? I would much rather have seen the famous gems at the Vaults.

The journey home was much the same as usual, and I shall not miss it. I am again in Edinburgh, and enjoying the fine weather. Birdie and I are taking long walks on Leith Links and along the beach at Seafield. It is summer and I do not have to decide straightaway about what I am going to do next. But I shall have to do something, that is certain.

This may amuse you as you know I am not much of a shopper, but Birdie was very keen that we go, as soon as I was home, to the new Jenners Department Store on Princes Street. You would not know of course that it was completely destroyed by fire just a few years ago. It has been rebuilt and is one of the most splendid buildings I have ever entered. The most impressive part is the upper two storeys which are galleries that wrap completely around the floor below, and the roof as well is made entirely of glass, so the light shines in and down onto the floor. And the store is so modern, Lottie, with hydraulic lifts and electric lighting everywhere. We are accustomed to electric lights in the theatres, but this is the most elaborate use of electric lights I have ever seen, with the exception perhaps of the Café Bauer!

Please write from wherever you are. I am sending this to Leipzig, but perhaps you will have already left for your long vacation.

~~~~~~~~~~~~~~~~

Seaview Villas No.7, Leith
Friday, July 12th, 1895

Dear Mr. Welsman,

I am home at last. I sent a postcard from Dresden, but there is more to tell than I had room for. A proper young lady would address you as Mr. Welsman in a letter, so I have done so, but I must say it feels it feels artificial to retreat into such constraints of etiquette.

First let me assure you that young Miss Ellerby was quite good company after all my doubts although I would not wish to share a room with her for many nights. I do not think I am an untidy person, but she was obsessively neat and also perhaps a little too timid in her outlook. In the old city I felt she was decidedly fearful about walking the narrow streets but for the most part, things went well. I did miss my friend Lily who is always willing to try just about anything. But to look on the bright side: we visited two museums, the
~~~~~~~~~~~~~~~~

Historical and the Zoological, which I would normally not have done, and I found a good deal to interest me in their musty old cases.

And how are you? May I venture that you are finding more hours for practising now that I am no longer there to tempt you into rambling around the parks and along the rivers. I was feeling a tinge of guilt these past weeks when I have had so few obligations and pulled you away from your work far too often. It being your first spring, I had so much to show you.

How delightful it was to rent that little boat and to go rowing. I have watched with envy whilst others did that but, as I did not know how to row, nor did anyone I knew, I had not had the lovely experience of gliding along the water. You were very patient with me and I thank you for giving me a turn at the oars, although it surely is awkward when one cannot see where one is going. I did not mind having you be my eyes, and I like to think I got on well enough.

Please write to me of your plans for the rest of the summer and whether you will return to Canada after all or spend your holiday in Devon. If it is to be the latter, I have the smallest beginning of an idea as to how we might meet. It is not suitable to suggest that you travel to Edinburgh, but being a young lady of some leisure now, surely I might be able to arrange a week or so in London with Lily and her family and it is possible that Lily might well persuade her mother to invite you to come to tea or some such. I am a schemer, aren't I? But I do like to have something to look forward to.

I do not think it is necessary that you write to Papa for permission to correspond with me. It may be a little unconventional, but I see no reason why one cannot correspond with one's male friends as well as with one's female friends. I like to think the dictates of society are a little more relaxed now than in the past. However, it would not be amiss if you were to do so. Papa is proud of his Courtenaye heritage and can be a stickler for the finer points of proper behaviour.

~~~~~~~~~~~~~~~~
~~~~~~~~~~~~~~~~

Imagining Violet

Seaview Villas 7, Leith

Sunday, July 22nd, 1895

Dear Mr. Welsman,

Papa has handed on your letter which arrived yesterday enclosed with your missive to him. As a result, he will like you even better when he meets you which I hope will not be at too far in the future. He says you seem to be a "nice young man, for a colonial."

I am sure I am happy for you that you will visit your family in Toronto this summer. I did not think my little scheme had any real chance of materializing. As it happens, Lily will go to the seaside with her family for several weeks so that part of my idea met with an obstacle straightaway. Papa intends to take us to Oban again for his holiday early next month. I had perhaps not been as enthusiastic about this as in the past. And Mama speaks about making a trip to Ireland and I know she would like my company this time. Are we never to meet again? Well, I am being melodramatic I suppose, but I had enjoyed imagining walking with you in Hyde Park or along the Embankment.

My goodness Edinburgh is dreary on a Sunday! We do have a time of it, trying to fill the day. Thankfully, the museum is open now on Sunday afternoon and the Botanic Gardens as well, but as the trams do not run, we must walk. I should not be so lazy, ja? But it is a long way for my sister and she is my best companion.

We are not regular church goers, although we went last Sunday to Saint Paul's and I did enjoy the organ playing and the singing of the choir. There is so little music here and I miss it. I am told there are bands playing at the bandstand on Leith Links on Saturday night, but Mama does not think it suitable that Birdie and I go by ourselves. I tell Mama that she must come with us then, but so far she has begged off such an outing.

~~~~~~~~~~~~~~~~~~
~~~~~~~~~~~~~~~~~~

Imagining Violet

Thursday, 1st August

Dear Lily,

Indeed it would have been delightful to visit you in London but our families do take over rather, don't they? Papa has booked rooms in Oban where we spent our holiday last year. We all enjoy the west coast even if it is a longer journey. We leave the day after tomorrow. A few years ago, when we went to North Berwick, the weather was dreadful, the sea was icy and there were no bathing machines. Not that I require a bathing machine, but Mama will not venture into the sea without one. Papa does not care to bathe at all, ever, so the existence of a bathing machine matters not a whit to him. The highlight of the day at North Berwick was the afternoon walk along the seafront when Mama insisted that Birdie and I dress in our good frocks and walk up and down, saying how do you do to people we knew. We felt rather on display, but at least it was something to do. Birdie and I much prefer Oban.

What am I doing to fill the days, you ask, and a good question too. One thing I am enjoying is the leisure to read the books that I choose to read. Birdie is always helpful, as she leads a somewhat studious life and directs me to various important works. I have particularly enjoyed Miss Bird's book, *A Lady's Life in the Rocky Mountains*, although Birdie did not recommend it, the librarian did. Adventure travel does not appeal to my sister. But anything about Canada is especially fascinating.

I have had tea with my school friend Margaret, who is now Mrs. Gerald Farquharson. She was married in May and we did not meet last summer as she was travelling in Europe. Well, if I thought we had little in common a few years back, nothing has improved that situation. Now her life revolves around her home, keeping it spotless, having delicious meals on the table on time and spending her afternoon hours paying calls and receiving visitors. I suppose that one day I may too find myself mistress of a household with limited means, but I am not in a hurry. I wrote to Frank about this and he thinks I should be more patient with Margaret.

Papa and Mama have not made the least fuss about Frank's occasional letters, thank goodness. He showed his customary courtesy and sensitivity and wrote to Papa asking permission to write. Frank's request was hardly necessary in my opinion, but that was dear of him. He has only written twice in any case.

I think though, that Mama suspects more than she lets on. As Birdie pointed out, his name came up very frequently indeed in my letters this past year. I told Mama how I admire him and that he had asked if he should request permission to write. And then his letter appeared and it made such a good impression. I would be a good deal less restless if I knew when we might see each other again, but I cannot let my feelings show. We will have to just be friends for some time.

Mama is glad to have me at home for I can be useful and I am willing to help. At fifteen, I probably resented the chores I was set. But now I see how hard she works and what a job it is to put three meals on the table every day, even when there is a maid. There is no end to the work. Thankfully, our Molly is a conscientious worker and healthy too and placid.

As I reflect on it, I do not know how Mama managed with the four of us growing up and only one servant. It seems we are a little better off now with Papa's promotion, and with Grandpa Courtenaye's passing four years ago, I believe Papa has come into some money, which of course I should not discuss outside the family, so I trust you to keep it to yourself. And indeed as one never speaks of money, even within the family, it is difficult to know exactly how things are.

I have realized too that both Mama and Papa are getting on in years. They are both nearly fifty, I think, although one can never ask directly. Mama is puffing a little on the stairs and Papa does mention chest pains from time to time. Of course, Birdie has always been here to lend a hand and as she still shows no inclination to marry, seeming to prefer her books to male company, it may well be her lot in life to look after our parents. She continues to have many days when she feels poorly although there is no clear explanation of just what ails her. Still, selfish beast that I am, Birdie's situation does give me the freedom to imagine a life for myself far away from here, in Toronto say?

With time on my hands, I have been thinking a little about the General Election next week, and realizing that I pay no attention to these matters whatsoever. If women were allowed to vote, would I take more of an interest? Have you been reading about it or do your friends talk about it – the election, I mean – or indeed, about women gaining the right to vote?

~~~~~~~~~~~~~~~~~

Caledonia Hotel, Oban

6th August, 1895

Dear Mr. Welsman,

We have come over to Oban on Scotland's west coast and are putting up at the Caledonia Hotel until the 11th inst. It is a five hour journey, but the coast here is very beautiful. The hotel is not the grandest hostelry, but happily it is located in the centre of the town. The better places are situated on top of the hill behind the town, and not so well placed for walking about, in my opinion. Seasoned traveler that I am.

The weather has been fine since we arrived yesterday afternoon and this morning we took a walk around the centre of the town which is one of the larger towns in the area. Not much has changed since last year. Now the clouds have rolled in and it is sputtering with rain, so I am in the writing room, writing.

Oban has a very pretty situation on Oban Bay, protected from the fierce Atlantic by islands, so it seems more like a lake than the seaside. The harbour is a busy place with ferries running back and forth to the islands and there are often steamers full of tourists arriving and departing. As well there are dozens of sailing yachts gliding around, or riding at anchor. Papa and my brothers and I can
~~~~~~~~~~~~~~~~~

watch all this activity for hours. There is something about the sea that is compelling. Mama and my sister find all this watery activity less interesting. For Mama, the town is too bustling and crowded and I dare say she would prefer a more tranquil setting, But the boys would be bored so she agrees to come here, because it is better all round if they are enjoying themselves.

There are several good walks to take, including a climb up to an old castle. We Leipzigers are familiar with old castles, nicht? I wish you could see this one. Dunolly Castle is mainly rubble, but there is a fine high square tower and the remains of the dungeon and part of the enclosing wall. We went there last year and will go again as it is magnificently situated on a steep knoll, on top of precipitous cliffs. There is a more impressive castle a few miles from here called Dunstaffnage Castle, and if the weather is accommodating, perhaps we shall see it.

My brothers, of course, prefer the beach, which is somewhat north of the town centre and sheltered from the wind by a nice curve in the shoreline. That will be our destination tomorrow. If one does not wish to walk both ways, and Birdie is unlikely to want to do that, there are usually young men with dog carts who will bring you back into town for a few pence. I am sure if you were here we would have no trouble making the walk, both ways.

Please do not tease me, but I found a copy of Susanna Moodie's book *Roughing It In the Bush*. Have you read it? Her life sixty years ago in the Ontario bush was certainly strenuous and rather frightening. It sounds as if Canada was not very civilized back then.

Papa says that if we are fortunate with the weather, we may make an excursion by ferry across the bay to the Isle of Kinnera. The hotel will put up a boxed lunch so we can enjoy the day without having to endure a restaurant dinner. That is something else to look forward to.

I hope my postcard reaches you in Toronto where I trust you are enjoying a well-earned rest with your family. Thank you for sending an address. It is nice to know just where you are. I am so glad that our Post Office has finally permitted the new picture postcards. Such a convenient way to send a quick if not a private message.

~~~~~~~~~~~~~~~~

Caledonia Hotel, Oban
8th August, 1895

Dear Lottie,

I am at Oban with the family on holiday, so have some leisure to reflect and to write. At this little distance from my studies, I can already see that Leipzig was valuable in so many ways, not just for the music and the friends but also the chance to live independently. What I did not appreciate fully, although I rather thought I did, was how everything there was relatively unaffected by concerns about class and one's position in society. Here in Britain one is back in a world where it is precisely the opposite. As a child, I took it for granted that some people were our betters and some people were not. When Mama would say of some child, "She is not the sort of girl we play with, Violet", I did not ask why. Did you have a similar experience as a child?
~~~~~~~~~~~~~~~~

But at the Conservatory where we were all thrown together and where talent was the most important thing, our lives were less restrained by these attitudes and little by little I forgot to consider whether someone might be of the same class or not. I took little notice in fact, when Frank spoke of his family, that his father owns a shop and that his oldest brother is a watchmaker. Of course I expected some comment or other from Papa on that subject, and now I worry that if the time comes, as I hope it will, that they meet him, that they may not accept him or may somehow make it clear that they do not consider him a social equal. They would never ever be impolite, I do know that. Do you think I need to be concerned?

Another thing. It is not easy, I find, to be a daughter of the house again, after being on my own for the better part of four years. Having to ask permission to come and go, having to take care that what I am doing is appropriate in my parents' eyes, well it is all rather vexing. It is not respectable, apparently, for me to take a walk by myself up Arthur's Seat. When Birdie and I were forbidden to go to Leith Links on a Saturday evening to hear the band play, I had to bite my tongue. Everyone here is so relentlessly obsessed with the appearance of things. I feel as if I had been put back in a box or put away on a shelf to be dusted off and brought out on special occasions.

Goodness, I am whining, dear Charlotte, do forgive me. I suppose my parents still see me as the young girl I was when I left at the age of sixteen. But I am not the same person.

I should add that I see them quite differently now. I notice that Papa is tired when he arrives home at the end of his work day, and I see that he needs to sit quietly with his pipe and a glass of sherry. Now I understand that that is not the best time to burst in with my news. And whilst I disagree with some of the constraints placed upon me, Mama and Papa are in many ways quite wise about things.

I was looking forward to renewing my friendship with Annie Gardiner, and alas, that opportunity has disappeared. She has recently removed from Edinburgh to Carlisle to take up a teaching position in a day school for girls. Her family is not best pleased. But Annie wanted her freedom, so off she went right after she finished her training. I met her mother in the street the other day and Mrs. Gardiner was stiff-lipped. It would seem she'd expected Annie would remain at home until she married and she does not have much to say for teachers.

I do not see why teaching is not held in higher regard. It is such important work. I was lucky that we came to Leith when we did and that I had the chance to go to St. George's which was and is a fine high school for girls. Sadly, my sister Birdie was already a little too old. I remember Mama saying, when we were still living in Gorleston, "I hope your father's next posting is Leith, because there are such good high schools for young ladies in Edinburgh." She herself did not have that opportunity in Ireland, and I am glad now that she wanted that for me and for my brothers, even if it was too late for Birdie.

You have been a good friend if you have read through to this, so I shall stop right now.

~~~~~~~~~~~~~~~~~

Seaview Villas 7, Leith

1st September, 1895

Dear Mr. Welsman,

I hope this letter will greet you when you reach Leipzig, and also that your journey was as easy as possible and that you had gemütlich travelling companions on that long train ride to Berlin. There can be such a fuss about the windows, when everyone doesn't agree.

For the moment, I am kept sufficiently busy accompanying Mama when she pays calls on Tuesday and Thursday afternoons. Now that summer is officially over, her friends have returned to town and the round of visits has started up again. I seem to be something of a novelty as not many of the young ladies in her circle have gone
~~~~~~~~~~~~~~~~~

as far as Leipzig for their studies. I have been invited to play at a small musicale at the home of Mrs. MacPherson, whose husband is also a senior Customs Officer. I was happy to accept, but I need an accompanist. I thought that might be an impediment but Mrs. MacPherson has a niece who plays the piano very well, according to her aunt. I am to meet Miss Fiona MacPherson one morning next week and we shall see what we might be able to play together. I shall have to apply myself over the next few days then, as I have been lazy about practising. The prospect of performing is once again the encouragement I need.

Classes at the School of Art commence at the beginning of October. I shall enjoy being more usefully occupied than at present.

~~~~~~~~~~~~~~~~~

Sunday, 27th September, 1895

Dear Mr. Welsman,

Many thanks for your kind letter which arrived on the 23rd inst. I was sorry to hear you had to endure a stuffy carriage most of the way to Berlin. It can indeed be awkward, especially when there is someone who insists on avoiding a draft.

I am, of course, full of questions and shall try to limit myself to a very few so that you do not feel obliged to write a long letter in return. I am sure you have very little time to spare. Please do not worry about smudges and blots. I know full well how tiresome it is to take the time to make a fair copy and sometimes one simply does not manage to do it, and the letter remains unsent. I would much rather hear from you with smudges than not at all.

How are you getting on with your new concerto? Is the final movement quite beastly? Is your rental piano adequate? Does Herr Krause speak of a recital for you? Will you be ready with a movement from the Beethoven? When it happens and it will, I shall long to be amongst the audience. Please also tell me about your classes and how you are getting along with Herr Schreck. Are you auditing the
~~~~~~~~~~~~~~~~~

history class? Your German is much better than mine at that stage, so you will have an easier time understanding Herr Prof. Paul. I used to take notes and often just write the words I thought I heard, even though I did not understand them, and then I would have to translate them after the class.

I lead a very quiet life here at the moment, my art classes begin next week at the Edinburgh School. I read a good deal and practise and sew, and so the days pass. I am reading all kinds of things. I found some interesting adventure tales in the boys' room, books by G.A. Henty that are the most exciting stories of exotic places. You have no spare time for frivolous reading I know, so I should not tempt you.

Miss MacPherson and I met last week and settled on a few pieces to play at her Aunt's musicale in October. I liked her very much and she does play ever so nicely, so I shall have to work hard to do my bit.

I help Mama in the kitchen and at the markets and accompany her on her calls. I helped at her At Home last week. She has third Wednesdays, and it was quite the to-do to have everything ready. We baked and baked. Of course I had to play a few simple numbers and Birdie accompanied, but she does not enjoy it.

I am sure you are looking forward to the start of the Gewandhaus season. It will be very different without Herr Reinecke on the podium, I expect. I wonder what changes Herr Nikisch will make to the orchestra, to the repertoire and of course, to the Conservatory. Perhaps someone younger and more vigorous will be a good thing altogether. I hope for a full report from you.

~~~~~~~~~~~~~~~~
~~~~~~~~~~~~~~~~

Imagining Violet

Sunday, 18th October, 1895

Dear Lily,

Thank you for yours of last week. I was sorry to know that your dear Mother has been ill again. Such a worry for you, but I know you take good care of her. You have not written a word about Mr. R. lately. Is he still a friend?

And let me congratulate you on your growing roster of pupils. With half a dozen this fall, you will be busy. And I do hope the appointment at Miss Truesdale's School is confirmed. You will enjoy that too, I suspect, being a little more out in the world.

It being the middle of October, I cannot help thinking of the musical season starting up in Leipzig. It is rather a musical desert here, and I confess to a feeling of envy when I imagine Frank sitting in the Gewandhaus concert hall. I spend more time than I should with that picture in my mind, thinking about him, missing him, and wondering what will happen with our friendship.

Of course, there is so much music in London. Here we await a short series of concerts next month when the ambitiously named Scottish National Orchestra comes from Glasgow to play.

Mama's friends are surprised at how much opera and theatre we attended in Leipzig. In Edinburgh they are lucky if a visiting opera company stops in twice a year. These ladies seem to find the idea of going to the theatre one or two nights a week almost self-indulgent. But this is Scotland after all, the land of Presbyterians, who probably do not think opera is respectable. They certainly have some old-fashioned views.

My classes have begun at the School of Art, and I shall not be critical, yet. I hope first impressions are not last impressions, that is all I shall say. I attend the popular mid-day class and there are more than a hundred young ladies, all vying for the attention of the one instructor and her assistant. Still, these instructors are women, and they are speaking English, so that is two points of improvement over my brief experience a few years ago at the Kunst Schule. At the moment we are making measured drawings which is sure to be helpful when one is sketching buildings. I have made some small acquaintance amongst my fellow pupils and not a few of them are ambitious to make art their profession. They tell me there are several women earning from their artwork now and that is encouraging, don't you think? The Edinburgh Ladies Art Club will hold their exhibition next month and I look forward to seeing it.

The principal excitement of my week was taking part in a small musicale at the home of Mrs. MacPherson. That lady lives in a fine large home not far from here, so it was a short walk there on a grey and misty afternoon. It is a good thing skirts may be worn a little shorter these days, especially when one is walking along rain-puddled streets. How I hate it when the hems of my skirts get damp and muddy!

Miss MacPherson and I had played though our selections several times, and we felt sufficiently prepared. We have taken to playing together once or twice a week and will continue to do so, I think. There were a few younger girls on the programme and her aunt graced us with two songs of Scottish origin. The idea of the musicale is to give young students the experience of performing. I suppose I was invited as an example of what one might achieve in four years' study in Germany. I hope I did not disappoint as I felt the responsibility of it, I can tell you. Next week I shall play again at Mama's day, this time with Fiona, for which Birdie is grateful.

Something mysterious is happening at our house. Mama and Papa have their heads together, talking intently, but the minute I enter the room, they stop and stoutly deny there is anything to tell me. They too often treat me as if I were a child still and it is exceedingly irritating. They both seem to be in good health, but I am worried.

~~~~~~~~~~~~~~~~
~~~~~~~~~~~~~~~~

Imagining Violet

Seaview Villas 7, Leith

24th October, 1895

Dear Mr. Welsman,

Your letter of last week was a pleasure to read. I almost felt I was there with you in Leipzig. I am grateful that you take the time to write such wonderful letters to me, when I know all your time is committed. I suspect you do not linger in the cafés the way I did.

You asked about the School of Art. To be honest, it is not a particularly inspiring place to study. The curriculum is very specific. In these first weeks we have been drawing from the flat and will shortly move on to drawing from the round. In these early stages, we use rulers and pencils and concentrate on perspective. In due course, we shall be drawing from Nature, but that lies in the unspecified future and unhappily may coincide with the chilly days of winter. In its favour, the School has a well-known collection of plaster casts of statues from antiquity and the Renaissance, and we shall be set to copying those, perhaps next month. We were allowed to peak into the Statues Gallery the other day, and they are well worth seeing. There is also a life drawing class in which, with Papa's permission, I may be permitted to enrol next year. But when I mentioned that to Mama, she said that I need not be too concerned about next year. She refused to elaborate, only to assure me that all is well and there is nothing to worry about. But when someone says do not worry, what does a person naturally do?

Until today, we have enjoyed some fine weather and Mama has come with me to walk on the Links. I enjoy having some private time with her. We <u>are</u> fortunate to have such a large park in our neighbourhood. Birdie and I have also ventured to the harbour and taken a stroll along the Pier beside the Custom House. Leith is a busy harbour and I like to watch the steam and sailing ships, tugs and fish boats moving here and there, wondering where they have been and where they are going. Perhaps I may sail away one day, who knows? There are usually some fellows fishing from the pier, but I would not care to eat fish caught in those oily black waters.

The musicale was a modest success. I thoroughly enjoyed playing with Miss MacPherson and we shall play together again at Mama's At Home tomorrow. I have also been invited to take part in the Waddell School's Christmas concert. It is a tradition to ask former pupils, after they complete their studies abroad, to perform with the string orchestra, and to play a solo piece. I had been expecting this invitation and was happy to accept.

I am glad you get on so well with Herr Krause. My friend Lily studied with him in her third year. He was demanding, Lily said, but fair in the way he managed his class, not favouring one pupil over another. Of course, you are studying privately. You may be glad though, that you are not with Herr Zwintscher. People said he was more interested in his own career than in his pupils. But I should not repeat gossip.

I look forward very much to your letters, and hope you will find a few minutes to write soon.

~~~~~~~~~~~~~~~~

Seaview Villas 7, Leith

November 3rd, 1895

Dear Mr. Welsman,

I am happy to say that some symphonic music is on our horizon. I should explain that since I left in 1891, a new orchestra has been organized here. To be entirely accurate, it is based in Glasgow, but they perform in Edinburgh in a subscription series of four concerts. It has been named The Scottish Orchestra which is politic, don't you agree? I am sure Glaswegians would not like it if it
~~~~~~~~~~~~~~~~

were the Edinburgh Symphony and vice versa. This season there is a new conductor, a M. Willem Kes, who may be Dutch. In any event he has come from Amsterdam where he founded an orchestra with great success. I read that he is very strict with his players, fining them if they are late to rehearsal, and making them stay "after class" as it were, if their playing is not satisfactory. The first concert is next week.

Mama and I went to the exhibition of the Edinburgh Ladies Art Club and were impressed by the excellent work of our local lady painters. There was nothing obviously feminine about the work; the subject matter was very wide-ranging. Naturally there were the usual floral arrangements but also some grand Scottish landscapes and a few beautifully rendered portraits. I was glad to see a few paintings with a "sold" mark affixed. It is heartening to know that there are women here earning a living making art. Mama said this would have been quite impossible in her day, when young ladies were not even admitted to the art schools.

The damp and drizzly days are upon us and there is NO SKATING. I hope you will soon be able to get out on the ponds. I have such happy memories of our times skating together last winter and I am jealously wondering whom you will find to skate with this year. Well, of course, you must skate with whomever you wish.

The family mystery is partially solved. Papa may be posted to London! I cannot let myself become too excited as it is not yet confirmed but ... it would be tremendous!

In the meantime, I am finding life quite satisfactory what with art classes and playing with Miss MacPherson. I did not know, just what I was going to do but life has a way of filling the gaps.

~~~~~~~~~~~~~~~~~
~~~~~~~~~~~~~~~~~

Imagining Violet

Seaview Villas 7, Leith

20th Nov., 1895

Dear Mr. Welsman,

I knew something was afoot as I wrote earlier. After several weeks of waiting, Papa has finally received news of his promotion to the London Customs Office. He will take up his duties at the beginning of the new year.

Mama has always taken these moves more or less in her stride as frequent removals are the lot of a Custom Officer's wife. Since I was born she has moved us at least four times. We came to Edinburgh expecting to stay for six years, and have been here close on eight.

Birdie has mixed feelings about this. On the one hand, she will be able to visit the British Museum at will, which pleases her immensely. On the other hand, she has several friends here and is the most regular church-goer amongst us, so it will be more difficult for her to leave all that behind.

The boys will miss their friends too but they may stay on at their school here. Reg works hard at his studies, but my little brother Jack, well Jack is no student and just wants to run away to sea or something else madly adventurous. I say he has been reading too much G.A. Henty. Gosh, here I am rambling on about my family and you have never even met them.

Needless to say, I am thrilled at the chance to live in London.

Yes, I am envious that you have weekly concerts to attend with such a superb orchestra to listen to. Your description of Herr Nikisch on the podium is excellent. His more restrained style might be a welcome change from some of the more flamboyant conductors. But it is nice to know that the King himself invited Professor Reinecke to stay on as a senior professor. He is such an excellent and valuable teacher.

Here we are not so well off for music, but I suppose I should be grateful there is symphonic music at all. Papa has generously bought a subscription for the series of concerts and we have now attended two of them. The first was on the 11th inst. Mama and I went and honestly it was not very good. I have been spoiled, I know, by four seasons of the excellent Gewandhaus Orchestra. Mr. Kes' men attempted the usually delightful *Magic Flute Overture* and did not redeem themselves.

Still, this new conductor is interesting. He insists that the audience remain quiet during the performance. It is possible that our silence, in this case, may have sent an unwelcome message. I overheard someone say that there are several newly arrived players in the orchestra, and that they had very little rehearsal, so that may explain the inconsistency of performance. Their second outing, one week later, was very much better, in my humble opinion. Mme Teresa Carreno was the assisting artist and she was excellent. She is an avid pusher of Grieg, and played his *A Minor Concerto*. If you have not seen her yet, you will undoubtedly have an opportunity, as she concertizes constantly. She lives in Berlin, so Leipzig is a regular stop. She may be a little past her prime – she is 42, I believe – but she does give a good show.

But when we remove to London, what musical treats await!

I hope you are looking after yourself carefully and not working too very hard and resting enough and eating well.

~~~~~~~~~~~~~~~~~
~~~~~~~~~~~~~~~~~

Imagining Violet

December 2nd, 1895

Dear Lily,

Thank you for writing back so quickly. Something I have realized is that starting fresh in a new city may help to resolve the predicament I find myself in here. The longer I have been home, the more awkward it has become to resist some of Mama's friends who seek to introduce me to their eligible sons and nephews. As I am not engaged, they cannot understand why I lack enthusiasm for their romantic projects. I cannot even say that I am keeping company with a student, one who has another year and half in Leipzig before he finishes his studies -- which seems a dreadfully long time to me now. As you are well aware that my feelings are more than just friendly, you can see that this might well have become a problem, not just for me, but perhaps a little embarrassing for Mama as well. Her friends seem to think that now I have finished with my Leipzig adventure, that I should want to marry and start a family. It is difficult to discourage them politely, to explain courteously that I am in no hurry at all to settle down.

I see Margaret once in a while and it makes me think that I shall never be a successful "angel in the house" as she tries to be. She came to tea last week and brought the darling baby boy. She has no nurse-maid, just a maid-of-all-work as we have, and Margaret does not wish to leave the child alone with her. The infant is a healthy little fellow, but he did fuss a good deal and that made conversation almost impossible, as you might imagine. As it is, we seem to have little of mutual interest to talk about in any case. I honestly do not care very much about the price of a mutton chop.

You and I have known so many young women who aspire to a life in music. But few succeed. However, on the 2nd inst., we shall hear one successful female artist in concert here. The American soprano, Miss Evangeline Florence, will perform and she is but two years older than I. And while I admit to some envy, the touring life of a solo performer does not have the appeal it once did. At the same time, I cannot see myself with a life like my friend Margaret's. And yet, you know how very fond I am of Frank. It is all more than a little confusing. In all honesty, Lily, I am not at all sure what I want.

One thing I shall not miss is the Edinburgh School of Art. We proceed so painfully slowly, repeating exercises and reworking each drawing. The classes are very large and the constant buzz of chatter irritates. We are crammed into a classroom which is not well lit and not very warm, and there is little instruction. The best thing was that it gave me a reason to forego paying calls with Mama.

The Waddell School Christmas recital is next week. I have been revising the Wienawski *Chanson Polonaise* and the Vivaldi and hope I shall not disgrace myself.

Oh, but I miss the Christmas Markets, don't you? It was always a pleasure to shop for little things for the family. And you can be sure there is no Glühwein in Edinburgh. Well, I shall enjoy a visit to Jenners and I shall go to the bookshops. At least this year I can buy books in English for Papa and the boys. Henty for Jack and I shall buy the new H.G. Wells book, *The Time Machine*, for Reg. I should like to send a small gift to Frank. Would that be appropriate and would notepaper be a good idea?

I am excited about living in London where you and I may meet regularly and not depend on letters. On the other hand, I sometimes want to pour out my feelings in a letter and say things I am probably too shy to utter in person. I find I must be so careful when writing to Frank, that I do not appear over-eager or sentimental.

~~~~~~~~~~~~~~~~~
~~~~~~~~~~~~~~~~~

Imagining Violet

December 17th, 1895

Dear Mr. Welsman,

For the first time in years, I am at home for Christmas. Goodness knows I had forgotten how dreary Edinburgh is at this time of year. I like to picture you roaming round the Christmas markets whilst I trudge through the grey and drizzly streets of Edinburgh. The Germans enjoy the Christmas season so much, with their gaily decorated trees and all the lights and other decorations.

I hope you are indulging yourself a little with the delicious Christmas baked goods, and the chocolate, and the mulled wine. By comparison, it is thoroughly gloomy here, and that is not just the fog. Christmas Day may be a Bank Holiday, but many people go to work as usual. It is mainly a quiet, reverent day, marked by church services and work.

Happily, our family follows mainly English traditions and we have a proper English Christmas dinner with all the trimmings including Christmas crackers, which I have missed. There are children's parties at the church, and we did attend them years ago but we have all outgrown them now. I am not unhappy that we are moving on from this chilly, damp city.

At least there is plenty of music here this month. We went to the third concert of the Scottish Orchestra when they gave the *Jupiter Symphony*, quite well I thought. Miss Evangeline Florence, an American soprano who is just my age, sang two arias. I mention this because I was impressed that someone so young has come so far in her career. Yet it makes me feel rather useless.

Everything is half in an uproar as Mama prepares for our departure early in January. She has been down to London with Papa and they have taken a house in Upper Tooting in a new development called the Heaver Estate. I am excited to see this new house which has six bedrooms and will seem quite a mansion. With the boys staying on here at school, we shall have heaps of room. Perhaps I may be able to set up one of the empty rooms as a practice room. And Birdie is to have a big room with a desk and book cases where she may pursue her studies in peace.

Mama says this is likely to be Papa's last move before he retires. She is content to settle somewhere without the prospect of moving again. We are all so proud of Papa and his promotion to Examining Officer First Class. I had forgotten that he lived in London in the late 60s whilst he was preparing for his Civil Service exams. Unlike the rest of us, he has had some experience of a large city.

I wish you a very happy Christmas. I do not know if we shall ever meet again. I hope that is not the case, I surely do. Perhaps next summer, but that is impossibly far away.

~~~~~~~~~~~~~~~~~

9th January, 1896

Dear Mr. Welsman,

Thank you for your beautiful birthday card and kind wishes for my twenty-first. You will notice that I am using the stationery you sent me for Christmas. How amusing that we sent each other notepaper. I had birthday cards too from Mr. Heins and Mr. Puddicombe and one from Charlotte Davis who has not written lately at all. We had a small celebration here, as Papa was to leave the next day to take up his new duties in London. For my birthday I am to have photographs taken and I shall send you one if you wish it.

Turning twenty-one does not seem to mean a great deal in the life of a young lady, unless, perhaps, she is coming into a legacy, which I, unfortunately, am not. A young gentleman might gain the right to vote and be given a latchkey to the family home. That is not how it is for young ladies, I am sorry to say.

Our Christmas Day was a good deal of fun after all. The only damper on our spirits was the terrible news of the lifeboat disaster off the coast of Ireland on Christmas Eve. There was a horrible storm,
~~~~~~~~~~~~~~~~~

and the lifeboat which set out to rescue people from a foundering ship, capsized and all fifteen crew members were lost. We could not help thinking about the grief-stricken families left behind, especially at Christmas. Papa was rather gloomy when he read the item in the newspaper, thinking perhaps of his younger brother John Drew, who was lost at sea more than twenty years ago. I do not know the full story and it was not the time to ask. You have lost a brother too, so you will understand.

New Year's was also pleasant with a house party at the MacPhersons. It is possible that I had a little more of the egg nog than was good for me. Still we were decidedly subdued compared to last year in Leipzig. Now that was a romp. I wonder if the three of you braved the streets again this year?

As I said, Papa has left, and we three have been working steadily packing everything into boxes and crates. It is always a good time to throw things out, but then one gets distracted, reading old letters and cards. We must be ready early tomorrow morning for the removal contractors and their wagons. Mama is grateful as she has never had so much help with a removal.

After all, I shall be a little sad to leave this house and to leave Edinburgh. The boys will go into a boarding house associated with their school and Mama, Birdie and I will stop with friends here for a night or two before taking the train to London.

Thank you also for news of Mr. H and Mr. P. I should think Mr. P will be glad to move on after five years in Leipzig. Will he seek a position in England or will he return to Canada straightaway? This reminds me that I owe Flo a letter. She kindly sent a Christmas card.

We shall be busy when we reach Ritherdon Road next week, unpacking and so on, so do not expect to hear from me for a while. But I shall let you know that we have arrived safely.

Upper Tooting, South London

78 Ritherdon Road, Upper Tooting,

January 20th, 1896

Dear Fiona,

I promised to write as soon as I could, to say we have arrived in Upper Tooting – or is it Balham? Apparently we are on the border, so I do not know which is correct. Perhaps Upper Tooting is a better address? In any case, we came to Ritherdon Road a few days ago and have been much occupied with unpacking and finding a place for everything. It is mainly up to Mama and me because Birdie tires easily and Papa is off early in the morning and not home until tea time. It is a long trip for him now. All these years he has been able to walk to his work. Now he can take the new underground electric train which brings him right into the city by London Bridge, and the Custom House is right there. I am impatient to take it myself.

We were immensely grateful for your Aunt's generous hospitality in having us to stay those two nights. It gave us some much needed time to rest and to say our goodbyes. Watching the men carrying our furniture out to their wagons did bring a tear to my eye, I will admit. Mama was pleased that she had time to settle the boys into their boarding house. I do not think either of them minds a bit being left behind on their own.

Our new house is very fine indeed. It truly is almost new, being built just four years ago in a new suburb in South London called the Heaver Estate. A gentleman named Mr. Alfred Heaver purchased a large old estate called Bedford Hill and divided it into city lots and there is still a good deal of building going on. I have not had a chance yet to go beyond the Balham High Road, but it appears that our road has some of the finest houses hereabouts.

Mama had written ahead to an agency for a maid, so we have Rosie now to help us. She is a young girl of about seventeen recently come down from the Midlands. I do not understand what she is saying half the time.

I am going to miss our musical afternoons, Fiona; I was fortunate to meet you last summer. I hope I shall quickly make some musical acquaintance here or I shall have to prevail upon Mama to sit down at the piano once in a while. When we were children, she played a good deal, and beautifully, but has not found time for it in recent years. Birdie can play, of course, but has no confidence and does not particularly enjoy it.

Well, it is all a new life and a new year, and beyond Balham and Tooting, and the countryside just down the road, there is all of London waiting to be explored.

I hope you will be able to pay us a visit before too long. I shall discuss with Mama what would be suitable, and perhaps we could go to a concert together in town.

~~~~~~~~~~~~~~~~
~~~~~~~~~~~~~~~~

Imagining Violet

78 Ritherdon Road, Upper Tooting,
London SW

January 20th, 1896

Dear Flo,

I am remiss in not writing sooner to let you know our new address. I believe I mentioned when I last wrote – late in November I am ashamed to say – that we were removing to London. As you can imagine, it has been a busy time.

We are in South London, practically in the country, which I do not mind at all, although it is not what I imagined when the prospect of living in London came up. Papa wished us to be as far away from the bad air and fog as possible.

My sister and I have begun to look around the neighbourhood. We are doing many errands for Mama, as there always so many little things to purchase when one moves. It has been a mild winter so far here in the south. I shall probably continue at an art school, but there are several such schools in London and I want to take care to find one that is suitable this time. It has not seriously occurred to me to resume violin lessons, although I know there are fine teachers here. I think I have gone as far as I can with my fiddle.

I shall not give up playing altogether, though, and hope I may make some musical acquaintances, but I am not sure how to proceed. We have joined the congregation at the nearby St. John the Divine where there is a fine organist named Mr. Lardner, and perhaps he might have some suggestions. I rather count on Lily too for advice and perhaps some introductions.

I expect you and Harry are still corresponding? Frank is generous with his letters given how busy he is. Oh how I welcome them, and I read them again and again. I find myself waiting for the postman all too often, and most days there is nothing, but then another letter arrives from Leipzig and I am happy again. Perhaps this is foolish, and I should accept that he is only a good friend and may never be more than that. But I hope that is not to be the case.

Please write and tell me your news. I hope you might make a trip up to town before long and stay with us perhaps. I have had little news of your dear brother of late, and trust that all is well with him.

~~~~~~~~~~~~~~~~~

78 Ritherdon Road, Upper Tooting
London SW

15th February, 1896

Dear Mr. Welsman,

I am so pleased that you are to have a recital. And at the Liszt Verein! I wish I could be there. Have you decided yet what you will play?

Yes, we have joined a church. There is one at the top of our road which is a large, new, red and yellow brick affair and not at all beautiful. But the old church in Balham village was bursting, so this is a "daughter" church. Mr. Henry Sutherland Dashwood Gill is the priest in charge, and he delivered a fine sermon last Sunday about our Christian duty to help the needy. Mrs. Henry Sutherland Dashwood Gill – it is amusing to write that all out – came to call the next day, which was kind of her, and invited Mama to join a group which does some kind of good works for the poor of East London. She suggested I might wish to come along too but I do not care to join a group of old ladies, not that Mama is old, but you know what I mean.

Mrs. Thurmond, who lives two doors away also came to call last week. It is difficult in a new neighbourhood where one knows no-one and it was kind of her to call on newcomers. And what is even better is that Mrs. Thurmond has a daughter, Henrietta, who would "love to learn the violin" or so her mother claims. She asked if I would consider giving her lessons. Apparently she had heard the sound of a violin coming from our house. Well, I have not taught small children, but as you know, I have had some experience
~~~~~~~~~~~~~~~~~

tutoring. Perhaps I shall look in my old books of technique to remind myself how to start. I dare say Miss Henrietta hasn't the least interest in learning the violin, but her mama thinks it is a necessary accomplishment for a young lady and I would not care to disoblige her.

I wrote to Flo and by reply, she sent an invitation to come down to Hereford early in April for a week's stay. I am ever so pleased about that. Lily has been to visit and we have had a couple of musical mornings together. She has a number of pupils now so does not have much free time.

We cannot complain of the weather this winter. It has been mild and we have seen the sun shine most days. What a welcome change from Scotland. And we are close to the countryside. At the bottom of our road one comes to the parkland of the old Bedford Hill estate, with its manor house now empty and doomed to destruction. The gardens all round have been neglected most terribly. It is sad as I believe it has been a handsome estate in its day. Fortunately, the Common is now managed by the London County Council and there are fine pathways, tennis courts and a yachting pond, so I do not miss the Leith Links as I had feared I might.

It is interesting to live here now, and imagine what it was like just a few years ago before there were any houses at all. Surely the streets around us will fill up with new housing little by little and the Heaver Estate will become crowded. For our family, it is very nice indeed to live in an almost new house where nothing is at all shabby. Mama could not be happier.

Summer and the long hols seems a long way off, but I do welcome your letters. In the meantime, I am sending a photograph under separate cover as you requested.

~~~~~~~~~~~~~~~~~
~~~~~~~~~~~~~~~~~

Imagining Violet

78 Ritherdon Road, Upper Tooting,
London SW

20th February, 1896

Dear Lottie,

Thank you for your letter. I am indeed grateful to have news of old friends at the Conservatory. Of course there will be fewer all the time to tell me about.

It is cheering to know that you see Frank from time to time and I am sure that as a friend you would tell me if there was anything important that I should know. I worry that he works too hard, now that I am not there to take him off skating and so on. We write friendly letters back and forth, but anything more personal is thoroughly hidden. That is the way things must be I'm afraid. But if these feelings lie buried for too long, will they wither away?

It is going to be wonderful living in London. And you are right to observe that it is a fine thing to have one's own room. Heretofore I have shared with my sister and when we were small, we were the best of friends. But with my absence of four years, Birdie became accustomed to her privacy, and of course, I lived in lodgings and had my own bedroom. These last months at Seafield Villas, Birdie and I felt somewhat cramped. Now I have my own room with my music stand and stool set up by the window, and Mama has promised to purchase some curtain material of my choosing.

I have been browsing at the draper's in the High Road and taken a fancy to some cretonne with designs of peacocks, dragons and poppies. It is the latest thing, I fancy, chinoiserie. Mama is teaching me to use her sewing machine, so soon I should be able to manage curtains. I tried to persuade her to create a Turkish corner in the parlour with an ottoman and a prayer rug, but she says Papa would find it too exotic. He may have grown up in Ireland, but he certainly is a conservative English type, I think, albeit a very dear father.

Indeed, we are close to the country here. The other day Birdie and I walked out the high road south beyond Tooting and on to the Merton Road. At first one sees the older estates with their parklands, much as Ritherdon Road was a few years ago. But before long you are in "olde England" with neat wooden cottages set close together. It is pretty and quite bucolic if you like the aromas of the farmyard. But it is also very dusty and noisy on account of the constant stream of carriages and dog carts and other vehicles, so it is not quite as delightful a walk as one might like.

~~~~~~~~~~~~~~~~
~~~~~~~~~~~~~~~~

Imagining Violet

78 Ritherdon Road, Upper Tooting

27th February, 1896

Dear Fiona,

Thank you ever so much for telling me about Herr Willy Burmester. Lily and I went to hear him at the Crystal Palace last week and he played a Paganini concerto. It was sensational! Is that the selection he played in Edinburgh? For someone not yet thirty, he was decidedly elegant in appearance, and his technical ability was superb. We were both taken aback that the audience was not enthusiastic. Perhaps it was too much bravura playing with too little emotion.

The Crystal Palace will deserve several more visits when the weather improves. There are splendid gardens, a maze and a pond with replicas of dinosaurs. As it was raining and the fog was very thick, we did not stay to see them. When my brothers come home at Easter, I shall take them there.

Rosie has left us for who knows what reason. Perhaps she did not like being out here in the suburbs. So whilst Mama hunts for a new maid, Birdie and I must help with housekeeping chores for a few hours every day, and this has curtailed our excursions for the time being. I do not mind in the least helping with the cooking, but the washing up is distinctly unpleasant.

Thank goodness there is a gas range in this kitchen which, in the way of new houses, is on the ground floor. I had not given it much thought until Rosie left, but it is ever so much easier having the kitchen closer to the dining room. I had never really thought about Molly having to trudge up and down, up and down, from the basement kitchen, morning, noon and night carrying platters and trays and jugs of hot water. There is also piped hot water upstairs to the bathroom. We are really very modern here at Ritherdon Road.

Still, I cannot see why the lamps must be cleaned every morning nor why I must dust every single thing in the drawing room, which we rarely use. At least all the laundry is sent out, and a man comes to do the floors once a week. I sincerely hope Mama finds a new maid soon.

Do you think it is awful of me to use the bathroom? It took a good deal of persuasion with Papa, I can tell you. But the boys are away at school, and why should only Papa have the pleasure of a good hot bath. I pointed out that it is healthful for Birdie to soak in a tub with Epsom salts, so Papa has finally agreed that Birdie and I may use the bathroom. Mama may yet be talked into bathing in the tub, but so far she continues with the old ways and has hot water carried to her room.

I have begun with my first pupil, Miss Henrietta Thurmond, and she requires all my patience. She is a stocky little miss of eleven who has had two years of piano lessons so has some rudiments of music. I looked in Spohr's Violin Schule for help, but I disagree with his advice advocating a daily lesson. Twice a week seems sufficient for a beginner. We tried to do an hour, but the lass became fidgety before our time was up, so she shall have half hour lessons.

My Canadian friend and I continue to write and his letters make me nostalgic for our time in Leipzig. At least here in London, I am not forced to discourage the attentions of potential suitors. But it is difficult to contemplate how it will end. Can we go on writing year after year after year and never meet?

As soon as my domestic duties do not consume so much of my life, I shall take up the search for an art class, but I do not wish to find myself in another school like the Edinburgh College of Art with its old fashioned rigid approach.

~~~~~~~~~~~~~~~~
~~~~~~~~~~~~~~~~

Imagining Violet

15th March, 1896

Dear Mr. Welsman,

I was completely delighted to know that your recital was a success. How thrilling to play in front of Herr Arthur Friedheim and Madame Schumann! I have always admired her very much. Were you introduced? Do tell me everything about it. You are fortunate that you do not get very nervous playing in front of an audience as Mr. Puddicombe does. Has he made plans yet for his return to Canada? I shall be visiting Flo next month and am naturally curious to know if Mr. P. will be in England at that time.

Yes, there are moments when I miss the student life very much. It was a good deal of hard work and not without its frustrations, but there were also times of immense satisfaction, when one finally got a difficult passage right, for example. I particularly miss the ensemble playing, but remain optimistic that I may find a few amateur musicians here, although I have had no luck thus far. In the meantime, Lily comes down one morning a week. We play duets and she stays to lunch. She has half a dozen pupils, but she did not get the position she sought at a day school for young ladies, so has her mornings free. This was no reflection whatsoever on her ability or qualifications, but it was discouraging, as they gave the position to a less qualified person, the younger sister of one of the owners. Mama is more tolerant of our music making than Lily's family, but that is mostly on account of Lily's invalid aunt stopping with them. She came for a short visit several months back, but Lily's dear, generous mother has urged her to stay on and so she has.

After two months of unusually fine weather, we have had nothing but torrential rain this past week, but it feels a little like spring none-the-less. We have had thunder and lightning and it was ever so exciting to watch the storm roll in. And the fog is unlike any I have ever seen. It can be so dense that one does not feel safe walking out after dark.

I had hoped for colder weather imagining that the pond at Tooting Bec Common might freeze for skating. But that has not happened. I miss the skating and envy you that freedom to strap on skates whenever the fancy takes you. There are two or three ice rinks in London, with "real ice" indoors and an orchestra playing which one skates to. I want to go but must persuade Lily to attempt it with me.

Despite the rain, Birdie and I have resumed our expeditions into town. Mama has hired a new maid and we are relieved of most of our chores. It truly is grand to be here in London where there is so much to do and to see. It takes some time to go anywhere, but the 'buses come every few minutes along Balham High Road and we climb aboard and off we go.

Miss Henrietta, the neighbour's child, has been coming for lessons for a few weeks now. The tutoring I did last year has helped, but teaching a child is something altogether different. I would value your opinion about Spohr's approach.

I have also been happily occupied sewing curtains for my bedroom and helping Mama put some finishing touches to the drawing room. And I made scones yesterday which were said by all to be entirely edible. Having been away at school for four years, I am behind more than a little when it comes to domestic skills.

Stay warm and look after yourself. I worry that you may take a fall on the ice and injure your fine hands.

~~~~~~~~~~~~~~~~~

8th April, 1896

Dear Flo,

I was so happy to read the comments that you copied from a Toronto newspaper about Frank's performance in Leipzig. There must be another Canadian there who sent a review to Canada. To think he played for Arthur Friedheim at the Liszt Verein! That was indeed an honour and much better than an old Conservatory Abend. Frank will never report praise; he really is far too modest. But for a
~~~~~~~~~~~~~~~~~

famous pianist like Friedheim to characterize Frank's playing of the Bach *Toccata* as "grossartig" – well that is an accolade.

I am very much looking forward to my visit with you later this month. I shall take the two o'clock train and should reach Hereford by four. Can I walk from the station? I could send for my bags later and would be happy to walk.

If you like, I shall look for a copy of Sarah Grand's new book when I am next in the city and bring it with me. Our local bookshop does not carry the latest novels by the New Women writers. Thank you for pointing out the work of Miss Caird; I enjoyed her novel, *The Daughters of Danaus*. I was heartily sorry, though, that the authoress concludes it is impossible to pursue a life as a musician and be a successful wife at the same time.

I did have my dreams, did not I? Perhaps I should regard it as fortunate that I discovered in good time that my talent as a violinist was modest. But goodness, for those of our former colleagues who were truly talented, what future awaits? My tutor, Miss Doyle, was determined to succeed on the concert platform. She was almost notorious at the Conservatory and I often wonder what became of her. And Miss Street as well. I hope she has pursued her dream. Still, we occasionally see women performing nowadays, and certainly some of them must be married.

~~~~~~~~~~~~~~~~~

12th April, 1896

Dear Mr. Welsman,

I was glad to read more about your Liszt Verein recital. I did not know you had met Herr Friedheim in Toronto. Was he surprised to find you in Leipzig?

My brothers were home over Easter and were excited to be in London. Reg is eighteen now and Jack is sixteen; they are no longer boys. Still, Papa tends to be cautious and did not wish them to wander about London on their own straightaway, so I was appointed
~~~~~~~~~~~~~~~~~

to accompany their first outings. They were dead keen about the Crystal Palace. In fact, the dinosaur lake fascinated us all. If creatures like that ever truly existed, how frightening for the ancient people who shared the earth with them thousands of years ago. The giant Megalosaurus impressed most. The boys estimated it was over thirty feet in length, plus its long tail. Its head is ferocious with long curved dagger-like teeth. I did not know that such animals had ever lived in England. We were warned that the models are not completely accurate, but that is not sufficient reason to disregard them.

My little brothers seem quite grown up. It has done them a power of good to be away at school and do for themselves. Still, Mama was happy to have her boys at home for the Easter vacation, and she spoiled them thoroughly. Birdie and I were expected to wait on their every need. I did not mind, for a week, but I would not be so accommodating if they were at home all the time.

Easter in London is nothing at all like Leipzig. It is mainly a time of church-going, and of course we attended service on Easter morning. I had saved some of my teaching money to buy chocolate eggs for every member of the family. There are so many more choices now, all beautifully decorated and Cadbury's does make such delectable chocolate. I hid the eggs around the drawing room, and even Papa entered into the spirit of the occasion and joined the hunt.

I had proposed to make an Ostereierbaum with painted eggs. Mama was hesitant but Papa was against it. He said he did not want us to look German, having such a thing in the front window. He did not forbid it outright, so I persevered. Jack helped by going off to the Common and fetching in some suitable branches. I cooked a dozen eggs with a little beetroot so they were a pretty shade of pink, and we used my watercolours to decorate them. I was not going to attempt to blow them out as we did at Fräul. Hohmanns. Devising a way to hang them took some doing. but Birdie created a sort of crocheted sling that was successful. Respecting Papa's concerns, we put the tree in the entrance hall, where we could enjoy it, but the neighbours would not think we were foreign.

There was an excellent Good Friday concert at the splendid St. James Hall on Regent Street. I am not sure my brothers enjoyed it overmuch, but I am sure it was good for them. St. James is London's principal concert hall and could stand next to the Gewandhaus with pride. The acoustics are first class and the décor is dramatic. Birdie pointed out that several features of the decorations are copied from the Alhambra Palace in Granada. It's amazing the things she knows.

Have you read anything about the Games of the Olympiad in Greece? Papa mentioned they were the first games of the modern era and we all followed the news in the newspaper with interest. England did rather well, winning in tennis and weightlifting and cycling. I read that Germany sent nineteen athletes; there were only ten from Great Britain.

Thank you for your advice regarding my violin teaching. I was lucky to find a lightly used copy of the *DeBeriot Violin School* at the local music store and I agree that it is a better method for a beginner. Miss Henrietta is, for the most part, coming along nicely. She has a decent violin that belonged to her late aunt and as she is a strapping lass, it is not too big for her. I hope her Mama will recommend me to friends and that I may acquire another pupil. If teaching is to be my lot, I may as well have another pupil or so.

~~~~~~~~~~~~~~~~~

"Rosslyn", Bodenham Road, Hereford

30th April, 1896

Dear Mr. Welsman,

How clever of you to write to me at Rosslyn! I did not expect any letters to reach me here, unless they were from Mama. I am sure I have Mr. Heins to thank for providing the address.

Flo has kept me so well entertained that I have scarcely had a moment to write a proper letter. I hope you had my postcard of the
~~~~~~~~~~~~~~~~~

Hereford Cathedral. Today it is raining heavily, so our expedition to Malvern has been postponed. Instead we shall spend an hour or so this afternoon making music.

It is delightful to be here so soon after their engagement. Of course, you knew all about it and did not tell me! You can keep a secret, which is an admirable quality in a man. How romantic of Mr. P. to come all the way to Hereford to propose. I thought perhaps they had come to some kind of understanding in Leipzig, but now it is official. Flo says they may not yet set a date as Mr. P. will have to have some assurance of steady employment. I expect that is why he will return to Canada soon and indeed, he has already written to people in Ottawa about possibilities there.

Flo is curious, excited and nervous all at once about living in Canada. It is fair to say that life in rural Hereford is a little too quiet and provincial for her energies.

Hereford is a pretty town though and their home, Rosslyn, is nicely situated on a height looking across a valley to the River Wye.

We have been busy with day trips here and there. Tomorrow, if it is fine, we go to Malvern, and the other day we ventured as far as Ludlow, twenty-four miles to the north. Ludlow Castle is deservedly famous, but I shall not bother you with the details as you have no doubt had your fill of castles.

Hereford Cathedral is the town's main attraction, as it deserves to be. There have been services there since the 8th century, although the present Cathedral is largely Norman and was built in the 13th century. One goes also to see their Mappa Mundi, the largest map of the world from that time. It is circular and painted on a single large piece of vellum and depicts Jerusalem as located in the middle of the world. Unfortunately, it is difficult to see it well, because it is hung, in its original frame, in a dark sort of corridor. I peered at it for some time; it is full of strange details, too much to take in all at once, but so interesting to see how people seven hundred years ago imagined the world. The other treasure is the collection of chained books in their original bookcases. Whilst the Cathedral was dimly lit, it was surprisingly warm inside. Flo pointed out four very large Gurney stoves which provide heat.

Flo will come to us in June. She has a good deal of shopping to do and I shall not mind going with her although I do not know the London shops. I have warned her that if she comes in the Season she might be disappointed as we are not in Society and will not have any interesting invitations. It would be splendid though, if we could go to Covent Garden!

I suppose spring has come to Leipzig and everyone is enjoying the parks and ponds again. I am glad you are enjoying your work with Herr Krause and that you are getting on better with Herr Schreck. I hope you will not mind my reminding you of the walks we took together a year ago.

~~~~~~~~~~~~~~~~~~~~

~~~~~~~~~~~~~~~~~~~~

Imagining Violet

"Rosslyn", Bodenham Road, Hereford

30th April, 1896

Dear Mama, Papa and Birdie,

I hope you will not mind sharing a letter. I have been made very welcome here and have been enjoying my visit immensely. It is lovely to see Mrs. Heins again, and Mr. Heins is most amiable. Flo has been taking me round the local sights. We have been of course to the Cathedral and have made one or two excursions further afield.

The other day we took the train to Ludlow, which feels a good deal like the mediaeval town it once was. There are dozens of old houses and inns, because Ludlow was a prosperous trading centre in the olden days. You can even see the remains of the town walls in places. Ludlow Castle is a grand old ruin. It was one of the castles built in the 13th century to keep the Welsh out of England, and it just grew and grew. I have sent a postcard.

My cough is much better, and I am sure that all the fresh air of Herefordshire has helped to cure it. I had almost forgotten what truly fresh air tastes like after just these few months in London.

I shall be home early next week, and shall make my own way from the station to Ritherdon Road. It is not necessary that anyone comes to fetch me, but thank you for the offer.

The gong has rung, so I must change for dinner. My refurbished spring frocks have done very nicely, I am glad to say, and the new yellow silk has been a hit with both Flo and her mother.

Fiona has written to accept our invitation to come to London later this month, and again, I thank you for offering our hospitality.

~~~~~~~~~~~~~~~~~
~~~~~~~~~~~~~~~~~

Imagining Violet

~~~~~~~~~~~~~~~~

78 Ritherdon Road

5th June, 1896

Dear Mr. Welsman,

We are enjoying an early summer with warm and sunny days. There has been scarcely any rain at all. And this year, I am free to enjoy it, without feeling guilty that I am not practising. That is some compensation I suppose. I expect you are staying well-disciplined and keeping to your piano many hours a day? I was happy to hear that there are no more complaints from your neighbours downstairs. Have they left or are you keeping the window closed?

As you correctly guessed, I have indeed been procrastinating about art school. What with visiting and being visited, and with such pleasant spring weather, I have put it off. Lily has been a help though with advice about choosing a school. She had good reports of the
~~~~~~~~~~~~~~~~

Heatherly School, so I went along with some samples of my drawing to meet the Director and to see the school which is some distance from Ritherdon. I am still getting used to the amount of time it takes to travel into the city.

The Heatherly School is one of the few that welcomes amateurs. I was shown the vast collections of casts, costumes, armour, pottery and even furniture, all of which are made available to the numerous young ladies who fill the afternoon classes. I think it must be a very progressive school. Indeed, it used to be the only art school in London which allowed women to paint from the nude model. Not that drawing from the nude is something I am keen to do. I expect it would be completely embarrassing to tell the truth. But I should like to study somewhere with a more modern atmosphere. One may also choose a short term of enrolment, which is what I believe I shall do.

My Edinburgh friend, Fiona MacPherson, has been to visit. We paid a visit to the National Gallery and had a small adventure. It is a huge place and of course Birdie wanted to look in the British galleries whilst Fiona and I were intent on seeing the Italian Renaissance paintings. We spent heaps of time gazing at the Tintorettos and Titians and no time at all in those galleries of Madonnas. One of the joys of my life is that the National Gallery is free, all the time, not just on Sundays.

Then Fiona and Lily and I went to the Philharmonic Concert at Queen’s Hall on the 3rd inst. Sir Alexander Mackenzie’s new *Scottish Fantasia* was on the programme to be played by Mr. Paderewski. . We were disappointed when they announced that Mr. Paderewski was indisposed, but the young man who replaced him was brilliant. This was a young Russian, a protégé of Paderewski's, named Mark Hambourg. He gave the Rubenstein *A Minor Concerto*. Do you know it? It is fiendish, but Mr. Hambourg played with dazzling technique and genuine emotion. Our disappointment rapidly turned to delight.

We had tea afterwards in one of those little tea shops that are springing up everywhere. It is deemed respectable, even by my father, for three young ladies to patronize them. Thank goodness! The tea was not fancy, but we were happy to find a cozy place to sit and chat. Lily and Fiona took to each other straightaway. We talked a little about making music together, wondering if there is any suitable repertoire for piano four hands and violin. That is probably a silly notion, but Lily offered to look in her local music shop. We had invited Birdie to come with us, but she did not care to, being happily occupied these days with the Bible Study group she has joined at our church.

Apparently we missed one of the great sights of the season, with all of our outings. The day we went to the Philharmonic was Derby Day at Epsom Downs. The local shopkeepers are still talking about the traffic that jammed the roads right up until ten o'clock that night. Papa said he did not think it would have been a proper spectacle for young ladies and I would not have wanted to expose Fiona to anything rough. Still, I shall try to be home next year as it must be quite a sight.

You are bound to be pleased that your parents are to come over this summer. It is difficult to be far from home for so long. Do you know how long they will stay or when they are coming or whether they will venture beyond Devon? I am happy that you think this might be an opportunity for us to meet in London. It has been nearly a year since I left Leipzig, a very long year indeed.

~~~~~~~~~~~~~~~

15th June, 1896

Dear Fiona,

Mama appreciated your note of thanks and the thoughtful gift. Now she will be writing you a note of thanks, and on and on it will go. Some of the finer points of etiquette seem a trifle foolish sometimes. Or should that be fossilish? Mr. Welsman is rather given to puns and he would like that one.
~~~~~~~~~~~~~~~

We write to each other with great regularity and I have every hope that we may meet here in London sometime this summer. His parents will travel to Britain this summer, so naturally he will come here to spend his holidays with them.

However, after being apart for a year, I am not sure what his feelings are. It seemed clear when I left Leipzig, that he cared for me, as I had come to care for him. But society demands that we are formal in our letters and I am not sure there will ever be a proposal. I must regard him as a friend although that is increasingly difficult. Surely there will be an opportunity to meet. Otherwise, is there any point to going on?

I so enjoyed your visit, especially the long rambles we took exploring the neighbourhood. Getting as far as Richmond Park and back in a day was an ambitious outing. Imagine building a wall around twenty-two hundred acres! And wasn't it great fun to feed the deer? I almost gave away my whole sandwich.

Will you go with your family to the west coast again this summer or have they decided? As we are newcomers to the south of England, there is quite a to-do in this house to decide where our holiday will be. Mama has been writing away for brochures and such and of course every seaside resort looks equally tempting. At the moment, I think they favour Eastbourne or Hove, but they are also considering Cornwall. Personally I think it would be more adventurous to go to Cornwall. That is where Lily is going with her family. It looks so beautiful in the brochures with those high cliffs and the turquoise sea.

Thank you for persuading me to go to a hair dresser to have my hair shampooed. It was very satisfactory altogether. I was able to talk Birdie into coming with me, and she enjoyed it as well. We can now both speak from experience and encourage Mama to try a hair dresser too. It was odd at first to have a man touching my head, but I quickly got used to it, and will happily go again in another few months.

~~~~~~~~~~~~~~~~~~
~~~~~~~~~~~~~~~~~~

6th July, 1896

My very dear Frank,

Yes, with all my heart,

Dein Veilchen

~~~~~~~~~~~~~~~~~~

6th July 1896,

Dear Lily,

I have tremendous news! I am verlobt – or I should say, "We are engaged!!!" At last! At last!! It has been a long, long wait not knowing what might happen or indeed, what to expect.

Frank has written to Papa. He acknowledges that his proposal might seem premature, and promises that he is prepared to undertake a long engagement, but says that he loves me and wants me to be his wife. And with this epistle, he enclosed a very sweet letter to me, asking me to marry him.

Papa is not enthusiastic, but has reluctantly given conditional consent. He is far from persuaded that Frank will ever be able to support a wife on a musician's income. Frank explained that he will return to Canada in a year's time and will set up in a studio to teach. He will also work at securing some recitals as he knows that establishing a reputation as a pianist will bring pupils to the door. He has thought this out carefully and that is definitely in his favour.

Papa is not much impressed with what I have told him about Frank's family. Sometimes I think he feels his Courtenaye heritage altogether too strongly. There may have been Dukes way back there
~~~~~~~~~~~~~~~~~~

in the middle ages but what does it count for now? My grandfather Courtenaye was a banker in a small city in Ireland, for goodness sake.

But Frank's father has a dry goods shop in Toronto, and is therefore not altogether a gentleman in the way Papa thinks of these things. His Uncle Bill is an innkeeper in Devon. I am sure they are all good decent Christian people and surely that is what matters. Mama, bless her, is gently optimistic that Frank will succeed as a musician. I suspect the idea rather appeals to her romantic side.

Flo Heins was here when Frank's letters arrived, and she burst into tears. Mama wept too when I told her, but I do not think they were tears of joy. She has been anxious for some time that my friendship with Frank might develop into something more, which would mean I would probably leave England altogether. And Canada is very, very far away. I thought she was accustomed to my absence, but in her mind, I guess, my time in Leipzig was temporary and of course I was home every summer. I feel sure that she expected me to come home, meet some nice young Englishman, marry and settle down nearby. She seems particularly upset about grandchildren saying, "Now I shall never know my grandchildren." Well that is a good way off in the future, if I can manage it.

Lily, I feel as if I have been waiting for this for ages. But ever since I returned home last year, knowing how I felt inside, it has been impossible to explain why I was not interested in meeting other young men. Even though I have been far from confident that Frank would ever propose.

For myself, as you know, I have been dreaming about this for a long time. The idea of leaving England does not upset me overmuch. Perhaps this is because we have moved from place to place throughout my life. My earliest memories are of Chester, then those happy years of childhood romping on the beaches of Gorleston. I was only in Edinburgh for two years before going to Leipzig. I hardly can say where home is, to tell you the truth.

And then there is our Irish heritage. Birdie feels more Irish than I do, being a few years older, but we were both born there. It does not mean very much to me, perhaps because I was an infant when Papa took the position in Chester, but Birdie has some slight memories of Ballina. Well, enough of this introspection; I do go on with you, don't I?

I hope the coast of Cornwall is every bit as beautiful as you had anticipated. And I trust you will not mind if I pass on your enthusiasm for it to my parents, although I think they have settled on Hove after all.

The wedding will not be for years but I hope you will wish to be a bridesmaid.

~~~~~~~~~~~~~~~

6th July

My dear Frank,

It was very brave of you to write to Papa and very wise to explain your intentions so forthrightly. I think he is impressed that you have thought it through carefully and see your way to making a success of music within a few years. Of course you know your city and how it is growing, but it is unfamiliar to us. So there you are, a dear, brave and wise man.

Before I let too much excitement take me over, I should tell you what a pleasant visit I have had with Flo Heins. We are such good friends, and now we have even more in common. She was here when your letters came and quite danced with delight.

We did get tickets to the opera; I think it was the highlight of her stay. We attended the first performance of *Carmen* which I never saw in Leipzig. I was sorry we did not manage to see the divine Mme Melba but her appearances did not fit with Flo's stay. *Carmen* is very different indeed from those light Viennese comedies we were usually fed in Leipzig. The lead role was sung with great effect by a not-so-young American soprano, Mlle. Zélie de Lussan, who makes a speciality of the part. She first sang it eight years ago and being so familiar with the character she gives a most convincing performance. However, Carmen is not altogether admirable, and the story was
~~~~~~~~~~~~~~~

confusing. Still, it is opera, so what can one expect? I always enjoy it no matter what.

Flo's father evidently agreed with mine about our travelling home late at night and he kindly provided a little extra to Flo's allowance which allowed us the luxury of a hansom cab. Papa had waited up for us, to open the door. I was sorry to keep him up so late, but he will not be persuaded to give me a latchkey. I have not given up on that though.

Flo was eager to visit our big department stores as there is nothing comparable in Hereford. We have Arding & Hobbs just two miles from Ritherdon Road, but it does not compare to Whiteley's in Westbourne Grove. Whiteley's boasts it can provide anything from a pin to an elephant! At the Universal Provider, which is what it calls itself, one can buy theatre tickets, do one's banking or even make travel arrangements. Flo made several purchases and I bought some gloves, and tired out by our shopping, we repaired to the charming refreshment room for tea.

She has invited me to come to Hereford toward the end of the summer, and I rather expect that you may receive a similar invitation from Mr. Heins. That would be ever so nice, wouldn't it?

We made the requisite visit to the Crystal Palace, but left the British Museum for another day. I think Flo finds the immensity of the city, the bustling crowds and constant traffic all very stimulating after the peace of Hereford. And so we did a good deal of walking about around Piccadilly and Oxford Street.

Mama and Papa would like to meet your parents when they are in England. She has suggested inviting them to dinner which I suppose is proper, although a dinner party feels a little awkward for a first meeting. I would appreciate your opinion whilst there is still time, and if you could provide an address and the date of their arrival, that would be helpful. I am delighted to know you will stop in London for a day or two when you arrive from Germany. I expect there must be a lodging house nearby. Might you be here by the 28th?

And yes, I have enrolled at the Heatherly School for a four-week session. I shall tell you about it in another letter. In the meantime, I am most happy to be your betrothed, and immer dein Freundin.

~~~~~~~~~~~~~~~~~~

Mrs. Ashton's Boarding House, Eastbourne

August 2nd, 1896

Dear Lily,

It has been a whirlwind these past few days, truly it has. I write this from a wee desk in our room at Mrs. Ashton's Boarding House in Eastbourne, where we have come for a fortnight's holiday. One of Mama's new friends at church recommended Mrs. Ashton's where Papa has taken three rooms. It is a few steps up from the Grand Parade and nicely situated. My brothers would much rather be
~~~~~~~~~~~~~~~~~~

in Brighton with all its attractions and much livelier pier. Obviously I was not successful in persuading the family to travel all the way to Paignton.

Frank has come and gone! And he came with the most beautiful engagement ring in the world. It is warm rosy gold with three small diamonds. I do not know how he managed it. He arrived from Leipzig on the 28th ult., and Mama promptly invited him to visit that very evening when Papa would be at home. My sister and brothers were on hand as well, so it may have been a little overwhelming, but in his own dear quiet way Frank behaved with such grace and charm that I think Mama fell in love with him too! Everyone was on their best behaviour and I had a time of it not throwing myself into his arms. It was so lovely to see him again after almost thirteen months! Indeed, we were more than a little shy. There have been times over this year when I wondered if he cared for me at all. One must be so proper in letters.

I was finishing up at the Heatherly School that week, which was tiresome, but I had work to complete. To my delight, Frank came to meet me at four o'clock and we walked home together; it was miles and miles to South London. My feet were tired, as it took us well over two hours, but we had the chance to become reacquainted and we missed tea. Mama forgave us and invited Frank to stay on to dinner, after which he sat down at our old piano and played Chopin. So beautifully. He had to leave for Exeter late the next day, so I went to Waterloo to see him off.

Although I had classes three days a week, I have been able to help this year preparing for our holiday. Goodness there is a lot to do! Last year, I am ashamed to say, I took no interest and just went on my way. There is all that sorting of clothes and packing; I had no idea it was such a project. Of course my brothers do nothing to help and Birdie tires so easily. And then there is all the unpacking at one's destination. Mama brings a large hamper full of things "just in case". I should pay attention to what she brings as I may be doing this myself in a few years. I feel badly now for all the times I have run off to the beach the minute we arrived at the seaside.

My dear Papa is in good health for a man his age and I am grateful for that. He and I tramped six miles across the South Downs this morning to Wilmington where there are the remains of an old priory. But much more fascinating is the famous Long Man of Wilmington, a giant figure cut into the side of the hill. The chalky ground gives the figure a strong white outline. No one knows for sure what it is or why it is there. Some say it may be of Celtic origin. It was restored six years ago, so is very visible.

Frank's parents are with family in Newton Poppleford and Mama has invited them to dine when they come up to London. I hope they will make that journey as it is almost a day's travel from Exeter. Bu I hope they are curious enough to come and meet this Irish Scottish English girl their son plans to marry! I wonder too how Canadian they will be after thirty years in Toronto. Frank does not seem English at all. He is always proper, but simply more relaxed about himself, not giving airs, not at all a snob. I do like that about him.

I just have a minute to pen a quick note to my betrothed before the dinner gong rings, so will catch you up on the rest of my news in another letter.

Mrs. Ashton's Boarding House,
Eastbourne

10th August, 1896

My dearest Frank,

I hope my postcards of Eastbourne and the Long Man have reached you in Newton Poppleford as well as the letters I wrote last week.

We are nearing the end of our holiday here. I honestly think Birdie and I are a little old for the family holiday, although we are grateful to Papa for giving us this time at the seaside. There are plenty of excursions one can take and the esplanade here is two miles long from one end to the other, so affords a pleasant walk. I was happy to have my fiddle with me though, and I am practising those duets we attempted when you came to dinner.

I hope you liked my family, mein lieber. I am sure they all liked you immensely. My brother Jack is a bit rambunctious, I admit. I want all the people I love, to love each other.

I am looking forward very much to meeting your parents on the 19th inst. They will be comfortable I am sure at the Bedford Hill Hotel which is close to us but is also convenient for going into town. I keep telling Mama that she must not overdo it and serve an elaborate seven course meal. It is summer and it may be warm, and I think she would do better to serve cold dishes. But she will not have it. I have, however, persuaded her that hiring a job cook is not necessary. Birdie and I will help and we have Sheila to serve.

Oh how lovely it is to write, "I'll see you in a week"! And later we shall be together again for a few days in Hereford. What a plenitude of blessings. But after that, another long, long year apart. Perhaps it will only be nine or ten months?

Immer deine liebende Freundin

~~~~~~~~~~~~~~~~~
~~~~~~~~~~~~~~~~~

Imagining Violet

Ritherdon Road

August 20th, 1896
Dear Fiona,

Many thanks for your letter and the postcards from Nairn. The glass-covered swimming bath looks grand. I expect the water might be toasty warm in that pool with the sun shining through the glass. Did you bathe? Eastbourne was pleasant enough but not a patch on the west coast of Scotland, even though it was generally fine weather. "They" say Eastbourne is the sunniest place in the United Kingdom, and "they" may be telling the truth.

I have met my future in-laws at last. They came to dine two nights ago. We were all a little shy, meeting for the first time, but it went off rather well, thanks mainly to dear Mama who is both capable and gracious. Mrs. Welsman is an energetic little person, rather short of stature, who sits up very straight – perhaps to seem taller -- oh, that is mean of me – but what a radiant smile. Mr. Welsman is quite the gentleman really, rather quiet and dignified. It is snobbish of me to say so, but you would never take him for a shop keeper. He and Papa got on famously – they are both stamp collectors – whilst Mama and Mrs. W. found plenty to chat about. The wedding, of course, may not yet be a topic of conversation, although I dare say that was exactly what they wished to discuss. Jack asked ever so many questions about Canada which suited me of course, as I want to know everything and did not wish to appear over-eager.

Birdie and I had helped Mama and Sheila in the kitchen and we prepared a delicious but not elaborate dinner which Sheila managed to serve nicely. I shall spare you the menu, but my savoury was tasty, if I do say so myself.

Frank and I were on our best behaviour and did not have a moment alone that evening. However, we remedied that yesterday. Mrs. W. and Mama and Birdie went off shopping, and Mr. W. had some business to attend to, so I finally had the chance to take Frank to the Crystal Palace. He was every bit as impressed as you were and we had a lovely time of it.

There are simply no concerts on, which was disappointing as I had wanted to take Frank to Queen's Hall at least, but he insisted, gracious as always, that he was content to have a complete holiday from music.

All too soon, we put them on the train for Exeter. But we have not had to say good bye, just "bis zum nächsten Mal", as we have both been invited to "Rosslyn" at the end of the month. We are having a good summer of it!

~~~~~~~~~~~~~~~~~

Ritherdon Road

7th September,

Mein liebste Frank,

It is barely three days since you set off on the boat train but after our many happy days together, it is difficult to accept that I shall not see you again for many, many, many months. I am a little comforted by having your picture in front of me, looking so handsome.

I hope your journey back to Leipzig was completely without incident. It may be the last time you make that trip. You will not miss it, I am sure, especially the long train ride from Flushing to Berlin. I hope you were not bothered at any of the border crossings by officious officials.

How interesting that Herr Zwintscher has left Leipzig. He may say he was tired of the politics and rivalries of the Conservatory and I do not mean to be unkind, but it is well known that he makes a good deal more money from private lessons. People used to say it was up to three times as much. It is a good thing you were not studying with him, only to be abandoned.

In a few weeks I shall be more usefully occupied when I begin classes at the Lambeth School. I have taken my samples and met with the headmaster who asked outright why I wished to enrol. I
~~~~~~~~~~~~~~~~~

was obliged to admit that I did not intend a career in art, that I am just another of the legion of young ladies who needs something worthwhile to do.

The Lambeth School is a good deal closer to home than the Heatherly and that alone is in its favour. If I had a bicycle, I could ride there, but no such luck and in any case the 'bus goes close enough. As I said to you, the Heatherly was a little too progressive for me. I imagine myself to be modern, but I did not fit in there. I am a long way from being a New Woman, you will be glad to know.

Birdie is in need of an occupation too and has suggested that we join the Streatham Choral Society which practises not far from here. I am sure she would not go alone, nor would Papa wish it. I hope she will meet some suitable people there, but be assured that making new friends is not the reason I would be going.

As Charlotte has gone off to Paris, you are now my only Leipzig correspondent. I shall have to rely upon you, my dear one, for the news. I do not expect you to pass on gossip, although I should dearly love to know everything. Lottie is determined to join the vibrato school and while I am not sure I agree with what seems sometimes to be a mindless and constant use of vibrato, it is nevertheless very much "en vogue" and any aspiring performer must know how to use it expertly. Or perhaps I am just envious that she is living in Paris? By comparison, Upper Tooting is very dull indeed.

I am impatient to know what you are studying and how your new lodgings suit and everything that you are doing, so I hope you will write a long letter soon. Or even a short one.

Gesandt mit meiner Liebe,

~~~~~~~~~~~~~~~~~
~~~~~~~~~~~~~~~~~

Imagining Violet

September 10, 1896

Dear Lottie,

It has been many weeks since I wrote to you and I feel more than a little guilty. I hope you will forgive your lazy friend. I have your letter of July 14th before me telling me of your plans. Well, you must be in Paris now, and about to start your lessons with M. Narcisse Augustin Lefort? What an interesting name. I do want to hear how you get on with vibrato. And of course I want to hear all about Paris too. Wouldn't I love to have a chance to visit you there!!

In Leipzig they used to say that one needed some time in Paris to smooth off the rough edges. And perhaps if things have cooled off with Mr. T., you were ready to leave Leipzig.

What a wonderful summer I have had! Frank came late in July and we have had three visits and as well, his parents came up to town to meet me and my family. Last week we were both house guests at Flo and Donald Heins' home in Hereford. Flo and I have a lot to talk about now that we are both engaged to Canadians and thinking ahead to a future in Canada.

Whilst we were in Hereford, we took some excellent walks along the Wye River and one afternoon we hired rowboats and took a spin on the water. Frank, as I knew from Leipzig, is an accomplished oarsman. He let me try the rowing, again, but it takes some skill to co-ordinate the oars and he got rather splashed from my efforts.

Another day we walked the good pathways up Dinedor Hill, just two and a half miles from town. At the top there are earthworks, the remains of a Roman camp they say, with excellent views all round the countryside. There is a circle of enormous beech trees in the centre of the fort which has been there for hundreds of years. We were told that there were a number of Roman camps in Herefordshire: I am sure I do not know why. Were they defending themselves against the Welsh?

We also went together to have our photographs taken. This was just the second time I have had mine done. And having a likeness of Frank cheers me up every time I look at it, which is very often indeed.

The Heatherly School of Art was not a success. In October I shall enrol at the Lambeth School, which should be more "gemütlich". But life will be very quiet here in Upper Tooting after what has been a delightfully busy summer.

Lottie, I do not have an address for you in Paris, so I am posting this to your family who will send it on, I trust.

~~~~~~~~~~~~~~~~~

23rd Sept., 1896

Dearest Frank,

I am sitting at my desk in my bedroom, a little too late at night, with your picture in front of me. I shall not make this a long letter as I do not want to oblige you to write all the time, and I give you permission to not reply to this one. I do not have much to write about in any case.

How nice that your old teacher, Mr. Field, has returned to Leipzig to assist Herr Krause. Perhaps he will be of some assistance to you when you have finished your work there, and are planning your return to Canada? Flo writes that Harry already has a number of pupils in his class in Ottawa.

I have one new pupil, Master Andrew, who is nine and has not had any music lessons, so I must begin at the very beginning. We shall go slowly with the violin, as I must first teach him the rudiments of theory and how to read music.

We are all looking forward to a visit from Aunt Kate and Uncle David in October. I have noticed that we are a good deal more popular with the Irish family since we came to London. Aunt Matilda travelled to Edinburgh once in a while when I was in Leipzig, but I am not sure that Aunt Kate ever did. I do not know my aunts at all well nor the associated uncles. Indeed there are cousins with whom I
~~~~~~~~~~~~~~~~~

played whilst on holiday in Foxford when we were small, but I scarcely remember them.

My classes at the Lambeth School start next week, as well as choir practice, so I shall be better occupied then. But even if I have little of importance to tell you, writing is rather like having a wee chat with you at the end of the day. And that makes me feel closer to you, my dear one, who is such a long way away.

Immer deine liebende Freundin

~~~~~~~~~~~~~~~~

78 Ritherdon Road
Upper Tooting

8th October, 1896

Dear Fiona,

Has there truly been snow in Edinburgh already? Come to think of it, the weather <u>has</u> been unusually cold for October, with nasty gales coming down from the north. Naturally we blame the Scots.

It was kind of you to inquire after my mother. She is much occupied these days with a Ladies' Group at St. John the Divine, and their pet project is most worthwhile. Every Tuesday they go into town to help with a Children's and Invalids' Dinner Table which is a charity to help people who have just come out of hospital. She had me come with her the first time, but I was the only young woman there and felt out of place. At the Dinner Table, the invalids receive a nourishing meal for several days in succession. They are often too weak or too poor to eat properly at home and the Dinner Table helps them to regain their strength. Members of the congregation purchase a one guinea subscription and that one guinea pays for forty dinner tickets. Mama says you can see from week to week what a lot of good it does. Papa was concerned at first about Mama being in such a poor
~~~~~~~~~~~~~~~~

area. She agreed that it is troubling to see the poverty, but as she is helping people back to health, she will go.

We are fairly settled into a routine here at Ritherdon Road. Birdie and I have joined the Streatham Hill Choral Society. You know I do not have much of a voice, but it is a way for Birdie to make some acquaintances. We practise on Monday evenings at St. Leonard's Church, a little more than a mile from home and a pleasant walk through the Common. For the concert in December, we are preparing Sir Arthur Sullivan's popular *Golden Legend*.

Mama's sister Kate and Uncle David have been to visit. I moved temporarily to the second floor whilst they were here, to let them have my bedroom, but I may make it a permanent move as it does seem more private up there. Mama had not seen her younger sister for some time. In honour of the occasion, Papa acquired tickets for the Lyceum Theatre where Sir Henry Irving and company were giving a new production of *Cymbeline*. You probably knew that Sir Henry was the first actor to be knighted by the Queen?

The theatre has certainly come up in the world since our parents' day, or so Mama says. *Cymbeline* was both spectacular and confusing. I found myself laughing in places, but I was not at all sure they were meant to be funny. The play is most fanciful, with ancient Britons and old Romans and a wonderful heroine named Imogen, played by Miss Ellen Terry. And that was a wonder of acting. Miss Terry is fully fifty years old, yet she was utterly believable as the high-spirited young Imogen. Her gowns were magnificent. Aunt Kate was thrilled to see Sir Henry Irving and Miss Terry, and I venture it was no accident that they came to us this month.

I have begun classes at the Lambeth School. I shall try to go three days a week, but with the teaching, it may be too much. I must help Mama with errands and in the kitchen, which does me no harm at all. I simply must learn to cook as I do not expect we shall be very well off when we are first married.

And no, I cannot tell you when that will be. If I had my way, it would be next June, as soon as Frank is completes his studies in Leipzig. But sadly, I fear that is out of the question. Papa will hear no talk of wedding dates.

~~~~~~~~~~~~~~~~~~

19th October, 1896

Mein liebste Frank,

Thank you, my dear one, for your very nice and ever-so-loving letter which arrived a few days ago. I surely am becoming sentimental, as I like to keep your most recent letter with me for a day or two before sitting down to write to you again. I am happy to know you and Don are comfortable in your new lodgings and that your landlady is tolerable. German landladies can be decidedly irksome with their strict rules about bathing and food and such.

The music season is upon us here, as it is in Leipzig. I am grateful to have Lily as a companion. She is almost always willing to go to concerts, and goodness, there are so many this month. We have been to the Crystal Palace to hear the violincellist Julius Klengel. We did not have classes with him, but even so it made us a little nostalgic for the Conservatory to hear him play. He gave a new concerto by August Klughardt which had some attractive melodies, but the audience was muted in their response. Klengel's own *Tarantella* was received with more enthusiasm.

We were there again, Lily and I, a fortnight later for Senor Sarasate's recital. I could not miss Sarasate and this was his only appearance with an orchestra. We thought it might be crowded, so went early to queue for tickets and thank goodness we did. Every seat was occupied. He played the Mendelssohn with great brilliance and took the last movement at a very fast tempo.

Birdie and I are faithful in our attendance at weekly choir practice. I enjoy the singing more than I expected to, but we have not had any notable success as of yet in making new friends. I suppose
~~~~~~~~~~~~~~~~~~

my beautiful engagement ring sends a message, and that does not help Birdie's situation at all.

At the Lambeth School, I have begun to work in the antiques room which is liberally populated by over-sized casts of statues and busts. These we are to copy using pencil. One may work right up close to the cast, which of course you could not do with a live model. I thought I had done my share of this work in pencil in Edinburgh, so I am hopeful they will soon see that I am ready to move on to chalk.

Headmaster McKeggie had explained at our interview that “the Lambeth course of training is adapted to each pupil’s special ability” and the school expects that one will make practical use of what one learns there. I did not like to say that I do not have any special ability. Nevertheless, it is gratifying that they try to treat each pupil as an individual. My principal teacher is Mr. Innes Tripp for drawing and painting, and I have Mr. Alfred Garth Jones for decorative and illuminative design.

I do not teach today, so I shall go and help Mama with tea and continue this later.

~~~~~~~~~~~~~~~~~

Sunday November 2nd, 1896

Dear Flo,

I am glad Harry is writing regularly from Ottawa. It sounds as if he has made an excellent start with the teaching. Frank is a good correspondent but I have learned not to expect long letters.

I enjoy my days at the Lambeth School although I am very much the dilettante. There is plenty of personal attention with the master stopping for a few words with each pupil in every class. Even the esteemed Headmaster makes an appearance with some regularity, as if he too takes a real interest in what the pupils are doing. How different this is from Edinburgh!

We spend our mornings in the cast room where we are allowed to talk, and the class, being composed mainly of young
~~~~~~~~~~~~~~~~~

ladies, is, as you would expect, a chatty one. One can see that the male students do not care for this more frivolous approach. But overall it is rather better disciplined than the Heatherly School, and many of the lady pupils are intent on doing something artistic with their lives.

Some are in training to teach art in the schools, and others hope to work in fashion-plate drawing or book illustration or painting miniatures. It is gratifying that making art is now an acceptable form of work for women and many young ladies are taking advantage of that. That is not my direction as I am better equipped to teach violin, but it is another kind of progress for women.

Last evening Papa took us to see *A Gaiety Girl* at the new and rather opulent Shakespeare Theatre in Lavender Hill. How nice to have a real theatre just a few miles from home. The show has been ever so popular in the West End, and I have never seen anything like it. It is not exactly an opera, nor is it a play. It is billed as a "musical comedy" and that describes it perfectly. There was a good deal of singing and dancing, and it was screamingly funny in places, poking fun at the military, the court and high society. Husbands are happy to go, as the Gaiety girls are very pretty, but in a respectable way, so that wives are not discomfited. I had seen pictures of the Gaiety Girls in their elegant gowns in the *Illustrated News*, so it was interesting to see them in person.

Will you come up to town before Christmas? You are always welcome here, you know, but perhaps if you are with your parents you will stay with them in the centre of London. If you were here on the 21st, I might persuade you to come to our choir concert.

~~~~~~~~~~~~~~~~~
~~~~~~~~~~~~~~~~~

Imagining Violet

Sunday November 15th, 1896

My dearest Frank,

It is late on Sunday evening after a chilly, rainy two days. I like to think that you, however, are toasty warm sitting by your stove. Perhaps you have been skating today? And perhaps you gave your poor arms a rest from practice.

How ever can I thank you for the delicious *Musette* you composed for me and my fiddle. You have a clear talent as a composer you know; I only wish you had more time to pursue it. The *Musette* is neither too easy nor too difficult; it is just right and such a pretty tune. Perhaps you may compose a piano accompaniment and we can play <u>your</u> music together over Christmas if you come to London. Is that truly a possibility? I do not want to get too excited until I know for sure.

We had a grand day yesterday. It was the day of "The Emancipation Run", a motor car race from London to Brighton. They called it "The Emancipation Run" because the speed limit has just been increased to fourteen miles per hour. Why would anyone want to travel that fast? Motor cars are a rare sight on our roads, and Papa was keen to go. And ever ready to try something new, I agreed that it would be thrilling to watch dozens of these new machines racing along at top speed.

I dressed as warmly as I could, as it was a nasty wet morning. Large crowds lined the Brixton Road, waiting and waiting and waiting some more. It always feels longer and colder when one waits in the rain. Finally a large band of cyclists appeared, followed by the motor cars which, to our dismay, were travelling at a very sedate pace. Soon we realized that the swarms of onlookers were getting in the way.

The variety of vehicles was a surprise. Some were like horseless landaus, others resembled dog carts and some seemed to be motorized tricycles. But they were all self powered, with the drivers and their companions sitting up proudly, wielding the steering stick or whatever you call it. I believe several were French but the Americans had an entry as well; naturally it was one of the larger cars. The newspaper said there would be more than fifty, but after all, we saw perhaps two dozen. The hundreds of cyclists formed a sort of flying or at least pedaling escort and I think they too got in the way more than a little. These horseless carriages may be noisy and smelly and will never be as reliable as a horse, but Papa does not think they will disappear from our roads. I should so like to ride in one!

Because the run had been delayed, I had to hurry home to change and make my way to St. James Hall where Eugen d'Albert was playing. We admired him so much at his concert in Leipzig, do you remember? He played one of your favourites, the *Appassionata*, and one of my favourites, the Brahms' *Quintet in F Minor*. He was superb and well worth rushing into town for, even in the rain.

Master Andrew is a regular little scamp and I doubt his fiddle will survive the year he is so rough with it. We go very slowly; the whole business of bowing and making a palatable sound is not easy. You'd think, having had young brothers, that I would remember how young lads do bang about. Master Andrew does not take it seriously and does not practise regularly. However, his mother is a formidable lady and thinks her darling boy can do no wrong, so it is not my place to dissuade her. Do you think some kind of reward system might help? And as soon as he can manage it, I shall set him some small childish tune, as he will never learn from repeating dull technical exercises.

When I read your letters in the quiet of my room at night, I imagine I am walking with you down the streets of the old city. I see you at your piano, or in a café. It brings you closer. And if your plans to come to London over Christmas come to fruition, I shall be walking the byways of Balham with the real you before too long.

Gesandt mit meine Liebe.

~~~~~~~~~~~~~~~~~
~~~~~~~~~~~~~~~~~

December 30, 1896.

Dear Fiona,

Thank you very much for your pretty Christmas card. I hope you enjoyed your Christmas as much as I did. My dear Frank did come to London, as promised, and although he had some obligations, I think he enjoyed having Christmas with our family. I surely enjoyed every minute of our time together. We grow closer and closer.

He came with a letter of introduction to Sir Frederick Bridge, the eminent organist at Westminster Abbey. I was terribly impressed. They had a fine visit, and Frank spent a few hours in the organ loft with Dr. Bridge during a service. Afterwards, Dr. Bridge showed him the Abbey's new electric organ which can produce all manner of sounds including gongs. Fancy, an electric organ doing that! Frank came back saying Dr. Bridge is "a jolly fellow, an out and out good Englishman," which I took to be high praise from a Canadian.

Whilst he was here, we went to the pantomime at Drury Lane. Papa did not think Mama would enjoy it, but I was sure my brothers would, and what a lark! It was a little crude in places, but all meant in a good-natured way. I think there were times when my brothers were not sure if they should laugh, but then they would glance over at Frank who was laughing out loud, so they knew it was all right. Papa sometimes forgets we are young adults and can tolerate a little roughness now and then. The famous Dan Leno was in it. He always plays the Dame and as he lives in Clapham, he is a South Londoner too.

Christmas Day was pleasant enough. Not as warm as Leith though. I was surprised to read that the thermometer reached 60 degrees there.

In my continuing attempt to acquire some domestic skills, I helped Mama with the Christmas cake and other baking. I love shortbread and Mama's is always excellent. I tried a batch by myself, carefully following her receipt, and it just crumbled. So disappointing. I must become a better cook by the time I am married!

It was kind of you to inquire about our choral concert. It took place on the solstice in Streatham Town Hall, and a grand new building it is too. Flo Heins was in town and came down for the evening. We sang the Sullivan piece rather well, at least my family said so. *Golden Legend* is a love story with a happy ending; it was truly romantic. Our soloists were more than capable – the two ladies have Royal Academy connections – and we choristers had nine numbers to learn.

Our second offering was the London première no less, of a new Irish ballad called *Phaudrig Cromoore* by Charles Stanford Villiers, who is Irish himself. It's a rollicking piece, but rather long and perhaps a little old fashioned. Frank had not yet arrived from Leipzig, so he was spared the experience.

Have a happy new year, Fiona. Please write when you can.

~~~~~~~~~~~~~~~~~~

8th January, 1897

My dear one,

How frightfully clever of you to arrange such a wonderful birthday gift. Birdie was very pleased with herself for keeping it a secret until yesterday and I still do not know how you arranged to acquire it. I shall read a few pages of *Canadian Pictures* every day. This evening I have been reading about ice-boating and skating and tobogganing. Do you toboggan in Toronto? And have you ever been ice-boating? I must say it sounds positively dangerous. How could you be sure you would not break through the ice? The Marquess' passion for Canada shines through the book and the drawings are very fine too. I thank you a thousand times, mein Lieber. I shall soon be quite the expert about all things Canadian.

I know it is terribly cold in Germany, but at least you do not suffer from the horrible brown fog which obscures our days far too
~~~~~~~~~~~~~~~~~~

frequently this winter. I heartily dislike it; it is clammy and dirty and odoriferous – isn't that a grand word? Honestly when it is very thick, I do not want to leave the house and I pity poor Papa who must do so, and breathe the foul air all day. In the shops here people say, "Oh it's never as bad as '92. There were days that year the sun never rose." Thousands of people died that winter, old people mostly They believe it is the fault of the fog, so they close their windows against it. I dare say my mood will improve when the fog lifts.

Ordinary life is about to begin again and I shall not bore you with a recital of my daily routine. Everyone is well here, though Mama has had a catarrh that she cannot shake. Birdie is busily engaged in preparing a paper for her Bible Study group which is more of an ancient history study group than anything very religious.

I go back and forth to the shops on the Balham High Road almost daily and just yesterday I noticed a curious building called the Swimming Baths Concert Hall that I had not stopped to look at before. What on earth can swimming baths have to do with a concert hall? There is a narrow entrance, and the front is no wider than that of an ordinary shop. Now I want to know what is going on inside, but there are no posters or billboards to enlighten me. I have not had the temerity to knock on the door to ask, but perhaps I shall do so another time.

I hold tight to the memories of your Christmas visit, and count the months until summer and your return to England.

~~~~~~~~~~~~~~~~
~~~~~~~~~~~~~~~~

February 8th, 1897

Dear Flo,

The art classes continue enjoyable. My favourite is Design Class. The teacher, Mr. Garth-Jones. is a fine looking young gentleman with a small reputation for illustration, which is what we do in his class. We are meant to study fabric design and other more practical things, and perhaps that will come. But we all crowd into Mr. Garth-Jones' class as he is such a charming fellow.

There was a social evening at St. John's last Saturday and Birdie persuaded me to accompany her. Goodness me, next she will want to go to a dance! There was an amusing speaker and a couple of comic sketches, but you would not have enjoyed the musical numbers. They were poorly done I'm afraid, and no I have not boldly offered to play my fiddle.

I have not yet met anyone in Balham with whom I can make music. Lily is busy with her teaching and she has a new young man with whom she is walking out most Sunday afternoons. I am happy for her, of course, but I miss her company. We still go to concerts, as I gather Mr. Anderson-Smyth, who is an engineer, does not have much appetite for music.

Have you read *Romance of a Shop* by Amy Levy? I found it at the lending library last week. It is New Womanish but in a common-sense way, a story of four sisters who must make their own way in the world. Their solution is to set up a photography shop. In the end – well I should not tell you any more, should I? It reminded me of the fine time we had in Hereford last summer having our pictures taken. Frank's photograph has been good company all this winter and I confess I talk to it from time to time. It is a good thing I sleep up here in a dachzimmer so no one is privy to my sentimental silliness.

~~~~~~~~~~~~~~~~~~
~~~~~~~~~~~~~~~~~~

Imagining Violet

February 20th, 1897.

Dear Mr. Heins (Donald)

I am exceedingly grateful to you for writing when Frank cannot. Of course I shall worry. It is silly to forbid it. I shall worry and hope you will write even a short note every day to tell me how my dear one is. I am glad to know the doctor has attended and that the medicine seems to be making a difference, but the prescription of two weeks' complete bed rest is surely a difficulty. Of course, by the time you receive this letter, everything will have changed, and I hope he will be well enough to write for himself.

I shall watch every post for your next message. Thank you again, Donald, for your kindness in writing, and I send my love to Frank.

Yours sincerely,
Violet Courtenaye.

~~~~~~~~~~~~~~~~~~`

7th March, 1897

My dear one,

I have been almost frantic, mein liebste. It was a great relief to see your own dear handwriting on the note that arrived this morning. I am very glad you are feeling stronger. It was kind of Don to write on your behalf, and three or four times too. Please thank him for me.

I scarcely want to write of trivial entertainments when I am so concerned for you. Perhaps though, our long-delayed skating expedition will distract you a little.

After several postponements, Lily and I at last ventured out to the skating at the Niagara Hall. What a splendid building! Inside there is a large circular ice rink and a full orchestra performs from a gallery above. The rink was exceedingly crowded with couples for
~~~~~~~~~~~~~~~~~~

the most part, who were all very well dressed. The lady skaters wore elegant satin blouses, wonderful large hats, gloves of course, and wool skirts that came just to the top of their booted skates. We enjoyed our skate – my goodness, it was good to be back on the ice, and we were both a little wobbly – but as we came away we agreed we felt somewhat out of place being two young ladies together. There were plenty of single men and we were invited to skate, but as we did not know them, nor have any mutual acquaintance there to make introductions, we naturally declined. Also, it was a little expensive and a bit fancy for Lily and me. We had to pay 3s for the morning session. In the afternoon, it costs 5s! All in all, I think I have given up on ice skating in London. One can go roller skating at the Crystal Palace, so that is something we might try.

My sketches in the cast room are improving slowly and I have decided to join the Saturday sketching group when it starts up in May. They go on weekly outings in order to draw from nature. What a nice change from the dusty cast room that will be! Between the men smoking and the young ladies chattering, it is not always an agreeable atmosphere. And no matter how I scrub, I always seem to have charcoal under my fingernails. Grubby fingers are not a good example for my small pupils. Well, perhaps that is a little too personal. But I wrote it, and I think I may be permitted to write to my dear one just the way I would talk.

Flo comes up to town next week to shop. And I shall go down to Hereford at Easter where I am to assist with her trousseau. The wedding is only a matter of ten weeks off. I should not allow myself to hope that you might be there, but you know what an optimist I am.

Gesandt mit viele Küsse,

~~~~~~~~~~~~~~~~~~
~~~~~~~~~~~~~~~~~~

Imagining Violet

19th April 1897
Easter Monday

"Rosslyn", Hereford

Mein Liebste,

Your postcards from Saxon Switzerland have indeed reached me here. Your tramp through the mountains sounds like a glorious adventure. It says something about these modern times does it not, that you can be hiking in the mountains and I can be out boating on the Wye River with Flo, and we can be in easy communication.

I am glad Mr. Cherrier was able to go with you. I dare say it might be dangerous to climb about on those mountains by yourself. I know you say you are completely well again, but you were very ill you know, and just weeks ago.

Donald is with us in Hereford. The three of us have had some good walks – we went to Dinedor Hill again – but Flo is dedicated to preparing her trousseau and I am here, after all, to help her. She still has a large pile of table napkins that want hemming and embroidering. I am not the best needlewoman but hemming is something I can do.

Flo tells me that Harry has a position at a school for young ladies in Ottawa. That will certainly please Mr. and Mrs. Heins, although they are rather more understanding about the uncertainties of a musical career than most parents would be. Flo is luckier than I in that respect.

Donald is happy to have a holiday here for a few weeks, at least until after the wedding, and later on he hopes to be taken on by Augustus Wilhelmj in London. It would be wonderful to have an old Conservatory friend in town.

You will be back for your last weeks in Leipzig and I expect you too will find it difficult to say goodbye to good friends and teachers. It is excellent news that Herr Krause has proposed a special recital for you in June. That will keep you hard at work right through May. I had harboured a secret hope that you might somehow slip away and come for Harry and Flo's wedding, but this possibility of a recital makes that possibility impossible. I shall have to wait as patiently as I can until July.

I have been reading the passages in *Canadian Pictures* about the Indians and although I remind myself that these stories are about the far-away west of your country, it is, after all, one country. The Marquess of Lorne seems to have a good deal of sympathy for the plight of the savage. He implies that it was the coming of the white man that caused so much strife and disease. He explains how the savages depended on the buffalo for so much of importance in their lives and he believes now, with the buffalo gone, they will only survive if they take up farming. He met one old chief who was persuaded with some difficulty, to plant potatoes! Yet, elsewhere I have read that the Indians of Ontario have always farmed, and have they survived? Does one see Indians on the streets of Toronto?

The choir has a concert in a fortnight and as I am missing choir practice, I have brought my music with me to study. We are singing Gounod's *Messe Solennelle* and Mendelssohn's *Athalie*, and we will have a professional orchestra to accompany us on the night. That should make for a better performance. The Gounod is growing on me, although I was not sure about it at first. The *Kyrie* is very long and rather dull, but the last minutes of the *Gloria* are glorious and the *Credo* is a powerful anthem-like piece. Birdie has become friendly with one or two of the choristers and I am glad for her.

My time is not entirely my own here. Flo is waiting for me to go for a walk by the river, so I shall say auf wiedersehen, my very dear Frank.

~~~~~~~~~~~~~~~~~
~~~~~~~~~~~~~~~~~

Friday, 4th June, 1897

My dear one,

I am home from Hereford and my goodness, I have been rushing around rather. I did not wish to cancel my pupils for more than a week no did I want to miss too many art classes.

I went down Monday – the wedding was late yesterday morning – and here I am home again. It was the nicest wedding ever, Frank, truly it was. Harry and Flo are so happy together and so brave, setting off for the new world. Well, it is not new to Harry, but what an adventure awaits them. There was a large attendance at the church as the Heins family is well established in Hereford. This will not be so with our wedding, whenever that is, mein lieber, as we scarcely know anyone at all in Upper Tooting.

As you would expect, Flo was a beautiful bride. The day dawned cloudy with a cool breeze, but just as everyone set off for the church, the sun peeped out. Wedding services are generally short, did you know? There was music, of course, with a fine organist and excellent choral numbers. Donald performed well in his role as best man. I know Harry had invited you, but he understands completely what your recital means to you. Who would know better! Don gave a very charming speech, and now that he is an experienced groomsman, well, I leave that to you. For twenty, he is quite the elegant young gentleman. Being away on his own since the age of fifteen has made him more poised and mature than my brothers at a similar age.

Mrs. Heins' garden was in full springtime bloom and we gathered there while the photographer fussed for a very long time taking photographs. As the day was fine, some tables were set out on the lawn, and some of us enjoyed the wedding breakfast al fresco. I shall omit the details of the menu, but you may be sure that as an engaged young lady, I was watching and learning what I could. I have not been to a proper wedding since I was very young and was then not interested in anything but the sweets.

I am so pleased that you are corresponding with the Toronto College of Music about a teaching position in the autumn. I know you wanted to wait until you could include some reviews of your playing, but surely that will not be a condition of taking you on. Does the College have pupils waiting for assignment to a teacher or would you be expected to find your own? I am not sure how it works.

All the same, I wish you would not completely abandon the idea of finding work here in London. At least we would be in the same city. And do you not think a year or so of teaching in London would stand you in good stead if you determined to return to Toronto later?

~~~~~~~~~~~~~~~~~~

4th June, 1897

Dear Fiona,

I imagine that you and I are both more than usually interested in weddings, are we not, especially the gowns? Flo was resplendent in ivory satin overlaid with chiffon, and her bridesmaids were gowned in white mousseline which is more elegant than traditional muslin, I think. It was a perfect time of year for a wedding as there were so many beautiful flowers in bloom, and the weather co-operated fully. Flo had three bridesmaids, two of her friends from childhood, and her young sister whom one might characterize as a "junior" bridesmaid. Little Elsie is ten and too old to be a flower girl, but she wanted so badly to take part in her sister's nuptials that Flo relented. Elsie took it very seriously and especially relished her task of handing out the wedding favours after the ceremony

Being such a musical family, the music was carefully chosen and beautifully sung as one would expect.

That whole business of wedding cards had been causing a commotion. As they are going very soon to Canada and do not have an address there, and in any case no one they know is going to call on them there, what is the point of wedding cards? It occurs to me that I
~~~~~~~~~~~~~~~~~~

may face the same dilemma, so I must ask Flo what they did in the end. One must send cards of some sort. Perhaps just a simple announcement of the happy event?

The newlyweds have set off on a short honeymoon to Cornwall. I expect Flo was nervous about everything to come, but it did not show and she was serenely composed. Don knew all along where they were going, but he was sworn to secrecy and did not let on until after their train had left. It cannot be a long honeymoon because they sail for Canada at the end of June. How will Flo feel, leaving her parents and brother for such distant shores? How will I feel when I do the same thing?

I was home from Hereford in time for Derby Day which we missed last year. It was quite something to see the vast crowds returning from the races. For more than four hours, the road from Epsom was jammed with a never-ending parade of all manner of decorated vehicles. You cannot imagine it – the noise, the colour – there were posh carriages, splendid landaus, ordinary traps, dog carts, donkey carts, even milk wagons – the more modest the cart, the more lavish the decoration – streamers and flags flapping along. Many people were dressed up too, with eccentric hats, and even the horses and donkeys were decorated. We saw one donkey wearing what appeared to be a lady's undergarment on its forelegs – so, yes, it was all a bit rough and rowdy. I had encouraged Mama to come along, but Papa was right; she did not enjoy it, nor did Birdie. But I told Papa I would not be knocked down by rough humour so we stayed a while longer. One does not often see the English enjoying themselves so wholeheartedly.

Frank writes that his parents will take a large house in the neighbourhood of the Toronto College of Music where he hopes to teach. It will be large enough that he will have the front reception room for a teaching studio. This is generous of them and represents a significant step along the path to his being established. You can imagine how pleased I was to pass on this news to Mama and Papa. Papa is not a skeptical man, but I know the idea of having a musician in the family is unsettling.

I am rather hoping to hear that you are yourself engaged. You hinted when you were here in March that you are fond of Mr McIsaac, so I hope your friendship has been progressing. As we have come to realize, there truly is little choice in life for us except to marry. So one may as well be in love and looking forward to it. I am blessed to have found Frank. We have a long way to go before we can marry, but my parents were very welcoming and friendly to him when they met last summer.

Please write when you can; I always enjoy getting your news. Especially if it is exciting news.

~~~~~~~~~~~~~~~~~

23rd June 1897

My very dear Frank,

This is but two days after your recital. I was thinking of you all the day and was with you in spirit. I hope it went tremendously well and that the German press will lavish praise upon you because you deserve it! Please send the clippings as soon as the notices appear.

This has been a momentous day in England – the celebration of the Queen's Diamond Jubilee. It is hard to believe she has been our sovereign since before my parents were born! There have never been such throngs. The newspaper said that more than three million people have crowded into London. We watched the parade for nearly two hours from the roadside near Westminster Bridge. It would have been grand to be nearer St Paul's or even Piccadilly, but Mama does not enjoy being part of a huge milling mass of people and Papa was concerned about pick pockets.

This Jubilee was about celebrating Empire. Instead of inviting all the kings and queens as they did ten years ago, for this occasion there were representatives from all the British possessions around the world marching and riding in the parade. We saw the very black Nigerian Constabulary and a militia group from Sierra
~~~~~~~~~~~~~~~~~

Leone was pointed out, wearing their blue turbans. Everyone cheered loudly for the North West Mounted Police impressive in their bright red tunics. I felt proud of my connection with Canada, I can tell you.

It was an exceedingly hot day and storms threatened but the "Queen's weather" held. I read later that severe hailstorms, tornadoes even, touched down in several localities around London, but thank goodness the heavy rain missed us.

The red, white and blue was everywhere; there were thousands of flags and banners and forests of plumes and lances. Every horse we saw had the colours braided into its mane. We all bought rosettes and waved small Union Jacks. Papa said there were motion picture companies filming the parade, but from our vantage point on the south bank we did not see them. The roar of the crowd in the distance told us the Queen would soon pass and so she did, in the state landau drawn by eight perfect cream-coloured horses. She was preceded by carriages full of various princes and princesses, and the Prince of Wales and the Duke of Connaught rode escort. It was a moving scene, the little old queen sitting up so straight and still smiling and waving after several hours. Westminster Bridge was close to the end of the parade route so she was probably tired by then. All in all, it was a grand day to be in London.

I was happy to get good seats for *La Traviata* which I did not see last year. I love Verdi, especially since he named his heroine after me. Violetta was admirably sung by an Australian soprano, Mme Fanny Saville, who made her debut at Covent Garden earlier this month. But I could not help recalling the wonderful Violetta of Mme Nordica that we saw together.

Your Doctor Torrington sounds like a loyal friend indeed, and it is encouraging that he wants to do what he can to get you started in Toronto. I know that you dislike the idea of puffing, but if I might venture an opinion, I think Dr. T. is correct to suggest that you put a notice in Toronto newspapers before you return to Canada.

Dein Veilchen is counting the days until you are here, mein lieber. I am delighted that you have accepted Mama's invitation to stop with us before going down to Devon. I have been saving a couple of expeditions we can make together. Birdie and I have little time to go sight-seeing these days and there is still much of London to explore. And I should very much like to come down to Devon to meet your uncles and aunts. An invitation from your Uncle William would be most welcome. We will likely go to Eastbourne again for Papa's annual holiday, but that is not yet entirely arranged.

~~~~~~~~~~~~~~~~~~

15th July, 1897

Dear Flo,

I am writing to the address in London, Ontario, hoping you and Harry have arrived safely at his parents' home, and that you had a safe and pleasurable voyage. Did you meet some interesting people on board? I hope you were not seasick.

I must brag to someone about Frank's recital and you are my first choice. It was especially arranged for him by Herr Krause and was reviewed in <u>three</u> German newspapers! His programme included the extremely difficult *Wanderer Phantasy* by Schubert/Liszt. He also played Bach's *Chromatic Phantasy and Fugue*, a good contrast with the Liszt I think, then two pieces by Chopin and the *12th Rhapsody* of Liszt as a finale. This is what the Leipziger *Tageblatt* had to say: (my translation) "Mr. Welsman played with a deeply developed understanding of the works; the audience was captivated by the exemplary clarity of the conceptional structure as well as by the proper use of dynamic nuances. The distinguished audience, among whom we could see Dr. Obrist, the conductor of the Imperial orchestra of Stuttgart, did not spare the applause." I am confident that this high praise will help him when he returns to Canada. The other good news is that there is a position awaiting him at the Toronto College of Music. Of course I am eager for him to have
~~~~~~~~~~~~~~~~~~

an early success so that we may set a wedding date. Papa is not budging on his conditions.

Frank will be here in a day or two and will stay with us at Ritherdon Road, and in August I am invited to Newton Poppleford for a week, Not only will I meet his family, but will see a part of England I have never seen before. After that, I wait, which I am not good at. Patience is not one of my virtues, which are few enough in any case.

Art school is over for the year. The Landscape Sketching Club was good fun. The school took a cottage near the village of Ewell about six miles south of here where people stored their bicycles and canvases. As it was not far from Ritherdon, it was easy enough to hop on the train to get there. If I had my own bicycle, it would have been even easier. I have been saving as much as I can from my teaching money but there are always other little demands on one's funds.

Ewell offered many pretty vistas for sketching. The willow-lined banks of the Hogsmill River have inspired painters for several years. Apparently Millais' *Ophelia* was painted there. I do not know that I was inspired, but it was a good experience to learn to sketch quickly in the constantly changing light.

I hope you will have the leisure to write a long chatty letter as I am eager to hear all about your new life.

~~~~~~~~~~~~~~~~
~~~~~~~~~~~~~~~~

The Breakers, Eastbourne

Thursday August 5th, 1897

Dearest Frank,

We are back in Eastbourne for our holiday, although not at the same boarding house. Mama declared the rooms from last year were musty and she wanted a better view.

It truly is a to-do going on holiday. Thank goodness the preparations did not commence until you had left us. Hauling the trunks down from the box room is just the beginning, and Papa does that. Then we must check through our summer clothes and, if there is time, sew new shirtwaists and put new trim on last year's summer frocks. Mama endures a flurry of shopping, mostly for my brothers, but both Birdie and I have new bathing costumes which are just as ugly as ever. I shall go bathing this year, but probably just in the swimming basins at Devonshire Park. We help with the packing of course, but Mama must do all the thinking and planning. It is Papa's holiday, after all. I do not think wives ever have holidays.

Imagining Violet

My brothers were saying again what a grand day we had at the Earl's Court Exhibition. Of course, the main attraction for them was the Great Wheel. I am glad I summoned up the courage to try it, but having you to hold on to helped a great deal. It was jolly good fun, wasn't it, to have them along with us, with their enthusiasm for everything? You were very gracious and amusing with them. They think your terrible puns are hilarious.

I have rather come to like Eastbourne, in part because it is not a large place. After a year in London, the peace and quiet and bracing sea air are welcome. The esplanade is fine and the Park at the one end with its gardens and bands is a delightful place to sit. And one can always walk out to the end of the pier and feel almost surrounded by the sea.

Yesterday we walked up to Beachy Head, and I do mean up, as it was a stiff climb to the dramatic chalk headland. The boys declared we were half a mile above the sea but Papa asked someone and was told it is 500 feet from the highest viewpoint. When we took the footpath along the edge of the cliffs I was gripping tightly to Papa's hand I can tell you, being so close to the precipice. May I add that long skirts are a distinct nuisance clambering up and down precipitous tracks?

Did you know that Beachy Head is a notorious suicide spot? What a disturbing thought that is. The local residents do not discuss it openly but I heard about it from a family staying at our guest house. Had I known this ahead of time, I should not have enjoyed the excursion as much. One can understand that a person might slip and fall and that would be a tragic accident, but to leap over the edge on purpose! What an alarming idea!

It was our good luck that the tide was out and thus we could take the steep path down the Cow Gap to the beach. Why is it called that? I cannot imagine cattle being led down that path!

It is one thing to look from the top of the cliff down, but to look up at five hundred feet of chalk cliff is breathtaking. The chalk is bright white with layers of flint running through it at intervals. Some people were searching for fossils, but as we did not know what to look for, we did not attempt it. I tucked a piece of chalk in my pocket though, and find it can actually be used to mark things.

As soon as the weather clears, we are all to go to Pevensey Castle which was built on the site of an old Roman city. The guidebook says the original Roman walls are still there and inside the walls, one finds the mediaeval castle. I shall send a postcard but shall wait until I see you to tell you about it.

I hope, mein liebste, that you and your cousins are finding heaps of jolly things to do. I look forward to meeting them in a short time, but until then, I am counting the days.

~~~~~~~~~~~~~~~~~`
~~~~~~~~~~~~~~~~~

Imagining Violet

The Exeter Inn,
Newton Poppleford

19th August, 1897

Dear Lily,

Your postcard awaited me at Ritherdon Road. I had only just arrived home from Eastbourne when I left again, or so it seemed. There was barely time to unpack and pack again, when I was on the train to Sidmouth Junction. I would not have had such a rush, except that Frank sails for Canada on the 24th inst., so this was my only chance to spend a few more days with him, and to meet his relations, of course.

The countryside here is lovely, all gentle rolling hills and green. Newton Poppleford is a good-sized village on the main road from Exeter, but I would have to say it is not particularly interesting or picturesque in itself.

Frank's Uncle Bill, who is Mr. Welsman's youngest brother, has the licence for the Exeter Inn, so that is where I am staying. The Inn is very old, but very homey and comfortable. They keep some of the rooms ready for visitors, but they no longer let them to travellers. Uncle Bill is also well known here as "The Poet", and he is most welcoming and friendly. He has been a widower for two years now. There are two daughters, close to my age, whom I like very much. Nellie is musical and we have spent some jolly evenings making music together. Nellie's sister Mary, known as Polly, married her cousin, so she is still a Welsman. The Welsman family has been in the district for hundreds of years and with the exception of Frank's father and his Uncle George, they have not strayed far from the nest. It is a close-knit family and a large one. In addition to Nellie and her sister, I have met countless other cousins and uncles and aunts. Uncle Alfred alone has had twelve children. I shall never get them straight, that is certain.

Newton P. is blessed by being just a few miles from the seaside resort of Sidmouth, which makes a pleasant outing. Frank was keen to go sailing and there were sailboats to hire for just 2s6d an hour. But Uncle Bill had told us a harrowing tale about sailing with Frank last summer, when the waves were ten feet high. His story was frightening and I did not like to think of Frank out on those waters. Frank assured me that his uncle "tells a good story" but I would not go with him nor would Nellie. Eventually he thought better of it. For compensation, we persuaded the donkey man to let us ride his donkeys although they are normally just for children. It was a great lark, and I do not think we taxed the donkeys overmuch.

Of course there is a beach, with the usual esplanade running along it. The beach is not long and has as "bookends", high red cliffs. We are more familiar with white chalk cliffs so this was striking. I must ask what makes them red. Nellie walks the four miles to Sidmouth for her music lessons but as we had taken a picnic and other beach necessities, we rode in the dog cart with Nellie driving. She allowed me to take the reins for a moment or two, but the pony must have realized it, because he chose to stop and graze on the grassy verge. He knew I was not in control.

I have gone on rather about the Welsman family, but coming from a small family, and having moved around so much, and with all Mama's family in Ireland, it has been quite an experience meeting the Welsman clan.

In just a few days, I shall say goodbye to my dear Frank for who knows how long. We are hoping that he will quickly establish himself in Toronto – he already has a position at the Toronto College of Music – hurrah! – and that Papa will be willing for us to marry, perhaps by next summer, if all goes well.

Well, you and I will be back to our teaching all too soon, and our town life. Perhaps we may have some musical mornings together very soon. I do need a reason to practise.

~~~~~~~~~~~~~~~~~
~~~~~~~~~~~~~~~~~

Imagining Violet

8th September, 1897

Mein lieber Frank,

I was much relieved to know you were safely back in Toronto, but your account of the fierce gale you endured on the St. Lawrence River was alarming.

I hope your parents are both in good health and happy to have you with them at home again. And I am very pleased that your studio is satisfactory and just one street away from the College. But now that you are so very far away in Canada, I can no longer "see" you in my mind's eye as I could when you were in Leipzig. Yes, please send postcards. And if your brother Fred is willing, perhaps he could take a photograph of your house.

Don has come up to London and found comfortable lodgings. He is to study with Wilhelmj and considers himself lucky to be taken on by the famous violinist. Wilhelmj no longer performs in public, but he is a frequent concert-goer and has been pointed out to me. What an impressive figure he is, with his flowing grey hair and dignified stature.

Shall I report to you on the progress of Mr. and Mrs. Harry Puddicombe? I wonder if you and Harry will correspond regularly even though you are both in Canada. Flo writes they have a lovely house in Ottawa and Harry has begun at Miss Harmon's School and has good prospects for another position at Ottawa Ladies College. There were only two pupils registered for music at Miss Harmon's, but with some flattering items published in the newspaper, Flo expects his reputation will quickly attract more advanced pupils.

Thank you heaps for the new duet. It was clever of you to dedicate it to Birdie too, and she has been learning the piano part willingly. I need some inspiration to keep practising, and learning your music provides that.

What a clever fellow you are to arrange for a recital so quickly. I hope a great many people will attend. It sounds like an excellent idea to give your Leipzig numbers. You will scarcely have time to get up anything new. And you mentioned a second recital in another town. Was it Brampton or Brantford?

Your modesty is part of your charm you know, but I must urge you to swallow your discomfort about puffing yourself. It simply must be done. I think you owe it to the world to let promising pupils know you are available.

I shall resume teaching next week. Miss Henrietta and Master Andrew go on with their lessons and I may have a third pupil. When art school starts up again, and choir practice, I shall be busy indeed, but not too busy to miss you and think of you constantly.

I believe I have enough savings to buy a bicycle, which I shall do very soon. I am not yet sure which one to purchase but I shall enjoy the search. I was trying to keep this letter short, and for once I have succeeded.

~~~~~~~~~~~~~~~~~

Ritherdon Road, Upper Tooting,
14th October, 1897

Dear Fiona,

I have been waiting weeks, but have finally enrolled in a life drawing class. It is for women only; the men have a separate class, and I am grateful for that. A fellow pupil, Miss Atkins, spent a few months in an atelier in Paris and her reports of the mixed life class there were almost shocking. Crowded rooms which were frightfully stuffy and over-heated, with the model dripping with perspiration, if you do not object to the word. On top of which, she said, there were too many other odours -- of human bodies, of tobacco, of paint and of damp clothes. It all sounds perfectly dreadful.

Fortunately, our life class is segregated and we are spared the odour of tobacco at least. Still it takes some getting used to. One does not wish to look like a silly school girl, all giggles and blushes, so one pretends to a sanguinity that one does not feel. The male model was appropriately draped, but still, Fiona, he was by no means
~~~~~~~~~~~~~~~~~

dressed. It was rather more of the male body than I have ever seen and it was unnerving. I was a little embarrassed to be sure, but Miss Atkins assured me that would soon pass. We were drawing from casts all last year and from live models in costume, but this was a wholly different experience. I found myself wondering how the model felt, having all those eyes on him. Every Monday we are to have a new model, and next week, it will be a female. Perhaps that will be easier.

Indeed, yes, Frank is nicely set up in his studio in his parents' home. I am inclined to think they took this house to accommodate him. And he has already played in his first Toronto recital! The pieces he is playing are fiercely difficult, but the programme was a success in Leipzig and that should give him confidence. In addition to having several piano pupils at his College, he has also been named Head of the Theory Department. He is getting on rather faster than expected. I did not realize that the people of Toronto would be so impressed by his having been to Leipzig.

I have mentioned I am sure that Frank is a dedicated punster and he occasionally includes one in his letters. Here is one that made me laugh and I simply must pass it on. "What do you call a musician who steals sheet music? – A cleftomaniac."

Here at Ritherdon, everything goes on much as before, except that I have at last purchased a bicycle, a Simpson, with the new lever chain. Travelling to the Lambeth School is ever so much faster now.

Birdie and I are singing again with the Streatham Chorus but I do not like the repertoire as much as last year's. Still one always feels ever so much better after singing for a few hours. Why that is I do not know, but singing does lift the spirits and we consistently make our way home over the Common in a better frame of mind.

You have not mentioned Mr. McIsaac in recent letters and it seemed indelicate to ask, but I am simply burning with curiosity. I had thought you nearly engaged. Please forgive my prying; it is just friendly concern.

~~~~~~~~~~~~~~~~~~
~~~~~~~~~~~~~~~~~~

20th October, 1897

Dearest Frank

Well, mein lieber, I am sequestered as always of an evening in my pleasant little room where I can gaze at your picture. Sometimes I even talk to you, out loud.

You have made your professional debut in Toronto! I am thrilled that it was so successful and that at last your dear parents had a chance to appreciate the results of your three years away. I have been watching the post for a thick envelope full of the notices.

Dr. Torrington has certainly been a great help in introducing you to the right people and arranging these recital bookings. I had not understood how the Brantford Conservatory fit into the picture, but now that you have explained its connection with the College, it makes sense.

My Irish Aunts have been for another visit, although this time, without Uncle David. Everyone wants to come to London to shop it seems. I went with them one afternoon and could not resist the very handsome muffler that should reach you in a few days. I want you to keep warm if you go skating. I am eager to hear that there is ice skating on some pond or river near your home.

My Aunts were talking a little this time of how things are changing in Ireland, or at least in Foxford. Naturally, they do not engage in politics, but like Mama, they read the newspaper and like to keep up with the world. They say land reform has made a big difference and that people seem more prosperous now that they are secure in their farms. The family's leases have largely been broken up and sold to the tenants, although dear Aunt Matilda has kept one of the smaller parcels for herself. She said she will in all likelihood appear in the next census as a farmer! I had the temerity to ask how they felt about Home Rule, and they seem to feel it must come. To my surprise, Papa agreed, but he has been here for so long, he thinks more like an Englishman, and a liberal one too, at least in that regard. My Aunts say they are still resented as English, even though the

Gawley family has been in County Mayo for more than two hundred years!

What with Lily being entirely taken up with her beau and her teaching, I had hoped to make some new acquaintances, either at the choral society or at the art school, just someone congenial to go to concerts with now and then. Mama enjoys the theatre in Clapham but the effort of getting to the concert halls is more than she feels up to most days.

The other night, we went to a new "sporting drama", which was truly spectacular. Papa especially enjoyed the boxing scene and the race scenes at Epsom Downs. One act was set at the Earls-Court Exhibition, complete with the Big Wheel, and was splendidly done. Birdie will go to a concert occasionally but I have become friendly with Miss Gertrude Atkins who is in my life drawing class. Perhaps we shall take in some concerts together.

I should tell you a little about that class. Naturally I was a little apprehensive the first day, not knowing what to expect. I had been told the model would be modestly draped, and indeed he was. There was no reason at all to be shy and in just a few classes I have grown accustomed to looking at and sketching the (almost) nude model. All that drawing from plaster casts prepares one with the skills for figure drawing, but a live model presents a new challenge every day. Miss Atkins said that our classes are much more agreeable than the one she attended in Paris. She said the daily scramble for a place and the over-crowding in the studio made concentration difficult. We are certainly not la vie de Bohème at the Lambeth School.

I wonder if you have any leisure to attend concerts and I would of course like to know what entertainments there are in Toronto. I like my bicycle very much; it makes me feel ever so independent.

~~~~~~~~~~~~~~~~~
~~~~~~~~~~~~~~~~~

78 Ritherdon Road, Upper Tooting,

November 15th, 1897

Dear Flo,

Thank you for yours of the 8th with all your news. I am grateful to have a friend in Canada as I shall be much better prepared when I finally get there, although we still do not know when that will be. Is it so very cold, then? You are lucky to have a canal to skate on. It sounds even finer than the ponds of Leipzig. What sport you will have whizzing along the ice!

It seems a little odd that you and I are passing news back and forth across the ocean, but I think Harry and Frank write only of music and their work, and not so much of the weather or other important matters, like your new house, which sounds very nice indeed. Was it difficult to know just where one should live in a new city, which neighbourhoods are suitable and which are not?

There is a drawing in my wonderful *Canadian Pictures* which depicts the Parliament Buildings in Ottawa, majestic and high up on a cliff, overlooking the river. They look very much like a castle or a cathedral or both. I wonder if they are as grand as they appear to be.

Yes, I am still taking classes at the Lambeth School, but there are days when I wonder why. I suppose I feel I must do something worthwhile, but just as I am not a musician, I am no artist. I wrote you last month about my first life drawing classes, and how I felt more than a little embarrassed. But I have quickly learned that one does not think of the model as a person at all. You are working so hard on line and shadow and light and skin texture and all manner of technical matters that the humanity of the model is quite forgotten. I suspect it is the same with the men when they have a female model. Now when I go to life class it matters little whether the model is male or female, young or old; I am working to solve other problems. We generally work with pencil, but also with pastels, and skin is so difficult to get right. Still, I make little progress and the tutor is not encouraging.

How busy Harry is already. Please pass on my congratulations on his appointment as organist. It is heartening to know that Leipzig training counts for so much. I am sure your parents are pleased that things are developing so well for you both. Frank seems to have a full class of pupils at the College and has had one recital already, with two more planned for early December. But perhaps you know this much from Harry?

If there is anything I might send you from London, I would be most happy to do so. I imagine that Ottawa does not have quite the fine shops that we have here. You have only to ask.

I look forward to your next letter. Your new life is ever so much more interesting than mine here in Balham. It is difficult to be patient. How much longer can Papa make us wait?

~~~~~~~~~~~~~~~~~

December 10th, 1897

Dearest Frank,

I am thrilled for you! We spoke so often of your dream of establishing an orchestra, but it seemed to be a distant possibility at best. To conduct the orchestral school's December concert is an honour and I hope you are as proud of yourself as you should be.

The wonderful Herr Dr. Grieg has been in London for a few weeks and I made a special effort to get tickets for his recital at St. James Hall. It was a good decision as it was fully subscribed. He played four of his *Lyrische Stücke* as well as a *Sonata for Violin* and of course there were songs. He composes so many different kinds of music. Lily was able to come with me and we had a good time together.

Is it very cold there yet? Flo writes that there is a great deal of snow in Ottawa. They are already skating on their canal. I may put away my bicycle for the winter as the roads here are very wet and slippery.
~~~~~~~~~~~~~~~~~

And, if I may ask, how do you find living at home again after three years away? It has been a few months now, and I have not read a word of complaint. I definitely found it difficult to resume my place in the family. They had not changed at all, but I felt that I had. I wonder if you are having a similar experience.

I suspect Don is not much of a correspondent, so I shall pass on his news. He is working diligently with Herr Wilhelmj, and enjoying it. As a private pupil, he can manage his time as he wishes, and so he has accepted a position as concert master of an orchestra in the Midlands.

Birdie and I went to his concert on the 8th inst., put on by the Westminster Orchestral Society. Their conductor is the same gentleman, Mr. Stewart MacPherson, who leads the Streatham Choral Society. Don played the Saint-Saens *Rondo Capriccioso* with great feeling and with his usual brilliance.

The Lambeth School and I may part company after this session. I make little progress and begin to think I am wasting Papa's money. I would be a better daughter if I were at home more and could be more helpful. Mama works too hard, and deserves a little time to herself.

Tucked away up here in my room – it is dark and drizzly outside – I am not as excited about the Christmas season as I was last year when I was looking forward to your being here with us. As it is, I do not know how long it will be before we are together again. I am hopeful, optimistic even, that in a few months Papa will allow me to set a wedding date. But should that not be the case, would you consider coming over next summer for a good long visit? That would be something at least. But when I am at my most optimistic, I like to think that a year from now, we shall be together in Toronto preparing for our first Christmas together.

Now that a life in Canada is almost imminent, I have been re-reading Susannah Moodie. Her anecdotes are amusing but her tales of the Ontario wilderness sound decidedly perilous. I know it all took place sixty years ago, but still, I am glad you live in a city.

The chapter about her Indian friends I found most engaging. She is generally respectful and sympathetic to the natives. And this passage in her 1871 introduction caught my eye: "Men are allowed, in this country, a freedom enjoyed by few in the more polished countries in Europe: freedom in religion, politics and speech; freedom to select their own friends and visit whom they please without consulting the Mrs. Grundys of society; and they can lead a more independent social life than in the mother country." It has been this idea of Canada that has appealed to me ever since I first met Canadian students at the Conservatory. Small wonder I would fall in love with one.

Your Christmas parcel has already gone to the post. I hope you like it. If it is a little extravagant, it is because I love you.

~~~~~~~~~~~~~~~~~

20th December, 1897

Dear Fiona,

Frank has sent a clipping about his recital in the town of Brantford. I had to beg him to send the notice, and isn't it wonderful? "A pianist of exceptional ability, possessing power, ambition and a rare sense of proportion." He has done <u>exceptionally</u> well these past months.

I am glad that you did not take it amiss that I inquired of Mr. McIsaac, and I do understand your growing unease with his extravagance, if I may use your word. I am sure it was very nice, at first, to have a little present with every outing and the very best seats at the theatre and fancy meals in restaurants, but I see your point, that if one is thinking of marriage, one should perhaps be saving, rather than spending lavishly. And I believe it is not a wise course of action to marry someone in hopes of changing them. At least that is what the advice columns say in the ladies' magazines. I hope you succeed in explaining your discomfort without hurting his feelings.

Did you read about the shocking terrible murder of the actor William Terriss at the Adelphi Theatre last week? Mama and Papa
~~~~~~~~~~~~~~~~~

had planned to attend that night but Mama wasn't well. How horrible it would have been to see him stabbed to death outside the theatre. They were very relieved they had not been in the audience.

Do write and tell me about your Christmas plans. No doubt Mr McIsaac will have something special planned. And please give Christmas wishes to your dear mother whom I remember fondly. I hope she is well enough to take part in the festivities. Her continued weakness must be a great concern to you and and your father. We shall be quiet at Ritherdon Road this year, and I shall miss Frank. It was so lovely to have him with us last year. But this may be my last Christmas at home so I am determined to enjoy it.

~~~~~~~~~~~~~~~~

2nd January, 1898

My dear one,

My garnet bracelet is simply exquisite. I wear it at every opportunity. I am relieved that you agree it is to be my birthday present as well as my Christmas present, as it is perhaps just a little imprudent of you to be so extravagant.

I have always loved the deep red of garnets, my birthstone. Did you know they are meant to bring the wearer tranquility, protect one against fevers and keep one safe from harm during travel? I am not sure I believe all this, not being very superstitious, but I like to think it might be true. It is the most beautiful bracelet ever and I thank you with all my heart.

Our Christmas time was thoroughly pleasant. The rain and fog let up for a few days and we took advantage of brisker weather to walk the Common. One evening we made a little family concert, and Birdie and I played your new duet. The family news is that my brother Jack has decided to go to South Africa. He has always favoured adventure stories and I guess the prospect of sailing down the coast of Africa has caught his imagination. Mama claims to understand his wish for adventure but I know how apprehensive she is. Papa does not care for travel himself, yet he seems proud of his
~~~~~~~~~~~~~~~~

younger son showing an independent streak. Jack has never been a good student, and would likely not even pass the civil service entrance. Reg is the steady one, and is hard at work preparing for his C.S. exams.

I have been, either with Lily or Miss Atkins, to a few of the popular concerts at St. James's Hall in recent weeks. It was mostly chamber music which I am coming to appreciate more and more. Lady Hallé has been performing regularly and she is wonderful to watch and to listen to. Every time I hear her I am reminded why I am in the audience and she is on the platform.

Honestly, I do not regret my decision to leave art school. As it happens, it was timely, as Mama has sprained her ankle and must rest with her leg up, if it is not indiscreet to mention that. Of course being Mama, she cannot sit still for long, but hobbles about in the kitchen. However, she cannot get to the shops, and she has never trusted the maid to do the marketing. Milk and bread are delivered, but we are not grand enough to warrant having the butcher call at our back door. Although I do not wish Mama to suffer, this is a welcome opportunity to learn a little more about managing a household. And I have a good deal to learn. It takes up most of my morning, as I like to shop around at the various greengrocers for the best quality and price, and that seems to vary from day to day. But now that I have my bicycle, the task is ever so much easier.

I hope I may have another pupil. It will be a temporary arrangement as the child's present teacher is unwell and it is no longer suitable for her to teach. I had been thinking also of auditioning for a string orchestra composed mostly of ladies, but until Mama is entirely recovered, I must not take on anything else.

I have kept my parents very well acquainted with the great progress you are making and I like to think Papa is coming to acknowledge that you are on the way to being able to support a wife and household. He will never completely accept that a musician's life will be as steady and secure as the Customs Service. Still, it has been most helpful to show him glowing notices, and I think he is almost ready to agree that we may marry this summer. Mama, bless her, understands better than I realized, how a long engagement can be taxing on both parties. She has never been as fussed about the niceties.

I am optimistic then, that we may soon be able to set a date, and for that I need your help. I know it is the bride's prerogative to choose the wedding day, but I should like to know how you may arrange your summer and when you might come to England. I expect your College shuts down for several weeks long holiday?

Also, would you mind if I asked my sister to be a bridesmaid. It is not entirely proper to do so, you know, as the older unmarried sister of the bride should not take such a role, but she is my only sister and if you approve, I shall ask her.

Papa continues to worry about where we shall live, and I have tried to reassure him on that count. I try not to get too excited just yet about our wedding. Not that it will be elaborate, as I know you would not care for that. And Papa will not be unhappy if we are modest in our wedding plans. But to think there is an end in sight to all these months and months of waiting is bliss, it truly is.

~~~~~~~~~~~~~~~~~

Ritherdon Road,
20th February, 1898

Dear Fiona,

How you must miss your dear mother. I know it has only been a very few weeks since she fell asleep. I wish I had some useful words of consolation, but I can only repeat how sorry I am.

It took courage for you to ignore convention and accompany your father to the funeral service. I completely agree that it was important that you were at his side and I am proud of you. Perhaps little by little the pain will ease. I truly wish that for you.

We also had a heavy fall of snow last week. It took days before we could get around safely, the pavements were so icy. I was glad I had kept my fur-lined boots from Leipzig. Even so, it was very
~~~~~~~~~~~~~~~~~

beautiful on the Common, with snow lying heavily on the branches of every tree. It is a good thing I spent four winters in Germany; I shall be quite prepared for Canada. Flo is enjoying her first winter there and that is encouraging. Ottawa may be a good deal colder than Toronto, but she is ever cheerful.

I hope you will not mind a little good news? Papa has finally consented that we may marry this summer and I am elated. I realize of course that there is no possibility of you joining the wedding party, and I shall miss you and your good advice. If you are in half mourning, would it be completely out of the question for you to at least attend the day? I am awaiting advice from Frank before we fix on a date. But with his approval, I did ask Birdie to be a bridesmaid and I am sorry to say she has declined. I know she is much more conventional than I am, but I thought I could persuade her to break with tradition, just this little bit, and say yes, to please me. But she will not do it.

My darling Frank continues from strength to strength and each letter brings new accomplishments. Most recently he has been appointed Examiner at the Brantford Ladies College which is affiliated with his own College of Music. And next month there are to be recitals in Ottawa, the nation's capital, and Quebec City, which is French and the oldest city in Canada. Harry Puddicombe has shown himself a good friend in helping to organize the Ottawa concert.

I do go on about Frank, do I not, and I suppose you may want to know what I am doing. Well to be honest, Fiona, life is a little humdrum, without my art classes to stimulate me. The teaching goes on well enough, and I think my three pupils enjoy the little pieces I compose for them, which are simple versions of nursery songs. Soon there will be wedding preparations to keep me occupied, but it is early days yet.

Mama has largely recovered from the sprain, thank you for asking, but both Birdie and I are needed to run errands and to help out generally. There has been another new maid to train, which has taken up a good deal of Mama's time. I have been busy in the kitchen and can say with pride that I can now make a decent white sauce, and I have also tried my hand at poaching fish.

I have not been diligent with concert-going of late, but I did not want to miss the Lamoureux Orchestra performing the *Choral Symphony*. In Leipzig, it was an annual event, closing the Gewandhaus season, so I was eager to hear how another orchestra would play it. Well, it was a fine performance, especially the choral section. I read that Lamoureux might bring his orchestra to Edinburgh? Shame on me, I should not tempt you; of course you could not go out to a concert yet. I do not know much about the etiquette of mourning so beg your indulgence if I have said anything untoward or inappropriate.

I shall not fatigue you with a long letter, dear Fiona, and hope to have something from you when you feel up to it.

~~~~~~~~~~~~~~~~

March 1st, 1898

Dear Flo,

How are you bearing up these days? I sincerely hope you are not as bilious as you were last month. I trust though that the prospect of the arrival of a little stranger must be in itself an interesting experience. You are still out and about are you, or are you already keeping home? I can understand that you would worry about slipping and falling on icy streets. I am excited for you both, and if I may say so, Harry will be a fine father.

You are not entirely alone, though, with your severe winter weather. We had a great snow storm here last month and it played havoc with the traffic. However, I am sure you do not wish to hear about crocuses blooming in February. Would there be any signs of spring yet in your garden? Well, you probably do not know what is in your garden, do you? It will all be a surprise.
~~~~~~~~~~~~~~~~

I am pleased that Frank will go to Ottawa to play for the Women's Morning Musical Club. Is it a prestigious organization? Have you become a member yet? Please do send me any notices in your newspapers, as I like to show them to my parents. Papa seems impressed that they write so generously about Frank. I know you will make him welcome and it is too bad that it must be such a brief visit. I cannot imagine how he can play in Ottawa one day and be in Quebec City the next. Is it not hundreds of miles away?

Wedding plans go forward, and goodness, even with a modest wedding, there are many little decisions to make. I am glad I could share your experience last year as it has prepared me a little. I had hoped Birdie would be one of my bridesmaids even though it would be unconventional, but she will not. Very sadly my friend Fiona's mother fell asleep last month and Fiona is in mourning and cannot take part. It will be Lily alone who precedes me up the aisle.

Mama and I think that Wednesday, the 27th of July would be a good date, but I await advice from Frank as to when he will come to England. We are still undecided as to whether it should be a morning or afternoon ceremony. I like the idea of mid-afternoon, so that one has the morning to dress, but noon hour seems to be the traditional time. I would likely not be ready if the service were earlier than noon. As well, if one is going away anywhere for a honeymoon, perhaps a midday service is more sensible.

Did I tell you that Mama had saved her orange blossom wreath all these years? Natural blossoms are unlikely to be available in late July or if they are they would be frightfully costly. Of course, we shall be married at St. John the Divine. The organist there is a most able musician and we wish to have plenty of music. Perhaps I should invite Donald to play. What do you think? Would that be suitable?

Birdie is being a wonderful help with her needle. Perhaps she feels a little guilty that she declined to be in the wedding party. I have not been as dedicated as I should have been in embroidering napkins and pillow slips and so on, and now I feel somewhat pressed for time. We have begun to work on some of the pretty undergarments for my trousseau. Mama is handy with her sewing machine, so she has run up a few night dresses and petticoats, and I am set to hemming and applying trim and lace and ribbons. That much I can do. Papa has been generous with the allowance for my trousseau and I thought it would be more than sufficient, but the fine lawn I wanted for night dresses has been very dear.

I was reading in an advice book that it is wise to make a few extra articles, shifts and petticoats and the like, with draw strings, in anticipation of a happy event, but I am not in a great hurry to start a family so I may ignore that advice.

Birdie is also much occupied with helping to organize the Choral Society's spring concert. She was invited to join the organising committee and she accepted, so is often out to meetings and the like. She is much too inclined to a quiet life, so this is good for her.

The family is surviving my attempts at cooking. Mama says I absolutely must learn a few more dishes beyond white sauces and poaching fish. She is giving me plenty of good advice about receipts and I am making a little cookery book of her favourites.

I certainly made the right decision about giving up art school. I should never have had enough time for it.

I look forward to hearing how you are getting on in <u>all</u> respects.

~~~~~~~~~~~~~~~~~

Sunday, March 20th,

Mein liebchen,

Here I am as always, squirreled away in my little room under the eaves with a small fire in the grate to take the damp off. I am counting the Sundays left until you are here again. There are sixteen of them. It seems a very long time since last summer, yet spring has arrived and summer will surely follow, and we shall be married.
~~~~~~~~~~~~~~~~~

Imagining Violet

It is indeed spring here, whereas I fear you are enduring the last gasps of winter, nicht? Flo writes that it may snow even in April in Ottawa. She is very well now, by the way, and expects the arrival of their little bundle of joy towards the end of June.

I am coming to realize that I have likely spent my last winter in England, and that is a curious feeling. I certainly shan't miss the fog. It truly is dreadful some days and unhealthy too I suspect. It lasts for days on end at times. I was relieved when you said Toronto may be a good deal colder, but not so foggy.

I am glad to know you have been ice skating on the bay; it sounds like good sport. For my part, I have been getting out on my bicycle every chance I get. Lily has one too now, and we have been meeting up near Clapham Junction one afternoon a week for a nice long ride.

Did you enjoy your travels to Ottawa and Quebec? I am sure you played brilliantly and I am impatiently waiting to read your impressions of both cities. The idea of a French city in Canada is difficult to comprehend. Perhaps it might be more useful in Canada to know French rather than German? I shall depend on Flo to send me the notices about Ottawa, so do not bother yourself with that.

That's very good news that you have as much as six weeks off come summer. What would you say to a wedding at the end of July? If you could sail in mid-July you would have time to go down to Devon for a visit before the happy day. Do you think it matters which day of the week and do you have a preferred time of day? If you would like to be back in Canada by the middle of August, we might forego a honeymoon here and treat our passage to Canada as our honeymoon.

I shall spare you all the news of wedding preparations but you might like to know that my Aunts Kate and Matilda have promised to send some of the family table linens. As the oldest, Aunt Matilda inherited some beautiful old pieces from her mother's family. And as I am the first to be married, she is kindly sending much of it to us, saying that she lives a simple village life and no longer needs fine naperies.

What nice news about the marriage of your Uncle Bill and your aunt, Miss Fry. He is a lovely gentleman and I am glad to know he has someone to look after his household. I suppose since your parents came over less than two years ago, they would not have come again for that wedding. In any case, I believe it is usual for an older couple to have a quiet wedding. Is there any chance your parents may make the journey for our nuptials?

I shall tell you about just one concert. As you know, modern Russian music is all the rage these days, so Lily and I went to the very first performance in London of a *Trio Elégaique* composed by a young Russian – he is exactly your age – called Sergei Rachmaninoff. The piece is an homage to Tschaikowsky, the themes are broad and expansive and very Russian in flavour, although I do not really know what that means. There was a large audience and the music was well received, which is gratifying for a new and modern work.

I am counting the weeks until you come in July. It has sometimes felt that my life is all about waiting, and now there is an end in sight.

Sending much love as always,

~~~~~~~~~~~~~~~~~

8th May, 1898,

Dear one,

Of course we shall send an invitation to your parents. I understand that they are not likely to make the journey but they must know that we wish them to share the day. As to your Newton P. relatives, you must decide whom we should invite, but please, my dear, do it soon. We should be sending out invitations any day now. Certainly your dear Uncle Bill and your new Aunt Mary and the girls, but perhaps not the little ones? How amusing that your Aunt Mary is now doubly your aunt. In fact, as she is your mother's sister as well as your uncle's wife, she might represent your parents all by herself.
~~~~~~~~~~~~~~~~~

Papa has been asking again where are we to live, and I was pleased to assure him that we will be welcome at 266 Sherbourne for the first months at least. I know you should like to find us our own accommodation, but there is no need to rush. I expect we can manage very well with your parents for a few months, and if you do not mind my opinion, it may be prudent to be a little better established before taking on the responsibilities of property.

Don has been down to Wales, to play with the Crickhowell Concert Society. Mr. Sinclair, the organist at the Hereford Cathedral, was the conductor, so I expect that is how it came about. Don played the Saint-Saens again which he gave late last year in London. He plays it brilliantly. I could never have attempted anything so difficult.

The concert season is about finished, but we have been to see Mr. and Mrs. Kendall in their new play, *A Cruel Heritage,* at the Shakespeare Theatre. Mama, Birdie and I went, and as the setting was meant to be a German watering place, I expected to enjoy it. But it was only a rather old fashioned vendetta story. The best part of the evening was Mrs. Kendall, who must be nearly fifty! She played a silly, talkative old spinster and was very comical indeed.

I look forward to hearing the news of your May recitals. Do not be shy to give me <u>all</u> the flattering details. Association Hall sounds like a very large room if it can accommodate a thousand auditors.

~~~~~~~~~~~~~~~~~~

Sunday 22nd May, 1898

Dear Fiona,

Thank you for your kind letter. I am glad to know that you and your father are slowly resuming your normal daily lives.

I hope you do not think this is boasting but I simply must pass on what the press said about Frank's Ottawa recital as I am bursting with pride. Thank goodness for Flo who sent the notices.
~~~~~~~~~~~~~~~~~~

"Mr. Welsman is a thorough master of the instrument, possessed of a delicate touch and that capability of grasping the full worth of the pieces he rendered." Isn't that high praise?

Now that better weather is upon us, Lily and I go further afield on our bicycles. There is a small cycling club in Balham which we joined and we have had some jolly good outings. I expect it would be unseemly for you to be cycling just yet, so you must make do with good long walks. Frank too has been about on a bicycle. He has joined the Toronto Clef Club, an association of musicians and attended their annual bicycle run last month. It was a ten mile ride from the Parliament Buildings to a hotel in the country where they stopped for their dinner. He reported he was considerably stiff the next day.

I am doing what I can to freshen up my old frocks and I am to have two new ones. I do not know what one will want exactly in the Canadian climate. Mama begins to talk about the wedding breakfast and what she should serve and how to prepare it and so on. I suggested that she get in a job-cook for the day or some additional help for young Betty who will decamp no doubt if she is the least bit over-worked. We shall be about thirty overall. It is a good thing that Frank and I do not have legions of friends here. I hope you know how much you will be missed.

Frank is thinking about taking his own quarters, but much as I would like to start married life with a home of my own, I have, rather unselfishly I must say, counselled caution. Goodness knows, he has only been home a year. I think it might be wise to wait a little.

My parents have decided on Bournemouth for their holiday this year. We shall be going for a fortnight in July, somewhat earlier this year because of the wedding. It will be a nice respite from the planning, and from the sewing. But right now, I should be stitching not writing, so I shall close.

~~~~~~~~~~~~~~~~
~~~~~~~~~~~~~~~~

Imagining Violet

19th June, Sunday, 1898

My dearest,

There are but a few Sundays left when I shall be writing to you, mein liebste. I have rather come to enjoy the ritual of rambling on, almost as if I were talking to you. But it will be ever so much nicer to be with you in person.

Papa's sister Aunt Clara and Uncle Ted came to tea last week. Aunt Clara brought a gift of bed linens which she had embroidered herself, and a table runner that belonged to her mother, whom I never knew. We shall be very well supplied with fine linens.

Aunt Clara asked if I was apprehensive about the sea voyage to Canada. "Ever since your Uncle Jack died," she said, "we have been anxious when anyone in the family goes to sea." I did not want to say that I knew very little about it. Later I asked Papa to tell me the whole story and thus I learned the sad tale of his brother's death. As a young man, Papa's brother Jack went to sea -- perhaps this is where our Jack gets his wanderlust – and had been promoted up the ranks to third officer on the steamer *Ismalia,* a cargo vessel plying the North Atlantic. They were just out of Halifax, Nova Scotia in October of 1874, when the ship foundered in a gale and all hands were lost. He was not yet thirty, the youngest of the family and his father's favourite. It was a great tragedy for the family.

Papa looked very gloomy as he related this tragic story, and I was truly sorry I had caused him grief. I apologized for asking, but he agreed I should know, adding that his brother had been a fine, bright young man who would have been a wonderful uncle. Father's other brother, Albert, died whilst I was in Leipzig. He had remained in Ireland and I did not remember him, but it is very unfortunate to have lost two brothers. One day perhaps, you will tell me about your late brother Walter.

Well, I did not mean to go on with such a distressing story. Let me move on to something more cheerful.

I had my little recital here last week with my three pupils. Miss Henrietta has grown up a bit since I began teaching her and I am ever so pleased with her progress. Master Andrew also acquitted himself nicely and played his little pieces without a mistake. I played a few things too, accompanied by Birdie, including your *Musette*. The piano part was a bit stiff for Birdie but she managed. The families all came and Mama gave us a nice tea afterwards. It was a pretty conclusion to my teaching career in Balham, but I expect I shall miss it and hope it is not the end of teaching forever.

We have been receiving replies to the wedding invitation and I am happy to report that your Uncle Bill and Aunt Mary will come with Nellie and your cousin William. Polly is unwell and cannot travel this summer and in any case little Frank is but four and too young for a wedding, in my opinion. Uncle Alfred and Aunt Joan have accepted tentatively, if Uncle Alfred's gout is not bothering him, and two or three of your cousins have been asked, as you requested. Then from the Gawley side, my dear Irish aunts, Uncle David and my cousin Eva whom I scarcely know, but she is close to my age. Aunt Clara is the only Courtenaye relation I know at all. We have also invited Miss Atkins and Lily's beau Mr. Anderson-Smyth to round things out a little. Perhaps our wedding may inspire him to propose to Lily. I know she is hoping he'll pop the question soon. He is well able to support a wife, but there is a semi-invalid mother in Oxfordshire who requires a good deal of his attention and time. Well, you will meet him and decide for yourself if you think he is a suitable match for my friend.

I had tea with Don the other day and he is flattered that you asked him to be your best man. I had the notion that we might ask him to play at the church, but I do not see how he could manage it along with his duties to you. But he <u>must</u> give us some music at the breakfast.

I am having a grand time with my bicycle. I do hope I may have one in Toronto, but I am learning the hard way to be more vigilant. The traffic in the High Street is busier all the time what with the 'buses, cabs, dog carts, an occasional motor and plenty of cyclists. I nearly had a collision yesterday with a dog cart whose driver was not being properly attentive to where he was going. This fellow came hurtling out of a laneway without a second glance right into the road as I was passing. At least that is the way I saw it. Thank goodness I was able to stop quickly.

I shall leave off now, sending my love, as always.

~~~~~~~~~~~~~~~~~

Sunday 3rd July, 1898

My last letter to you, my dearest Frank, for a very long time, I hope.

Thank you for sending news of your last recitals. I can scarcely imagine what it must feel like to play before a thousand listeners.

You have made the right decision to defer any move until the autumn. And, truth be told, I should like to be with you when we look for a home. Knowing we may stay at 266 Sherbourne for as long as need be means there is no hurry in this regard. I should like to get to know Toronto a little before settling on where we are to live.

Your appointment at Havergal Ladies College is another feather in your cap. Congratulations! Again! With Miss Veal's, St Margaret's and now Havergal, you will be quite surrounded by adoring young ladies. Shall I be jealous? With the three schools, the College and your private pupils, you will scarcely have a minute for me. Well, I am teasing, of course.

Apparently a sense of adventure resides with the Welsman family,nicht? Your father has bought an entire island? Just where is this Muskoka and what is it like? Is it bush country as in Susannah Moodie's book, or more rugged and rocky? Have you ever been that far north yourself? I am full of questions, and must save them for when you arrive as you will not have a chance to answer this letter
~~~~~~~~~~~~~~~~~

before you leave. But if you do, tell me, are there trains to the north? Is it cold there in summer, with snow?

The arrangements for the "day" are largely complete, and I hope you will be pleased. I may not tell you anything about my wedding gown; it must be a surprise, but Mrs. Thompson, Mama's dressmaker, is a wizard with her needle. I may tell you, though, that you are to take special notice of the seed pearls decorating the bodice. They are ever so pretty and rather precious as they come from a necklace that belonged to Mama's late Aunt Matilda.

There is a great deal of fuss attendant to a wedding, rather more than I had expected. Do you mind if I say I am looking forward most of all to being quietly just with you. I suppose all brides feel anxious about many things, and I am no exception.

Now I am set to looking ahead, I wonder what it will be like to leave home. I am not particularly attached to this house as we have not been here for long. But to leave my dear family, not knowing when I shall see them again, will surely be difficult. Will we all be very tearful, or will we be brave and hide our emotions?

What is exciting, most exciting, is the prospect of the sea voyage and seeing Canada. I have been reading what I can about Canada and Toronto and I am curious to see if what I have imagined is at all like the reality. I hope to have a letter from you soon with news that you have booked our passage, the name of the ship, our embarkation date and as much as you can tell me.

I am so in the habit of committing my thoughts to you to paper. I save them up in mind for my long Sunday night visit. I shall hardly know what to do when I can talk to you from morning to night. So much that has passed between us has been carefully composed in these epistles. I hope you will remember from our months in Germany that I am not always careful and composed, but inclined to be a little impulsive.

Sending my love, by post, for the last time.

~~~~~~~~~~~~~~~~~
~~~~~~~~~~~~~~~~~

Imagining Violet

The Garrison House, Bournemouth,

July 14, 1898

Dear Flo,

What wonderful news arrived in the morning mail yesterday. Thank you for writing so promptly, even from your sickbed. Your ordeal is over and you have a bonny son! And born on Dominion Day too! He will be a thoroughly Canadian lad. How proud you must both be!

Mama, Birdie and I have nearly finished my trousseau and we make weekly visits to a nice dressmaker Mama found in Balham. She is sewing my wedding dress and my going-away outfit. After a great deal of discussion – Birdie would say "dithering" – I chose ivory silk, trimmed with chiffon and seed pearls. I remember that you found your satin gown rather too warm even in late May and as the end of July can certainly be uncomfortably warm, we concluded that heavy satin was not necessary or even sensible. The gown will have a plain skirt with little puffs at the shoulders, but tight sleeves. The seed pearls are from a necklace that belonged to Mama's late aunt. She left them – and her money! – to my Aunt Matilda, who has passed them on to me to use as I wish. I mean the pearls, not the money.

I wish I had thought of this sooner, as it is now likely too late, but I wanted your advice about the wedding breakfast. Yours was sumptuous, but I must be more modest in my expectations as we do not have as much help in the house and I do not want to exhaust Mama. I suggested we have a few of those delicious jellied dishes your mother served – I am altogether ignorant of fancy cooking and do not know the proper names – but Mama fears that in the heat of the day they will not keep. What do you think? And may we do without hot dishes? Mama says not. Please be candid.

I have been reading Annie Swan again, as I think you did. She counsels, "The ideal wife must be careful not to lose her individuality, to become merely an echo of her husband, to render herself insipid." That seems like excellent advice, but then she continues, "The ideal wife may never seek to usurp his place as head of the house." – I agree -- but "she will delight to keep herself in the background." <u>That</u> may not be so easy. You have been married for more than a year now. Are you happily able to "keep in the background"?

And naturally I am anxious about a great many matters, although I take comfort in knowing how much you are enjoying married life. There is nothing in the advice books about the wedding night itself and I do not know how I am supposed to behave. And now you are a mother, another of life's great thresholds has been crossed. I hope you will write fully about it when you are rested.

We have had a pleasant but rainy week in Bournemouth, and it was a welcome holiday from the busyness of dressmakers and such. I had time to do a little drawing and enclose one poor effort, just a family I saw on the beach.

Frank will arrive in England in a week, first to visit his relations in Devon, and then up to London for our special day. I do not know what is planned for a honeymoon and I am not to know. I had had a mad wish to take a short voyage aboard the new paddle steamer *Yarmouth Belle* and sail to Great Yarmouth as I thought it would be grand to visit the shores of my childhood in Gorleston, but I have been voted down. Frank says the wedding trip is his surprise and in any case as we sail from Liverpool on the 4th of August, it would not do to go off in the opposite direction. I imagine we shall just go to the south coast. Of course he is right. Perhaps I should learn to be more deferential. But I believe many young couples now plan their honeymoon together, so it is rather charming of him to follow an older convention, don't you agree?

~~~~~~~~~~~~~~~~~

The Queen's Hotel, Manchester

28th July, 1898

Dear Fiona,

Frank has gone to the station to see to the luggage and fetch tickets so I have a few minutes to write to you. I did miss you yesterday.

Frank arrived on Sunday and oh my goodness how happy we were to see each other again after all these many months of being apart. But it was such a busy time at Ritherdon Road that we scarcely had a moment to ourselves.

Truly, Fiona, it all went swimmingly yesterday. It was cloudy in the morning and there was a sprinkle of rain, but when the carriage came near noon, the sun broke through, exactly as it was meant to do. A wedding is meant to be sunshiny.

Papa made a very gracious speech and said too many nice things about me and about Frank and how he is confident we shall have a long and happy marriage. I know he is not entirely at peace with the idea of my living so far away, so his words were welcome.
~~~~~~~~~~~~~~~~~

Mama has an uncle who emigrated to America years ago and there are other members of the Gawley clan over there too, so for her America feels somehow less distant. Papa worries that he will never see me again.

Frank responded equally graciously with only a few of his outrageous puns and Donald was a first-rate best man, and quite witty in his toast to the bride. Lily looked charming in her large picture hat and pale blue gown, but to have had you there with me would have made the day just a little more perfect.

We did have to dash to the station to make our train. I had assumed we were going to Victoria, to go to the coast, so I was lingering over my adieus. It was harder to say goodbye than I expected – not to see dear Mama and Papa, Birdie and my so grown up brothers – for who knows how long.

Well, I was quite teary. I could see that Frank was a little agitated, pacing up and down and "ahemming" if I may invent a word. Once I was in the carriage, waving and waving, Frank told me we were going to Euston Square, a good deal farther than Victoria, hence the rush, so I knew or guessed we were going all the way to the Lake District after all. I had written him that I had always wanted to see the lakes and mountains. Clever Frank had made the point that the south coast was more practical and I had concurred, all of which made it an even better surprise.

We were barely in time for our train, but as there are dozens every day to Manchester, we need not have fretted so. We had rooms at the Queen's Hotel here, the very nicest hotel ever, and arrived a little past eight in time for a late supper. I was tired by this time, although I had dozed off on the train and delighted in laying my head on Frank's shoulder. Just to sit close beside him and know that I could, was a joy. It is lovely to be able to show a little affection, within limits, in public.

I will say, Fiona, that we were shy and awkward, but we were so terribly happy to be together that it was all all right and we slept soundly until the morning tea was brought in. Today we continue on to Windermere. I believe we are to stop at the Old England Hotel, to which you might wish to address a card to Mrs. Frank Welsman. After twenty-three years of being Miss Courtenaye, it will take some getting used to, being Mrs. Welsman. When the doorman said "Good morning, Mrs. Welsman" I did not respond straightaway. It took a moment to realize he was addressing me. That may be one of the smaller adjustments to married life. We shall see.

~~~~~~~~~~~~~~~~~~

~~~~~~~~~~~~~~~~~~

Imagining Violet

The Old England Hotel,
Bowness on Windermere

July 28, 1898

Dear Mama, Papa and everyone,

We are safely here, arriving a few hours ago, having put up in Manchester last night. Perhaps you knew what our destination was all along, but for me this has been a lovely surprise. It is so beautiful here! I believe I have an affinity with water somehow, so to look out our window across the lake to the hills and mountains is a treat, even if it is cloudy and there is a cool breeze.

I know I said many thank yous yesterday, but let me repeat them. It was a wonderful wedding and we are both grateful to you all for making our special day so perfect. All my favourite people except Fiona were there. I thought the aunts and uncles from both sides got on very well.

Frank is waiting for me to take a walk around the town before tea, so this will be a short note. I shall do better in a few days. There is a great deal to do here, so I shan't have much time for writing, but I will send postcards.

~~~~~~~~~~~~~~~~~

The Old England Hotel,
Bowness-on-Windermere

31st July, 1898

Dear Lily,

You were a beautiful bridesmaid and I thank you again and again for helping to make our wedding day a success. I hope Mr. Anderson-Smyth enjoyed himself. I hope too that he was inspired and will propose very soon.
~~~~~~~~~~~~~~~~~

Imagining Violet

Frank is at the post office sending postcards to Canada, so I have a few minutes to write. Then we are off on an expedition, to take the little ferry across the Windermere and walk up to a smaller lake called Esthwaite Water. Frank thoughtfully suggested that today I might wish to stay behind whilst he went off tramping. Is that what brides are supposed to do? Yesterday we climbed up to Orrest Head where one has a fine view of the whole south end of the lake. Perhaps he thought I was tired out from that. From the top, you can see the surrounding mountains and the small islands that dot the lake. Frank is ambitious to climb one of those mountains, but I shall decline that opportunity.

Our hotel is one of the oldest in the town and faces the lake and the boat station, so we can watch the steamers come and go. Tomorrow we shall take a day excursion and tour the lake. Windermere, as I expect you know, is the longest lake in the country with mountains all round. It may be the most beautiful scenery I have ever seen. The mountains in Germany were magnificent, but the places I saw in Saxony did not have lakes. Frank says he thinks Muskoka – the lake country north of Toronto where his father has bought an island – is like this.

Goodness me but Windermere is popular with honeymooning couples. There must be a half dozen like us in the dining room and there is rather a lot of surreptitious glancing back and forth. I suppose we all know we are having new experiences.

Altogether it is the busiest time of the summer here; the streets and shops are crowded; there are long queues for the lake steamer. Besides the Old England, there are at least two other large hotels and well over a hundred lodging houses.

Well, this is our honeymoon, even if it is only a week long, not a month. And we are having such a grand time. To think it was just a few days and nights ago that we were married, and already we grow comfortable and relaxed with each other. We are already thinking back to our wedding night and laughing, now that we have both admitted we were just a little nervous.

Imagining Violet

I wonder what day to day life with Frank will be like. After nearly three years apart, our only brief times together have always had a holiday feel, each day being precious and too short. Although perhaps we know each other rather better than many couples do, as one may write what one might not say out loud. Still, I learn new things about him daily, such as the important discovery that he does not care for strawberry jam but will only put marmalade on his toast.

And although I had counselled otherwise, I confess I find myself a wee bit disappointed that we are to live with his parents. I think I should like the privacy of our own home. But it may be easier to get used to a new country in the shelter of his family.

~~~~~~~~~~~~~~~~~~
~~~~~~~~~~~~~~~~~~

Imagining Violet

The Old England Hotel,
Bowness-on-Windermere

1st August, 1898

Dear Flo,

Mama kindly sent on your letter which reached me here. Frank joins me in sending congratulations on your choice of name. George Beverley Puddicombe has a fine ring to it.

I was glad to hear you are well on the road to full recovery from your recent travails and soon to resume your domestic and social duties. It cannot be pleasant to be confined to bed in the middle of summer when one longs to be out of doors. Good for you for insisting on sitting out in your garden at least.

We are comfortably installed here in Bowness and savouring all it has to offer. I especially enjoyed our steamer trip around the lake, although it was extremely crowded and difficult to find a place to sit. It was a long climb up the road and then on to a little place called Hawkshead where Wordsworth attended grammar school. I shall not be one of those brides who stays behind whilst the new husband goes off on adventures. If I am a little fatigued at the end of the day, I simply allow myself a short rest before dressing for dinner.

Mama advised that we avoid hurry and bustle on our honeymoon and how right she was. We do not rush from place to place trying to see everything, nor is Frank climbing every mountain. Other young couples in the dining room seem to sit through dinner without much conversation. We are in no danger of running out of things to talk about. There is so much to know about Frank's life in Toronto, his family, his work and his dreams of an orchestra. I am full of questions and now he is right there across from me, to answer.

Every day we grow more at ease with each other. It is a new experience to be with someone, someone you love dearly, every hour of the day and night.

I am sure I blushed all through that first breakfast, as if everyone in the room would know we were just married. Yet I hear of couples, and there may be one or two in the hotel, who stay for a month or more and invite family members to come and join them. I cannot imagine doing that! The privacy of the honeymoon is much to be valued. I am happier than I have ever been.

We leave tomorrow for Liverpool and sail aboard the *S.S. Yorkshire* on the 4th. We shall be well-rested though and able to withstand any rough seas, although I believe we may expect calm waters in August. Frank tells me it is not a large vessel, and I hope we shall meet some congenial people on board to help pass the time.

~~~~~~~~~~~~~~~~

Adelphi Hotel, Liverpool
3rd August, 1898

Dear Mama,

This morning we came down from Windermere, and tomorrow we go aboard our ship. We are stopping tonight at the Adelphi Hotel. It is a favourite with Canadians when they arrive in England or so Frank tells me. This is my last night on English soil, and I am a stew of feelings. We have had such a lovely time in the Lake District; I did not want it to end, but the ship must sail. Yes, I worry that I shall be seasick. It will be embarrassing and I shall be ashamed of myself. It never occurs to me that Frank might be seasick. I just imagine myself being ill.

I shall write as we go, but I do not expect to be able to post anything until Quebec. You will have to be patient as it will be about three weeks before you have any further news.

But you and Papa are not to worry. We shall be safe. Truly, I am not afraid of crossing the ocean.

~~~~~~~~~~~~~~~~

Afterword

Violet Alice Trant Courtenaye was born in Foxford, County Mayo, Ireland on January 7, 1875. Her parents were Anglo-Irish. Her mother, Alice Marian Gawley, was a daughter of Dr. Eccles Gawley, of Foxford, Co. Mayo. Dr. Gawley had a successful medical practice and also held leases on three large parcels of land amounting to about 160 acres. Alice Gawley had several sisters, including Violet's Irish Aunts, Matilda and Kate.

Violet's father, Philip Allan Trant Courtenaye, was likely connected to the aristocratic Courtenaye family but his branch was by no means landed gentry. Philip's father, Albert, was in banking, at first in Banbridge, near Belfast, and later in the town of Clogheen. Philip joined the Customs Service in 1871 at the age of 26, and an early posting took him to Ballina, where he married Alice Gawley on 10th July, 1872. Their first-born, Clara (Birdie) arrived in 1873.

Customs Officers were moved around regularly, and soon Philip was posted to Chester, England where Violet's brother Reg was born. In 1879 the family moved to Yarmouth, where Jack was born. In 1886 Philip was promoted to the Customs Office in Leith where the family was living in 1891. His final posting was indeed to Head Office in London.

There are two more parts to Violet's story: *Imagining Violet Married and Imagining Violet Blooming.*

.

Thanks and Acknowledgments

I am sincerely grateful to the following: The InterLibraryLoan Volunteers at the Salt Spring Island Library; my violin teachers Suzanne Hunter, Joan Blackman and Carolyn Hatch; Paula Kiffner and Carol Wright for allowing me to play second violin with Salty Strings; Anke Hofman and Ingrid Jack, of the Leipzig Hochschule für Musik und Theater for giving me their morning to go over documents regarding Violet's time at the Leipzig Conservatory; my cousin Penelope Cowman for her knowledge of Sidmouth, Newton Poppleford and environs. Thanks also to early readers Julia and Emma McIntyre, Anita Hunter, Keegan Campbell with special thanks to Kate Merry and Kathy Marks.

~~~~~~~~~~~~~~~~

About the Author

Born and educated in Toronto, Mary E. Hughes came to writing fiction by a circuitous route. Early careers in theatre and television production were followed by several years in association management. She has written and self-published two works of non-fiction: *Frank Welsman, Canadian Conductor and The Life and Times of the Floathouse Zastrozzi,* as well as dozens of articles in Canadian trade magazines.

Several years ago she acquired a copy of the flyleaf of her grandmother's Bible. Violet Courtenaye had recorded some key facts about her early life. "Went to Germany, May 1891", wrote sixteen year old Violet. This was an irresistible invitation to explore Violet's world and to imagine her life.
~~~~~~~~~~~~~~~~

Books that helped me imagine Violet

For information about travel in the 1890s, I was happy to find the following: Clarissa Sands Arnold, *Four Girls in Europe;* Karl Baedeker, *The Rhine and Northern Germany Handbook for Travellers, 1868;* Eva Marie Kroller, *Canadian Travellers in Europe 1851-1900;* Jack Simmons, *The Victorian Railway;* Sandra L. Singer, *Adventures Abroad – North American Women at German Speaking Universities 1868 – 1915;* Emily Murphy, *The Impressions of Janey Canuck Abroad.*

For Violet's life in Leipzig, I was delighted with Katherine Mansfield's *In a German Pension;* Nancy Reagin's *Sweeping the German Nation, Domesticity and National Identity in Germany, 1870 – 1945;* and Henry Handel Richardson's *Maurice Guest.*

Being woefully ignorant of all matters Irish, I found the following useful: Susan Campbell Bartoletti, *Black Potatoes, The Story of the Great Irish Famine;* Elizabeth Bowen, *The Last September; Rhys Bowen, In Dublin's Fair City;* Constantine FitzGibbon, *The Irish in Ireland;* David Hey, *How Our Ancestors Lived;* Jennifer Johnston, *The Old Jest;* Molly Keane, *Time After Time;* Derek Lundy, *The Bloody Red Hand;* Edward Rutherford, *The Princes of Ireland;* and Edith O. Somerville, *The Real Charlotte.*

To learn more about the lives of women in late Victorian England I read Eric Bligh, *Tooting Corner;* Patricia Branca, *Silent Sisterhood: Middle Class Women in the Victorian Home;* Louise Creighton and Covert, James Thayne, Eds. *A Victorian Family as seen through the letters of Louise Creighton to her mother, 1872 – 1880;* Yaffa Claire Draznin, *Victorian London's Middle Class Housewife, What She Did All Day;*Judith Flanders' *Circle of Sisters* and *Victorian House,Domestic Life from Childbirth to Deathbed;* Molly V. Hughes, *A Victorian Family; Elizabeth Lee, The Diary of Elizabeth Lee, Growing Up in Merseyside in the Late 19th century;* Shirley Nicholson, *A Victorian Household, based on the Diaries of Marion Sambourne;* Jane Ellen Panton, *From Kitchen to Garrett: Hints for Young Householders;* Daniel Pool, *What Jane Austen Ate and Charles Dickens Knew;* Emily Post, *Etiquette in Society, in Business, in Politics and at Home;* Routledge's *Manual of Etiquette;* David Thomson, *England in the Nineteenth Century;* John Tosh, *A Man's Place; Masculinity* *and the Middle Class Home in Victorian England* and Angus Wilson, *The World of Charles Dickens.*

For background on the Edinburgh art world in the mid 1890s, I am indebted to Janice Helland's *Professional Women Painters in Nineteenth-Century Scotland* and Sian Reynolds, *Paris –Edinburgh, Cultural Connections of the Belle Epoque.*

For period language, I read George Gissing and revisited E.M. Forster. And for verisimilitude, I read novels that Violet might have read including some by Katherine Thurston, Alice Mona Caird, Sara Jeannette Duncan and Amy Levy.